ONE
LAST
BREATH

(A TARA MILLS MYSTERY—BOOK TWO)

SARAH SUTTON

Sarah Sutton

Debut author Sarah Sutton is author of the TARA MILLS mystery series, which includes ONE LAST STEP (Book #1), ONE LAST BREATH (Book #2), and ONE LAST UNVEIL (Book #3).

Sarah has always been fascinated by the mystery genre and loves to write suspenseful books with complex characters. Sarah would love to hear from you, so please visit www.sarahsuttonauthor.com to email her, to join the mailing list, to hear the latest news, and to stay in touch!

BOOKS BY SARAH SUTTON

TARA MILLS MYSTERY SERIES
ONE LAST STEP (Book #1)
ONE LAST BREATH (Book #2)
ONE LAST UNVEIL (Book #3)

Prologue

He stood on a mound of sand formed from the deep pit he had just dug. There was no one around. No one knew what he was doing. No one had seen him—just as he had planned.

It was nearly three in the morning, and the homes lining the beach were just a row of shadows, dark and silent. They were the vacation homes of the wealthy, used to escape the fast-paced city life for days of tranquility. People were resting their weary heads, only to awake and rest some more under the sun and atop the sand. Little would they know what would be buried nearby or that they would soon hear another girl went missing.

He smiled at the thought of their concerned faces glued to the news as they stepped into their vacation homes for lunch the next day, unaware that they sunbathed so close to her body that very morning—that their children played right where he had carried her in a trash bag.

He could picture them in a panic as they questioned their own safety and gathered their things. It was the type of town where crime was rare. A person going missing was not supposed to happen here, but it would now be the second time. His eyes drifted down the dunes, along the row of houses, to where he had buried Alyssa White just about a year ago. She was still there; she still had not been found. He smiled at the memory—at the panic her search had caused—and at the realization that it was now going to happen again.

The town was just starting to get back to normal, but he couldn't let them get too comfortable. It would be a huge news story, he could feel it, and it sent a flurry of excitement through his body.

He stared back into the hole he had just dug. *It's deep enough*, he concluded as a gust of wind swirled around him, scooping up the fragments of sand until they struck the beach grass like shattered glass.

His forehead glistened with sweat in the moonlight as he sliced his shovel one last time into the walls of the sand, making the hole wide enough.

He was done now, but not completely, and a sudden tinge of excitement flowed through his body once more at the thought of what lay in his car. He was ready to bury her, and he knew he was so close to getting away with it. This had all gone so perfectly to plan.

He had already backed his car up onto the sand, and he quietly walked toward it. The trunk was cracked slightly, and he opened it wider. He had already disabled the light, but he could still see the outline of her body—curled unnaturally within the trash bag he had stuffed her in.

He stared at the bag for a moment. He had envisioned this for weeks, each time he watched her walk to and from work, each time he interacted with her. Every time, his mind wandered to this very outcome. At first, it was just a fantasy, but then it became a need as it seeped into his mind during everything he did. It became an urge so strong that he felt there was no other choice. He wanted all of her. He needed her. But it wasn't for his own enjoyment. What he wanted was indirectly associated with her. She was a flame that attracted anything in her path. She was polite. She was smart and beautiful. She would smile and blush at the slightest compliment. She was innocent. She was perfect.

And that was when he knew she was the flame that would spark a fire.

He reached for her with his gloved hands and cradled her in his arms as he turned back toward the beach and walked across the sand. When close enough, he kneeled before the hole he had just dug and placed her body deep into the earth.

He reached for the shovel and pierced the mound of sand with it, tossing what he scooped on top of her. He did this over and over again as her body slowly disappeared into the sand.

And when done, he took a step back, staring at his work as a whole.

He smiled again. She was nowhere in sight, and he was certain no one would ever find her.

Chapter One

One week later

Tara flinched as another roll of thunder rumbled. She had just placed the casserole she had made onto the table, but no one was sitting at it. John and his parents stood by the window, staring out with eager eyes.

"It's getting pretty bad out there," John said as he turned back to the table, letting the curtain fall.

The storm had just started brewing within the past hour. It was a low-grade hurricane that had just been upgraded from a tropical storm that very morning.

The dinner had been planned before there was even a mention of the storm, but after they heard of it, Tara extended the invitation for them to stay over. After all, John's parents' condo was located right along the Potomac River—a flood zone.

John's mother, Claire, was still staring out the window when John and his father, Tommy, sat back down at the dinner table.

"Got any beer?" Tommy asked as he pulled in his chair, his round belly grazing the edge of the table as his deep-set eyes scanned the room for a sign of any.

John began to stand up, but Tara was quicker.

"I got it," she said as she placed a hand on John's shoulder, causing him to settle back down in his seat.

Tara was always well prepared for when his parents came. She always carefully chose a dish they would all enjoy, and she always had Tommy's beer of choice. One thing she had learned very clearly over the years was that once Tommy liked something, he never wanted anything different. He was the type of man who would buy the same pair of shoes over and over again, each time they wore out. And he was certainly the type of man who only liked one brand of beer—Sam Adams.

Tara grabbed one from the fridge and placed it on the table in front of him. He thanked her as she settled down in a chair across from him.

"I hope this clears up by morning," Claire finally said with concern as she too moved away from the window. "Do you still have work in the morning?" she asked, turning to John as she pulled out her chair and took a seat at the table too.

"They're letting me work from home."

His mother nodded. "I just hope this doesn't ruin any other plans," she added casually as she reached for Tara's casserole with her long, bony fingers.

Awkwardness momentarily swept through the room, and John and his father shot Claire a quick look, as if she had said something she shouldn't. But then they looked toward Tara and their eyes quickly fell.

John reached for his water glass, taking a sip. "Well, the only plans I have other than work is band practice, and it's not a big deal if I have to cancel."

A look of confusion momentarily crossed Claire's face. But then it just as quickly vanished, as if she suddenly understood something he couldn't say. She nodded.

It was certainly true that John did have band practice. Music was something he got back into recently. He had played drums in college, but that was over four years ago, and then life had gotten in the way. John had started his Master's in the city, while Tara started working in the NYPD before starting her training at Quantico two years later to join the FBI, where she now worked as a general special agent for the BAU. There had always been something pulling him away from his drums—earning a living, soaking up the time with Tara before she left—but now their lives were settled, his more so than Tara's. After meeting some local friends who needed a drummer for their classic rock cover band, John and Tara agreed that it would be good for him— that it would be a good distraction if Tara had to get up and leave again on assignment—and it also added excitement to his life that he had been missing for quite some time.

But Tara knew very well that band practice was not what Claire was referring to. Normally, Tara would ask what was meant by her comment, but she had sensed it was not something she should question. In fact, she had this strange feeling for the past few weeks—that all three of them knew something she didn't.

It had all started with John acting odd. He didn't want her to look at his phone, and he would step out of the room when certain people called—including his mother. Meanwhile, Claire had been smiling way more often than usual, which made Tara suspicious. She had always been exceptionally kind, but Tara knew that when Claire held information, she showed it in everything she did, and lately she looked as if she was ready to burst at the seams.

The only person who was acting normal was Tommy, but he was always mostly quiet, often overpowered by Claire. But John and Claire's behavior was enough for Tara to suspect that a proposal might be on the horizon. And while it certainly excited her, the timing made her uneasy, and she didn't quite understand why John would think it was good timing either.

She wasn't sure if she could handle the pressures of planning a wedding right now. She had just finished her first big case only a month ago, when she had come face-to-face with the Appalachian Trail Killer, barely escaping with her life. And while her arm that he had slashed had healed, she was still recovering emotionally. Meanwhile, she still had yet to face her biggest obstacle of all: visiting her father.

"How are your new jobs going, by the way?" Tommy asked as he took another bite.

He was a tall man, with a thick head of gray hair. He leaned forward, his arms resting on the table, and looked across the table at the two of them. Tommy was someone Tara greatly respected. He was a retired lawyer with a big heart. He was smart and kind and always gave the best advice.

John opened his mouth to speak as another rumble of thunder sounded, followed by a flash of lightning. The windows momentarily illuminated brightly, and John's eyes wandered to them before directing his attention back to his father.

He sighed. "It's all right," he said with a shrug as he looked back down at his plate and took another bite. "I'm starting to like it a bit more," he added.

"That's great!" Tommy replied. "I knew you just needed to give it more time."

It was something he and Tara had discussed multiple times already. It was true; he was starting to like his job as an accountant a bit more. He was starting to enjoy working with his clients, and he had made some friends in the office too. But he admitted that he was envious of Tara's action-packed career. He needed something more, which was why they decided that getting back into music in his spare time would be good for him.

"I'm just so happy to hear you're playing the drums again," Claire chimed in. "You always had a talent for music." She took another bite before turning her attention to Tara. "And what about you, dear? I know that last case took a toll on you." She paused a moment and sighed. "You're a brave woman, Tara, and I admire it. But I have to say, I worry about you. Not just physically, but emotionally with everything, you see."

Tara felt heat rise to her face.

"Mom, stop," John suddenly said.

He knew his mom was stoking a delicate subject, much more than she was even aware of, and he wanted to save Tara the discomfort. In reality, her job did affect her emotionally, but it wasn't the details of the case that affected her most. It was the trauma of her childhood that would surface without warning at the slightest trigger—and she still had yet to deal with it fully.

Tara forced a smile. "There's no need to worry. I'll be fine. I actually really like the excitement of it all."

Another flash of lightning caused Tara's head to spin, a loud boom sounded in the street, and then the lights went out.

***

The flashlight from Tara's phone guided her as she made her way to the bed. After dinner, she and John had tried their best to clean up the kitchen in the dark with just the light of a lantern they kept in case of emergency.

Once John's parents left the room, Tara and John barely spoke, yet Tara sensed that John had something he wanted to tell her. Each time she handed him a dish to dry, she had caught his eyes, fixated on the sink—on the soapy water—until Tara said his name.

But she also knew it wasn't the place to ask him. Their apartment wasn't very large. Their kitchen and living room were situated in the center, divided by a barstool counter. There was a hallway on either side of the living room. One led to Tara and John's bedroom and the other to the guest room, where his parents slept. She knew that they could most likely overhear whatever was said in the kitchen. It was an unspoken understanding that sat loudly in the air.

Tara had a feeling it was related to what his mother had said, that she was worried about her. It was most likely a triggered reminder to John of what Tara revealed to him and that they had barely spoken about it since her nightmares stopped. It was during that time— when they were regularly occurring, when they bubbled into anxiety during the trail killer case—that she realized why she was having them at all. They weren't just recurring nightmares. They were memories from her childhood, when she was only six years old and her father took her mother's life. They were memories of when Tara walked into the room, when she saw her mother's body. But there was always one piece of the nightmare that had taken Tara time to admit to herself and then to John—that her father wasn't alone, and she had sensed someone else was in the room with him.

Tara and John had agreed that she should go see her father—that it was necessary for her to get answers in order to battle her trauma. But it had now been a few weeks since they last spoke about it, and she still had yet to decide when she would go. At first, she just wanted to wait until her injury healed, but then once it did, she needed to heal mentally. The nightmares eventually stopped, but now she was beginning to question if visiting her father was truly necessary at all.

Tara pulled back the covers and slid into bed. John was already lying down, his eyes fixed on the ceiling in the dark. As Tara lay down, he shifted closer to her. She braced herself for whatever he was about to say.

He spoke in a whisper. "Sorry I was a bit quiet in the kitchen before."

"Yeah, what was that about?" Tara asked, already anticipating his answer.

John sat up, his back pressed against the headboard. The storm was still brewing, and at each flash of lightning, Tara could see his face, staring off in front of him, deep in thought.

John had always been someone who thought clearly before he spoke. It was something Tara had always admired about him—his self-control, his restraint. Of course, he wasn't always perfect, and there had been a few moments when he had acted out of emotion and said something he later regretted, but it was always a rare occurrence. And when it did happen, it would eat away at him. He hated being the cause of someone's discomfort.

Tara knew he was choosing his words carefully.

He sighed. "Sorry if I made you feel awkward when I told my mom to stop…I just…I was trying to prevent you from feeling uncomfortable, and I feel like I did exactly what I was trying to prevent." He let out a slight chuckle.

"It's okay," Tara replied, now sitting up as well. "I know you were just trying to protect me, but you don't always need to do that. I can handle replying myself."

Tara leaned over and kissed his cheek, and he smiled. But even though she reassured him that there was no need for him to feel like he had to protect her, deep down she was glad that John said something.

In reality, his mother had caught her off-guard. Tara had a feeling that if John didn't step in—if the lights didn't go out—her discomfort would've been written all over her face. But she refused to admit that to him. John already had enough reason to worry about her.

But Tara knew that wasn't all John wanted to say. There was something else on his mind. He was now turned fully toward her. Concern swirled in his eyes as each flash of lightning filled the room.

He sighed. "We also haven't spoken about you going to see your dad in a while. I feel like you've kind of been avoiding it."

It was exactly what Tara anticipated. But at the same time, she felt very unprepared for the conversation. He was right; she had been avoiding it. Because deep down, she had doubts. What if she was wrong about what she saw? The question had been rolling around in her mind for weeks. And she had wondered, if she were indeed wrong, would seeing her father be worth it? What if it only opened her psychological scars wider?

"I'm just starting to wonder," she started, "if it's really a good idea." She looked down at her hands, clenched anxiously together in her lap. She couldn't see John's reaction, but she sensed him lift his head up.

"Why?"

His question stirred a strange feeling. Because, in reality, she could think of so many reasons why she shouldn't go see him. But she also knew that deep down, her biggest hesitation was just *seeing* him. She didn't know if she was ready to open that door.

"What if I'm wrong?" she finally said. "What if I allow him into my life and it only makes everything more complicated? What if I'm not ready?" The questions poured out of her mouth, and when she finished, John moved closer to her, grabbing hold of her hand.

"I don't think you're ever going to feel completely ready," he started. "But I also know you, and I know you wouldn't even have thought of doing this if you didn't feel a strong need to."

He was right. Tara knew that something had always felt off to her about the night of her mother's murder. It was something that had been eating away at her for years, and she had finally admitted what troubled her. But now that it was out in the open, it had stirred a new level of anxiety. It was the thought of seeing her father after all these years. It was the fear of opening a door she had tried so hard to close.

When she was younger, he had written to her for years. Her grandmother had allowed her to make the decision herself if she wanted to read the letters—and a few she did. In some odd way, she felt like she needed to. Her life had changed so drastically as a child, and she missed her old life, her family, her mother. His letters were mostly questions for her—asking how she was doing, what she did for her birthday, and so on. At first, she read her father's letters because she craved her old life. But as she grew older, that craving turned into anger, and she eventually stopped reading them. She never wrote back, and he eventually stopped writing too.

Tara feared that by visiting him, she would give him new hope, and then she would have to painfully push him out of her life again.

"It's going to be strange seeing him." John's voice caused her to look up, realizing that she had been absorbed in her thoughts. "But just because you see him once doesn't mean you ever have to again. I think you'll regret not trying to get some answers."

Tara nodded. "I just worry that he's going to try to weasel his way back into my life, and I don't want that. I don't want anything to do with him except to find answers."

It was another fear of hers. What if she was right? What if someone else *was* in the room? Who could it have been? What would it mean? Would it mean she would need to see him again? And what if finding the answer was more painful than not knowing? Those thoughts danced frantically around in her head.

She was very young when her father went to prison, but her memories of him in general were not positive. He was an angry drunk who would take everything out on her mother. She didn't know what secrets he kept buried, but she knew it was possible that he did.

"Well, you don't have to do anything you're not ready for. You don't have to let anyone into your life that you don't want in it. But if you need answers, don't let him hold that power over you. You owe it to yourself to get them."

Tara nodded again. "You're right."

She did need answers, or she'd be plagued with nightmares once again, and it would inevitably affect her job.

"You're in control now," John added, squeezing her hand.

His words suddenly sparked something within her, and she sat up straighter, a moment of clarity bursting in her mind. *I'm not a scared child anymore,* she told herself. *I'm an adult. I'm an FBI agent.* And at the thought, she reminded herself that if she needed answers, that was what she would get. Nothing more, nothing less. She was in control.

"I think I just need to do it," she said. "Tomorrow."

Tara could see a slight smile form on John's face, filled with relief and worry swirled into one.

"Do you want me to go with you?"

"No," Tara replied. "I think I need to do this on my own." She knew this was a solo journey. She needed to face her father all on her own.

14

Chapter Two

T ara opened her eyes but then quickly squeezed them shut as the ceiling light glared down at her. She turned her head sharply, opening her eyes slightly once again.

The thunder and lightning from the night before were now just a memory, replaced by a flicker of sunlight peeking through a break in her silver curtains. The electricity was clearly back on, reminding Tara that they had forgotten to flick the light switches before bed.

John was still sound asleep, as usual, and Tara quietly peeled back her cover, treaded across the floor, threw some clothes on, and flicked the switch for him, sending the room into near darkness.

She grabbed hold of her phone, checking the time as she quietly crept into the kitchen. It was 6:00 a.m. Normally, she wouldn't get up for another hour, but she knew if she was going to keep her promise to John, if she was going to visit her father that day, she would need the extra time to plan.

At the thought, she could feel her stomach grow queasy, but she couldn't dare let herself cave in to emotion. She needed to do this; she knew that now. For so long, she had seen visiting her father as a window to more pain, but now she knew it held the possibility of freedom—the freedom of knowing what happened that night. But most importantly, of not being controlled by her demons anymore.

But even though Tara felt mentally ready, she knew there was another hurdle. Her father was imprisoned in New York, over two hundred miles from Washington, D.C. It would not be easy to get to with less than a day to plan. But she had to try because she didn't know how long her mental clarity would last before the fear would take hold again.

Tara placed a filter and coffee grinds into the machine as she began to search on her phone for flights from Washington to New York. She knew it could be an easy day trip. After all, she had taken a similar trip when she was in the FBI academy in Quantico, when her grandmother was diagnosed with cancer. It was only a week into Tara's training when she had received a call from her grandmother. She didn't tell her at first. Her grandmother was always the type to hold things in—especially if she knew it would cause Tara the slightest discomfort. But she was also not someone to keep things completely hidden either. It was something she often struggled with—when to shield Tara from more pain and when to tell her the cold, hard truth, because in the end she deserved to know.

Tara had sensed that something was wrong that day. She could hear the same passivity in her grandma's voice, the same hesitation and conflict from the first time Tara's father wrote to her—when she decided that even though it would be painful, it was ultimately Tara's decision if she wanted to read the letter.

It took Tara a few times asking before her grandmother cleared her throat—something she always did before saying something that troubled her. It was then that Tara learned of the cancer.

Tara had wanted to fly back home that very day, but her grandmother begged her not to. She was afraid it would disrupt her training—that it would disrupt the one thing that had gone right in Tara's life. Tara knew very well that flying home would cause her grandmother more stress than she needed. And so she decided to stay, under the condition that her grandmother would call her if things worsened.

Two weeks later, Tara received the worst call she had ever gotten. It was her grandmother's live-in nurse. Her situation had worsened, and her doctors didn't think she would make it through the night. Apparently, her cancer was much further along than she had led Tara to believe.

Tara flew home immediately, but her grandmother was already gone. That was the last time she went to New York. It would be strange, she thought, to be back in the city after all these years.

Tara took a sip of coffee as she took a seat on a barstool and continued to look down at her phone. There was a flight leaving at twelve. *I can probably make that*, she told herself, but she would have to call Reinhardt first and see if she could take the day. She hasn't had a major case since the trail killer case, and they'd been keeping her on local smaller cases while her arm healed.

She reassured herself with those thoughts as she searched his contact and then placed her phone to her ear. He picked up almost immediately.

"Mills, what's up?" There was a softness in his voice, tainted with concern.

Over the past few months, Tara's relationship with Reinhardt and the entire division of the FBI, had grown much more comfortable. They respected her more; she could feel it. They no longer just saw as a rookie.

However, it was still unusual for Tara to call Reinhardt this early. She glanced at the clock on the stove—it read six thirty. This was early, even for Reinhardt, who didn't get to the office until seven.

"Sorry to call you this early," Tara started.

"Everything all right? How'd you make out in the storm?"

"Yes, everything's fine. We're all okay," she replied. She had almost forgotten about the storm. "What about you?"

"All good here. A few agents called and said they had some home damage, though, won't make it in."

Tara hadn't anticipated that before this call, and she suddenly began to question if maybe Reinhardt would need her more right now, and maybe it was an inappropriate time to ask to pick up and leave. She felt the phone grow slippery in her sweaty palm.

"I'm guessing that's not why you called?" Reinhardt finally asked.

Tara was quiet for a moment, trying to determine if she should still ask.

"I just wanted to check in with you early and see if you have anything urgent for me today." She paused, deciding how she would word what she was about to say. "I have a bit of a family matter I'd like to take care of in New York today. If it's not a problem, I'd like to take the day."

Reinhardt was silent for a moment. "You want to fly all the way to New York? You sure everything's all right?"

"Yes, everything's fine," she replied quickly, but she couldn't think of anything more to say without telling the truth. *He's going to ask me what type of family matter,* she thought as her heart rate picked. She quickly tried to think of an excuse.

"Yeah, should be fine," he finally said hesitantly. Tara sensed his suspicion but that he didn't want to pry, and she relaxed. "Because of the storm, there's not a whole lot going on today."

Relieved, Tara thanked him and was soon off the phone. She was about to book the flight when she heard footsteps and felt the presence of someone in the doorframe where the hallway met the living room.

Tara raised her head to see Claire entering the kitchen, already dressed for the day with a duffle bag around her shoulder. She struggled to carry it into the living room before dropping it down on the floor and looked up at Tara, out of breath. She always had a habit of overpacking.

Tara was surprised to see her up this early, and she felt a sudden anxiety bubble up at the thought of Claire overhearing her conversation with Reinhardt.

Tara stood up from her bar stool. "You're up early. Do you need help with that?"

Claire pushed her bag neatly into the corner of the room. "No, dear, but thank you," she said as she stood up. "I wanted to get over to the condo early and check on it," she added as she walked into the kitchen. "Any coffee?"

Tara poured Claire a cup before settling back down in her seat, and the room fell into silence. She looked back down at her phone. She was almost finished booking her flight, and she quickly finished the transaction before looking back up at Claire.

Tara hadn't even realized that Claire was staring at her skeptically until she looked up.

"Doing something for work?" Claire asked as her eyes moved to Tara's debit card sitting on the counter.

Tara placed her phone down as she felt her face begin to flush. She didn't like to lie, especially to John and his family, but she knew she certainly couldn't tell the truth. Claire did not know about Tara's father. As far as Claire knew, Tara's parents were murdered during a break-in gone wrong—it was the story John and Tara had stuck to when his parents spontaneously asked about her family a couple of years ago. Even though John insisted that Tara could tell them the truth—that his parents wouldn't look at her differently—she refused to tell them. She knew no matter who she told, a change in perception was inevitable, and she certainly didn't want that to occur with John's parents.

"Yes," Tara started before hesitating. "Well, I was, but then I was just buying something I needed."

Tara knew Claire wouldn't ask what it was. She was respectful in that way. But Tara also knew that if she were concerned about something, she would push.

Claire reached for the handle on the fridge before grabbing some milk. As she poured it into her mug, she turned halfway to Tara.

"Is that who you were on the phone with before— work?" Claire asked. Her eyes moved from Tara to her mug, which she was now stirring anxiously, awaiting Tara's reply.

Tara's heart sank. She had overheard. *But how much?* She knew she couldn't now lie. Depending on how much Claire had overheard, she would catch her in it.

"Yes, it was my boss," Tara replied.

Claire nodded. She opened her mouth briefly as if about to speak before hesitating and twisting her mouth, as if deciding what she was about to say. She placed the milk back into the fridge.

"I don't mean to pry, but I couldn't help but overhear. It sounds like you're going to New York?"

Tara's stomach twisted into a knot. It was one thing about Claire that always irked her—she didn't have many boundaries. In Claire's eyes she was treating Tara like a daughter, but at times it was overboard, and it certainly wasn't something Tara was used to. She was independent. She kept things to herself unless she wanted to speak of them, and she wanted to keep it that way with Claire. But Claire would never allow it, and it was clear that she had overheard the majority, if not all, of her conversation. And if that were the case, she would know that Tara did ask to leave work early—that she wanted to fly to New York later that day for a personal reason.

Tara searched in all corners of her mind for a response. She needed one that was believable but still kept her father's imprisonment a secret. *My grandmother*, Tara thought. *I'll make up something about her estate.*

"Yes," Tara finally said. "My great-aunt has some things of my grandmother's that she wants me to go through."

Claire nodded. "That's a long way to go on a weekday."

"I kind of just want to get it over with," Tara shot back.

Tara was growing irritated by the incessant questioning, and she couldn't help but question why Claire was pushing so. It had to have been clear that Tara was uncomfortable with the conversation.

Claire moved closer to the island counter until she stood directly across from her. Tara could sense her movement, but her eyes remained focused on her coffee mug, trying to deter any further conversation. But all of a sudden, Tara felt Claire's hand clasp hers and then give it a gentle squeeze.

Tara looked up.

"You know you can tell me anything, right?" Claire asked. "I see you as family, Tara—as a daughter. I want you to know that you can always confide in me."

Tara nodded, but she didn't know what to say. It was clear that Claire knew she wasn't being truthful. Tara knew Claire meant what she said, and it gave her a sudden surge of belonging—one that she had always searched for. Tara knew very well that she put walls around herself, and it was likely that Claire sensed that too. But as much as Tara wanted to grow closer to John's family, she was in no way ready to tear this one wall down.

"Thank you," Tara replied. "Yes, I do know that."

There was brief silence, and Tara's hand squeezed Claire's on instinct, without even meaning to do so, and then she quickly pulled away. But Claire only smiled. It was as if Tara had said something without even speaking a word—that she was grateful, but she wasn't ready yet to tell her what she held deep inside.

Footsteps interrupted the moment as their eyes darted to the hallway entrance that led to Tara's bedroom. John stood in the doorframe. He looked at them sleepily.

"Good morning," he said as he trudged into the kitchen.

But Tara was already looking at the clock. She needed to get ready, and she quickly excused herself before leaving the room.

***

Tara sat in the passenger seat of John's car as they made their way to the airport. She had already told him of the awkward conversation with his mother, but he wasn't surprised. He had already sensed it from Tara's awkward exit from the kitchen, and how she seemingly stayed in their bedroom until they left—only leaving the room for a quick goodbye.

"I think she knows," Tara finally said as she sighed and looked back down at her phone, double-checking that there were no delays with her flight. There weren't. "It was like she was trying to pull it out of me."

John's eyes moved briefly to Tara before shifting back in front of him.

"She just loves you, Tara, and she just wants to make sure you're okay." He grasped her hand and slid his fingers between hers. It was something he had said numerous times already. "You have nothing to be ashamed of," he added as he gave her hand a gentle squeeze. "Your past doesn't define you. You never did anything wrong. Your dad did, and that doesn't say anything about you."

Tara sighed. "But it does, John. You know that."

John remained silent. She had explained her reasoning to him before. And although John had always respected Tara's feelings on the subject, he could never quite grasp what it felt like to be in Tara's shoes. She knew it wasn't his fault. No matter how hard he tried to empathize with her, no matter how hard he tried to understand, he was always limited because he never actually had the experience. Part of her envied that about him. He had a loving family—a normal family—and because of that Tara was certain that he didn't fully understand the depths of shame.

To John, Tara was merely the victim of a tragedy. She was an innocent bystander. And because she didn't play a part in the events that unfolded, in his eyes she had no reason to feel ashamed. But Tara knew different. Her past *did* define her, because no matter who she told, she would always look damaged.

She placed her phone back down and looked over at him. She could see him growing flustered, the way he knitted his eyebrows, evaluating his next choice of words carefully.

His display of distress suddenly made Tara feel sorry for him. He was trying so hard to say the right thing and to make Tara feel better, but there was no right thing to say.

John finally sighed. "I just don't think you should worry about that right now. And I promise you, there's nothing to worry about with my mom anyway." He raised her hand to his lips and kissed it.

"You're right," Tara sighed.

She wasn't going to keep pushing the subject, and she could see John relax slightly at her words. He knew that he didn't have to keep reassuring her now. But he was also right. Tara had something much bigger to face, and it suddenly occurred to her that maybe she was using the situation with John's mom as a distraction.

Tara's phone beeped, interrupting her thought. It was her work phone, and as she picked it up, she could see Warren, her partner's name, light up the screen. She had a text from him.

How is everything?

Tara assumed he was asking in regard to the storm. It occurred to her that she hadn't even checked in with him to see how he was. Reinhardt mentioned that some agents had damage to their homes, and it didn't even cross her mind at the time that Warren could be one of them. She felt guilty.

Everything's fine. We didn't have any damage. How about you?

No damage.

Tara was about to write that she was glad to hear it, but then Warren started typing again, and a message came through.

Reinhardt said you're going to NY?

Tara's heart sank. She wasn't prepared for Warren to know. Ever since the trail killer case—since she proved herself to him and revealed the details of her past— Tara's relationship with Warren had become much more level. Instead of seeing her as an inferior rookie, he now saw her as an agent with potential. He seemed to feel like he had a new role, to mentor her, which often required him to check in with her if he was concerned. And Tara knew that was exactly what he was doing. Warren knew that Tara was from New York, and that given her past, there were very few reasons why she would be heading back there. It quickly occurred to her why Warren had texted her at all. It wasn't to check on her about the storm. It was because he heard of her plans.

"Is that work?" John suddenly asked as his eyes moved from the road to her.

Tara looked up. They were close; she could see the exit sign to her terminal, where John would be dropping her off.

"Yes," she replied. "It's just Warren."

She looked back down at her phone.

Yes, I'm just going for the day, she finally wrote.

Warren was quick to reply. *Everything OK?*

Tara's fingers hung heavy over her phone as John veered off the exit and then slowed down as he neared the drop-off.

Yes, everything's fine.

She sent off the message and then slipped her phone into her purse as the car came to a stop. She turned to John, whose dark brown eyes were heavy with concern. It made her realize just how quiet he had been throughout this drive, and that he was probably torturing himself with worry.

"I can still come with you," he said.

Tara shook her head. "This is something I need to do by myself."

John opened his mouth, about to protest, but then he closed it as his reason caught up to his emotions. He wanted to respect her decision.

"Well, if you change your mind when you're there, just call. I'll hop on the next flight."

Tara smiled. It felt good to have someone so supportive and devoted to her, and that she felt the same about. It was something she had always craved as a child. And now it felt almost ironic—how she would've done anything to find this type of love and leave her life behind, and yet here she was, leaving John behind as she faced what she always wanted to escape.

"Thank you," she replied. She would never ask him to do that, but it was still nice to hear that he would.

He leaned over, placing his hand gently on the back of her neck as he pulled her in for a kiss.

Their lips parted ways, but he still held her there, their foreheads touching, his hand still caressing the back of her neck.

"You'll be okay," he added. "You're the strongest person I know, Tara. You can do this."

His hand slid off her as they settled back into their seats, and she nodded. She could feel a newfound strength swim through her at his words, but then her father's face surfaced in her mind and butterflies burst into her belly.

She took a deep breath as she pushed the image out of her mind and said her goodbyes to John. She then gathered her things and stepped out of the car.

Chapter Three

W endy Stern closed her eyes briefly, letting the salty wind brush against her face. It was refreshing—just what she needed. She could taste the fragments of the ocean that it had swept into the air. But she also knew the wind was moist from the storm—that it carried the last bits of rain.

She took a deep breath and looked ahead of her, hearing the laughter of Stella, her six-year-old daughter. She was a bit farther up the beach, digging in the sand. Each time her hands touched the sandy earth, their Golden Retriever would join in, kicking the sand up into Stella's face and sending her into joyful hysterics.

A smile seeped onto Wendy's face. "Remember, don't get too close to the water," she reminded her daughter.

Stella nodded, only half listening, too consumed by laughter. But Wendy knew that Stella already understood. She had told her numerous times before they even left the house, warning her that the currents were still strong from the storm.

Wendy knew she would listen, because Stella loved the beach, even on a day like today. She wouldn't risk her chances of being there by defying her mother's orders. Stella had begged her to go, and she had agreed. But it wasn't just her daughter that convinced her; she also saw it as an opportunity to survey the damage.

We're lucky, she said to herself as she scanned the homes lining the beach. She could see the damage to some of the siding and roofs, where it looked as if branches or some other physical objects had whacked the homes. Her eyes fell upon a man in the distance in front of one of the perfectly lined houses. His salt-and-pepper hair danced at each flick of the wind. He was bent over, wearing knee-high rain boots as he collected the fallen debris around his home. As Wendy walked past, he caught her presence from the corner of his eye and looked up briefly. He stared at her a moment until they locked eyes and he briefly shook his head. It was clear what he was saying—*what a nightmare*—and even from afar, Wendy could see the defeat, the exhaustion in his face. She felt sorry for him, and she nodded back at him as if to say *I know, I'm sorry.*

Wendy, Stella, and Stella's father were lucky that their home was inland. It was their main home. They weren't fortunate enough to own two. Today was the first time Wendy had actually felt grateful that they didn't have a beachfront summer home. For so long it had been her dream to own one—to be able to watch the sunset from her protruding porch, to wake up to the sound of waves crashing on the beach, but not today. Today, she was grateful.

She scanned the beach for Stella, and for a moment a panic swirled within her when she couldn't spot her instantly, but then she saw her curly head bobbing at each playful step. She had made her way over to the sand dunes, a few houses back from where Wendy had just walked.

"Stella, stay off the dunes!" Wendy called out.

She had lived in a beach community long enough to know that you weren't supposed to let your kids play there, that they could ruin the dune grass planted to combat erosion. The storm, Wendy was sure, already gave it a beating, but she didn't want to add to it.

Stella stopped in her tracks as she turned to her mother, her hair whipping her face as the wind blew full force, and she pointed in front of her at their dog Charlie. He was a few feet in front of Stella, digging desperately in the sand.

"Charlie, no!" Wendy called out as she picked up into a run toward where they stood. "Stella, don't let him do that," she called out again.

Stella ran toward him as well, scolding him, in her usual playful scold. But just like every other time Stella tried to stop Charlie from doing something, it was ineffective. And Wendy chuckled slightly at the sight of it—her daughter trying so hard and Charlie knowing very well that he could get away with it in her presence.

But all of a sudden Stella grew quiet as she stared down at the sand Charlie was frantically digging away. Wendy was already almost near them, and she slowed down to a brisk walk as she called out again for Charlie to stop. This time, Stella didn't echo her mother's words, and as Wendy looked at her, she could see her daughter's face morph into something she had never seen on it before: terror. And just before Wendy could ask her what was wrong, her daughter let out a shrilling, pained scream as she ran toward her mother.

Panic and confusion pulsated through Wendy's body as she instinctively scooped up her daughter, who buried her face into her mother's neck.

As she approached the dog, he stepped back, almost as if he knew she needed to see what he had done. Her heart pounded as she peered into the hole. A large white object gleamed in the sand. Her mind swirled in confusion; she couldn't quite make out what it was. But then her eyes moved down the object to where it joined another and splayed into short, smaller white objects. It was bone—a leg, a foot, toes. Wendy gasped for air.

She looked up into the distance to the man she had caught eyes with moments earlier. She wanted to call to him, to ask for help. But as her eyes moved toward him, she could see that he was already reaching for his phone in his pocket as he picked up into a run toward them—as if he already understood.

Chapter Four

Tara stepped into a narrow lobby of white walls as her heart thumped. She had arrived at the prison moments ago, only to hesitate at the door. The reality of where she was and what she was about to do slammed into her at full force. But she forced herself through the threshold as her mind gave her every reason to turn around.

She walked up to a large, protruding desk, scribbled her name down on a visitation log, and slid her ID and the clipboard into a slot under a large Plexiglas window. She didn't even bother to look in front of her at the officer who grabbed the ID from the other side. She was too preoccupied with her thoughts, in keeping herself grounded with strength, and pushing every thought out of her mind telling her to leave.

"Tara Mills?" the officer asked.

It wasn't just a question. A stroke of familiarity played in his words. As he spoke them, Tara realized too that his voice sounded familiar.

She raised her gaze and was met by a face she had certainly seen before. It was Owen Reiner, an officer she had trained with during recruit training at the NYPD academy. He had the same clean-shaven face and muscular arms that always made the shirts of his uniform look too small. Tara had always thought he would be intimidating if it weren't for his height. Even seated, Tara could tell that he was still the same short man she remembered. The majority of his body was barely visible behind the desk. Training was the last time Tara had seen him, but he was a difficult person to forget. He always seemed to be at a disadvantage because of his height, and Tara knew he overcompensated by working out. He was one of the strongest and fastest during training, and had run a mile and a half in 8:15. It was a record.

His smile was wide. "Not a place I'd expect to run into you."

Tara forced a smile. It was not a place she would expect to run into him either, or anyone for that matter, and it was certainly not a place she would hope to. They were an hour outside the city. Last Tara had heard when she left for Quantico, Owen was still in the NYPD, stationed in the Bronx. She was just as surprised to see him here at a state prison.

"When did you leave the NYPD?" she asked.

"About a year ago. My wife's family lives up here, so we moved after we had a kid. I was able to get a nine-to-five."

"Congratulations," Tara replied before an awkward silence fell between them. He was a father now, and the mention only twisted the knot in Tara's stomach tighter. She had remembered Owen always helping other officers in training, showing them how to increase their strength, their speed, going to the gym with them on weekends. He was always willing to devote his time to those that needed it, and Tara couldn't help but assume he was a good father. It was a realization that made her suddenly feel like an outsider. She knew that as soon as he knew she was here to see her father—a man convicted of killing her mother—he would never look at her the same. He would pity her. He would dissect everything he knew about her. He would suddenly make sense of all her life choices, of all her reactions in every situation he had witnessed. It was what everyone did once they knew her history. He would assume he knew her, when in reality he knew nothing about her at all.

"Who are you here to see?" he asked as he grabbed hold of the clipboard that Tara had just written her name on moments ago. He scanned the names.

Tara's heart thumped harder. "Richard Mills."

The officer nodded as he found Tara's name. He then looked up again.

"What's your relation?"

Tara could feel every instinct telling her to turn away, to run. She could feel her palms begin to sweat. "Father," she started. "He's my father."

It was strange saying it out loud. Even though it was an undeniable fact, he didn't feel like a father to her at all, and it felt odd calling him that.

Owen's face fell. She could see the pity surface in his eyes, and Tara couldn't help but feel ashamed as a frustration boiled within her. He only nodded as he motioned to the metal detector and Tara focused on her breathing. She focused on controlling every piece of her being as she stepped through. *You can do this*, she said to herself. She knew very well how her anxiety worked.

It would creep up, and if she didn't fight back, it would seize her lungs, her body, and her mind.

Another officer stood on the other side of the metal detector. Unlike Owen, he stood tall and showed little emotion, his face stoic. Tara followed him as he opened a large, barred metal gate and continued to walk down a dimly lit hallway. It was lined with brick white walls and a concrete floor that gave off a musty smell. Tara focused on her surroundings, trying to keep her mind preoccupied when it suddenly occurred to her that she had no idea what she would say to her father. She had been so focused on keeping her emotions at bay, and then her interaction with Owen, that she hadn't even considered how she would broach the subject of her mother's murder.

It was as if she was a child again, controlled only by emotion, and it irked her that she would allow that to happen. So many times as a child she had approached her father with the intention to ask him something—to get ice cream, to go play with a friend—but then she would see his mood twisted into a scowl as she entered the room. His dark brown eyes that were so dark they looked like one large pupil would stare her into intimidation. She would stare back at him like a deer in headlights as he took a swig of his Budweiser.

"What?" he would bark, and Tara would shoot her eyes to her feet at the realization that she had been standing there quietly for too long.

Eventually, she would mumble that she had nothing to say, or she would lie and say something else that wouldn't irritate him—something that didn't require him to take her anywhere or do anything for her—and then she would eventually cower back to her room.

The officer reached the end of the hallway and scanned his ID before opening a large steel door. Tara quickly followed behind. *You will just feel it out*, she told herself. *You got this.* As she said the words to herself, she could feel her heart drumming, and a trace of doubt seeped in, but she quickly reminded herself that she wasn't leaving until she asked.

They came to another door, and the officer stopped before turning around to Tara. He motioned to a small window cutout in the intimidating door.

"He should be a minute. You can go in now," he said before opening the door for her.

Tara took a deep breath and held the air in her lungs for a moment, as if about to jump into a pool. She stepped into the room, and the door slammed shut behind her. She exhaled. The room was small, about six feet in every direction. It was bare except for a single chair, which sat in front of a glass window. A short steel desk jutted from beneath it.

Tara took a seat as her mind swirled into a haze. No one was in the room opposite the glass window, but she knew that any minute her father would walk through the door. She continued to reassure herself as she sat there. *He's in here, you're free*, she reminded herself. *He can't hurt you. You have every right to ask questions. You're strong. Don't you dare look weak in front of him. You came for one thing, and you're going to get it.* She told herself that over and over again as she stared at the doorknob to the room across from her, as if in a trance.

She wanted to look away, but she couldn't. It was instinctual—like staring at the door in an active shooting, hoping you won't be found. Even after coming so far, there was still a part of her that hoped he wouldn't want to see her and that they wouldn't come face to face. But it was a hope she kept pushing away, swatting at it each time it surfaced. She needed to be here. She needed to see him in person.

The doorknob began to turn, snapping Tara out of her trance. She sat up straight, took a deep breath, and tried her best to look as relaxed as possible. The door swung open, and in stepped a tall, lanky officer with jet-black hair. His keys dangled from his belt loop, and they clanked at each movement, almost synchronizing with the pulsating that suddenly started in Tara's head. He held the door open, looked toward Tara, and nodded—as if to say hello—and then turned toward the door frame.

Every muscle in Tara's body stiffened. The pulsating in her head roared in her ears. She stared at the door as everything else darkened around it. It felt like minutes were going by, when it had only been a matter of seconds. She could hear movement, then a figure stood in the doorway. She noticed the orange jumpsuit first, but then her eyes moved up his body, and she noticed that someone else stood behind him—an officer, escorting him in. They stopped walking once the door was closed, and Tara stared at the man in the orange jumpsuit's wrists as the officer removed his cuffs.

The officers then stepped back as the orange jumpsuit moved toward her, and for the first time she looked up at his face, at her father. He had the same dark brown eyes that had intimidated her as a child, the same large, sharp jaw, and the same large, masculine nose that always reminded her of Robert De Niro. But he also looked different. He had lines on his face that showed the passage of time; his skin was no longer tight and youthful but hung slightly under his chin; and his brown hair was now speckled with white.

He smiled at her as he took a seat, and Tara could feel the tiny hairs on her arms suddenly stand up. It was the smile that had given her nightmares, that had always stuck in her mind. It was the smile he had given her as a child as he stood over her mother's body.

He reached for the phone, and Tara did the same. Her hand was slick with sweat, and she held the phone tightly in her grip.

They sat quietly for a moment, both unsure of how to even start a conversation, but then he spoke.

"Tara," he said in one exhale, like a sigh of relief to be able to say her name.

He stared at her a moment, studying her face. A look of pain momentarily washed over him. Tara knew it was because she was grown. It signified how many years he hadn't seen her. After all, she was six years old the last time she saw him, when he was charged with her mother's murder, and she was now twenty-five. But she also knew it was because of the woman she'd grown into. When her grandmother was alive, she'd told her many times how much she resembled her mother. She had her green eyes, her long lashes, her petite little nose, and her olive skin. She could see that her father saw it too. He knitted his eyebrows, and his mouth hung slightly open as he studied her face—it was shock and sadness.

His eyes momentarily fell, and then he looked toward her again. "Well, how are you?"

Her hand that gripped the phone shook slightly. "Fine."

A smile formed on his face, and Tara could feel anger rise within her. He had a look of satisfaction, a moment of happiness, but he didn't deserve even a fraction of it. She wished she could slap the look off his face. It felt like a betrayal that she caused it—her mother's daughter. Her stomach twisted into a knot at the thought. What would her mother think if she saw this moment? Would she be hurt? Would she feel betrayed?

A fire swirled within her, but then she felt his eyes studying her, and she remembered her purpose. *It's not betrayal*, she reminded herself. *I'm here for the truth. My mom would want me to dig deep and find it.* At that thought, she knew that making him feel flickers of happiness was exactly what she needed to do. She needed him to feel comfortable. She relaxed slightly in her chair.

"How are you?" she finally replied. He smiled again, and Tara quickly extinguished her natural emotional response.

He shrugged. "As good as I can be," he started and then hesitated, as if afraid to speak what he was about to say. "But I have to say, my day just got a lot better," he finally added.

An awkward silence fell around them. *That's odd,* Tara thought. *To see him not drunk or angry.*

She knew he wanted to ask her why she was here, but he didn't want to ruin the moment, and she let him enjoy it.

"So, what have you been up to in here?" she asked. It was a stupid question. What could anyone be up to in prison? But she had to keep the conversation going, and she didn't want to be the subject of it.

He let out a chuckle. "Well, just trying to keep busy," he started. "I get my plumbing license renewed every year, so that's something I help out with around here."

Tara nodded. Her dad had been a plumber. She clearly remembered him coming home each day, his clothes tattered and stained, as he reached for a beer in the fridge before wanting anyone to say a word to him.

"They try to give us each a job around here," he added. "Certainly saves them a few bucks." He smiled. "But I can't complain. I'd rather be doing that then lying in my cell all day."

Tara nodded again.

"But enough about me, what about you?" he asked. "You working? Married yet?"

His eyes moved to her finger wrapped around the phone, and she suddenly felt vulnerable.

She shook her head. "I'm working, but not married yet." She didn't want to go into detail. She didn't want to tell him about John, about how good he was to her. It would bring him too much joy.

"Where do you work?" he asked as he stared at her with eager eyes.

She shifted slightly in her seat. She didn't know if she should tell him, and she felt a slight panic wash over her. She knew if she told him the truth, he would be less likely to confide in her about the details of the night of her mother's murder.

"I'm an accountant," she replied. It was the first occupation that popped into her head because of John.

"Ahh, a number cruncher." He sat back in his chair, letting his body relax. "Good for you, Tara."

Tara forced a smile as the room fell silent.

He suddenly stiffened, moving closer to the window, as if about to tell a secret. "You know, I was surprised to hear you wanted to see me…after all these years." He met Tara's eyes, clearly hoping she would reply before he had to ask the question. But she didn't. "What made you want to?"

Tara's mouth was dry. This was it: it was time to ask. A moment of doubt seeped into her mind. *Maybe I shouldn't. Maybe I should just go.* But then she remembered the promise to herself. She couldn't allow herself to leave unless she asked.

"Dad, I have to ask you something." It was her first time addressing him as "Dad" since she was a child, and it tasted sour rolling off her tongue. But she knew she had to. She couldn't be cold to him if she wanted him to give her an answer.

He raised his eyebrows, waiting, but she could see a tinge of worry in his eyes.

"I've been having these dreams," she started. "About Mom…about you."

He stiffened. "About what?" he asked, loud and proud. He was trying to play dumb, but Tara could see the complete panic in his eyes. He wouldn't blink; he wouldn't dare lose focus with her. He was afraid to miss the slightest hint of what would come next.

His reaction fueled her. He was afraid she would bring something up, she could feel it, and it only solidified her desire to ask.

She leaned in closer. "It's always about the night it happened," she started, being careful how she worded it. "When we lost Mom," she added.

Small beads of sweat glistened on his forehead, but she was careful not to look at them. She knew her father would never be receptive if he felt he was being attacked or purposely made to feel uncomfortable.

Tara swallowed hard. "It always starts out with me in the closet, but then I come out and I see you in the living room, standing over Mom. But you whisper something to the corner of the room, which I couldn't see. It almost seems as if someone was—"

She was about to say "there" but he abruptly spoke. "Dreams are dreams, Tara," he spat with annoyance. "I don't think I can help you. I'm not a psychologist." He looked toward a camera in the corner of the room and waved at it, signaling he was done with the meeting.

Tara began to panic. She knew he heard what she was trying to say, that someone was in the room, and now he was acting odd. She was on the brink of something; she could feel it.

"Wait," she said as an officer began to open the door. "It's not just a dream. It's a memory. Someone was in the room, I—"

Her father stood up. "We're done here," he uttered as the officer entered the room and began to place the cuffs on him.

Tara stood up. She knew now; there was something suspicious about that night. There was someone there. He wouldn't be acting this way if there weren't.

"Who are you protecting?" she yelled. "Who else was there?"

Her father acted as if he hadn't heard, but she knew her voice was still slightly audible through the glass. The officer looked at her for a split-second, but then her father leaned in closer, whispering in his ear. As he pulled back, the officer nodded. It was clear that her father was telling him he wanted to leave the room now, that he didn't want to reply to her, and he got what he wished. The officer led him to the door, reached for the knob, and was soon escorting him through the threshold. The door slammed shut behind them.

Chapter Five

T ara stood in the lobby. They had led her out of the room and down the hall to where she first checked in. She had nowhere else to go but leave, and she was heading to the entrance of the building until her feet stopped short. She was still trying to make sense of what had just occurred. Her head was spinning. She had come for answers, but her father only refused to hear her. *What did I expect?* Deep down, she knew her father wouldn't react welcoming to the memory, but she was so busy preparing herself for how to confront him that she hadn't prepared herself for the outcome.

Now what? Her skepticism was heightened more than ever. Her drive to find the truth was now in full gear. She had touched a nerve. So much so that he couldn't even formulate a response. She just hoped that she didn't ruin her chances of being able to see him again, to ask him once more. She knew he could always deny her future visits, and she had a worried feeling that he might.

"Everything all right?" she heard.

Her head turned to Owen, still sitting behind the counter where he had checked her in when she arrived. He was staring at her with a concerned look, reminding her that she had been standing there, consumed by her thoughts, for a moment too long. She turned to him as it suddenly occurred to her that she had signed her name on the way in and that everyone who had come to visit an inmate had to do the same. It was an obvious thought, but it was motivated by something she knew might help her. She had come all this way, and she didn't want to leave empty-handed. Maybe she could see the visitation records. She couldn't think of anyone that would come visit her father, but maybe there was. It would give her a lead, if so.

Owen continued to stare at her, his bushy brows raised, confused. She moved closer.

"Sorry," she started. She looked around her; no one was nearby. The few chairs placed in the center of the room, where visitors waited for the name to be called, were unoccupied. The room was empty except for the two of them and the armed guard by the metal detector. She lowered her voice as she reached into her pocket for her badge. She didn't want it to be known that she was an agent, because she didn't want her father to know, but she was desperate now, and she could only hope that he wouldn't find out.

She flashed it in front of Owen. She wasn't sure if he knew she was now in the FBI, and his face only confirmed that he didn't. His eyes opened wide.

"I need to see the visitation log of Richard Mills," she said as she leaned in closer.

"Of your father?" he asked skeptically.

45

"That's correct," she said. "I'm looking into his case." She knew she was bending the truth. This was a private matter. She was not on a case for the FBI, and her words were misleading.

Owen sighed, and Tara realized that it was too obvious it was personal, and she could see the same pity once again surface in his eyes. Visitation logs were not something they readily handed over. He looked up at her in an endearing way, and Tara could tell he felt for her.

"Do you have a subpoena?" he asked.

She didn't, and she shook her head, hope evaporating as she anticipated his next words.

"Tara, you know I can't give it to you then. I'm sorry."

She had known it would be difficult, if next to impossible to retrieve them, but desperation was pulling at her hard.

She leaned even closer, her voice now a frantic low whisper. "Owen, you don't understand," she said. "It's extremely important that I know who's been visiting him. Something is not right with this case." She could feel emotion rising within her. She steadied herself as she pulled back from the counter. She didn't want him to see, but it was too late; he had sensed it. He could hear the panic in her voice, and his face scrunched even more into concern. A half smile formed. He pitied her, it was obvious, and it gave Tara another spark of hope.

But then his eyes moved to the stoic officer standing by the metal detector. He was staring at them, studying Tara, as if waiting to step in.

"I'm sorry, Tara," Owen finally said. "I can't help you if you don't have a subpoena."

Her heart sank. The last bit of hope had finally gone out inside her. But she understood. He had no authority to hand over those documents unless there was an active case and she had a subpoena, but her father's case had been closed for many years. In his eyes, she just looked like any other desperate family member. Her eyes moved to a camera in the corner of the room. He was doing his job, and Tara would never want to sacrifice that for her own benefit. She thanked him, finally giving in to defeat. Hopelessness swirled within her belly as she turned to the door and exited into the parking lot. She had no answers, nowhere to look, and now she would have to take a plane home empty-handed.

Her only option would be to try to confront her father again.

***

Tara waited as John unlocked their apartment and opened the door. As soon as they stepped inside, she dropped her bags on the floor and collapsed on the couch. It had finally hit her just how exhausting the day had actually been.

The whole plane ride home, Tara had been replaying the meeting with her father, and she still couldn't quite make sense of it. The only thing she was certain of was that he was hiding something—he had to be.

"I just don't get why he would be covering for someone," she finally said. John stood in the kitchen, filling up the kettle. He nodded.

She had already told him everything that unfolded as he drove her home from the airport, and he had agreed that it was suspicious.

"I don't know what to do if he won't tell me," she admitted, feeling totally defeated.

John turned on the burner and then moved toward Tara and took a seat on the couch next to her.

"Do you think your dad speaks to anyone else?"

It was something she had considered, but Tara shook her head. It was unlikely.

"He doesn't really have anyone else," she said. "He just had Jennie, and well, I told you what happened to her."

The only sibling her father had was a sister who lived in California, but she didn't live there very long before becoming addicted to drugs and overdosing. Tara's father never spoke of her much, but from what Tara understood, they never had much of a relationship at all. Her father grew up in a family similar to the one he created—he had a drunk, abusive father and a mother who was scared for her life half the time. It was an environment that made those within it feel the need to fend for themselves. And so, when his sister was eighteen, she took a bus across the country and cut ties with everyone who reminded her of where she came from.

The kettle began to whistle, and John quickly got up to attend to it, but Tara only stared in front of her. She had to get answers. There was something being kept from her—she could feel it pulsating through her body. She had seen it on his face the moment she mentioned she wanted to ask him something. She could see the fear—a fear that he had held all along but bubbled to the surface at Tara's words.

John placed a steaming cup of tea on the coffee table in front of her, but she only stared at it. She was searching in every corner of her mind for answers, for a lead. *I can go back to where it happened*, she said to herself. *Maybe a neighbor saw someone leave the house that night. Maybe they saw someone lurking around the area.* It was worth a shot, but she also didn't want to waste time. She knew it was possible that her old neighbors didn't live in the same house anymore. After all, it had been over twenty years.

John wrapped an arm around her. He pulled her in close and kissed her on the top of her head. "Maybe you should get some sleep," he said as his lips parted on her forehead.

Tara nodded. She was exhausted, and she knew that whatever she needed to find, she wasn't going to find it tonight. But she also knew that this wasn't over. She had hoped that by seeing her dad, she would find answers, but now she only had more questions—more suspicion.

Her head was now resting on John's chest, and she finally looked up, meeting his eyes.

"I'll have to go back," she finally said. "You understand, right?"

John looked down at her and nodded. "Yes," he said as he stroked her head. "Do what you need to do."

At his words, Tara relaxed slightly. She hadn't even realized just how stiff she was. She lay down, resting her head on John's lap. She wanted to go to sleep, but she knew her mind was still too awake.

"Let's just watch TV for a little," she said.

John agreed and turned it on. They watched in silence until Tara's mind caught up with her exhaustion, and she couldn't hold her eyes open any longer.

Chapter Six

Tara's eyes fluttered open, but before she could even make sense of her surroundings, her phone vibrated on the nightstand. She sat up quickly, still in a daze, as she scanned the room. She was in her bed. John was next to her. Last she remembered, she had fallen asleep on the couch, but John must've woken her.

Her phone pulsated again, and John began to stir.

"Who is it?" he asked. "What time is it?"

She looked to her nightstand and squinted in the dark to read the name flashing across the screen—Reinhardt, her boss. Her heart leapt, and she felt instantly awake. She didn't even take a second to reply to John before springing out of bed, grabbing the phone, and tiptoeing across the cold floor. Just as she exited the room, she picked up.

She was about to say good morning, even though she wasn't quite sure if it was still late in the night. But before she could even utter a word, Reinhardt spoke.

"Good, you're up," he started. "I got a new case for you."

"Yeah?" Tara tried to sound as awake as possible.

"A skeleton was found buried under the sand dunes yesterday after the storm passed, down by Dewey beach. They think it might be Alyssa White. She went missing last year, but the case went cold after a while."

Tara felt a pit in her stomach. She remembered the news stories last summer. Alyssa was a straight-A student who had just gotten accepted to some Ivy League school. She had taken a trip to Dewey Beach with her family to celebrate, but then one night she disappeared. It sent a shock wave throughout the whole community.

But Tara also knew that she wouldn't get a call just for developments in a cold case unless there was suspicion of a serial killer.

"And what, they think it's a serial killer?" Tara asked.

Reinhardt sighed. "That's what it's lookin' like. Homicide has been searching the area all night for evidence, and they just found another body about an hour ago."

"You want me to head over?"

"Yes, I just got off the phone with Warren. He's already on his way, so the sooner you can get there, the better."

Tara agreed, and they were soon off the phone. She had only been to Dewey Beach once since she moved to Washington, D.C. It was about a two-and-a-half-hour drive from where they lived. Her eyes moved to the time on the stove. She hadn't even taken a moment to turn a light on when she got the call, and the green light of the time stung her eyes—it was five thirty. If she left in twenty minutes, she could get there just short of eight thirty.

The light fixture above her suddenly lit up, instantly making her squint. John was standing in the doorway between the kitchen and the hallway to their bedroom.

"Everything all right?" he asked as he fully moved into the light-filled room.

"It was Reinhardt. I have a new case out by Dewey Beach. I got to head over there now."

Concern washed over John's face, but she could see his struggle to control it, not to let it show.

"You're going to be okay?" he asked. "With everything going on with your dad?"

Silence filled the space between them. Tara knew it wasn't ideal. She had wished and hoped that she could lay the issues of her past to rest before embarking on another case. But she also knew it wasn't realistic. Her past was way too complicated, more than she probably understood, and she would have to chip away at it to get to the center. She most certainly couldn't put her life or her career on hold.

"I have to be," she said firmly. "I can't put everything else on hold until I get answers."

John nodded. "If you get any nightmares, though, if it affects your ability to perform, to stay safe…"

"I know," she interrupted. "I haven't had any nightmares—not since I admitted what they stemmed from. I'll be okay."

"And you'll tell me, right? If you have them again?"

Tara could feel herself hesitate before she could speak. It was always something hard for her to be open about. She had always wanted to protect John from her pain, afraid she'd pull him down. And it was also something she had kept to herself for so long before she even met him. Learning to be open was exceptionally difficult. But she had promised him that she would be, and she knew their relationship depended on it.

"Yes, I promise."

John moved closer to her, giving her a quick kiss before pulling away, and her eyes drifted to the clock.

"I have to get ready."

John nodded again, but she could see another question rising within him.

"Are you still going to visit your dad again?"

"Yes," she replied. "As soon as I get a break from work."

Her words trailed behind her as she walked to the hallway and shifted her focus to the case.

***

Tara stepped out of her car as the salty wind brushed against her face. She had just arrived at Dewey Beach, and she could already see that Warren was there, his car parked amongst the row of police vehicles and forensics vans. News crews littered the street, some doing live shots while others looked toward her as she made her way to the beach.

She stepped over the yellow tape that lined the entrance and then trudged up the walkway as sand snuck into her shoes. She could see Warren just over the hump, speaking with a man in a sheriff's uniform whose jet-black hair danced in the wind. As she saw Warren, it reminded her of the texting conversation they had yesterday. He knew about her visit to New York. He was concerned. It was only a matter of time before he would bring it up in person, and Tara didn't yet know what she planned to say. But she also knew she had time, since this case would be their focus now.

Warren and the sheriff kept looking toward her, and then their eyes would veer off to the side of her. She followed their gaze to the right to see forensics and a detective standing atop the sand dunes. As she moved closer to Warren, his eyes turned to her again and remained there. She could see a slight smile form at her presence.

"This is Agent Mills," he said once she was close enough.

The sheriff nodded and then reached out his hand to introduce himself. "Sheriff Patel," he said.

Warren assured her that he had just gotten to the scene only fifteen minutes before she did, and he was just getting filled in.

"Well, what do we know?" Tara asked. Farther down the beach, she could see yellow tape whipping in the wind.

"A woman was on the beach after the storm yesterday with her six-year-old daughter," the sheriff said. He had a short beard, salt-and-pepper, with a whiteness that shimmered at the touch of the sun, now beginning to peek through the stormy clouds. "Their dog ran up onto the sand dunes and started digging. The daughter followed. Turns out he was digging up the leg of the victim, which is just a bone at this point."

"Oh my god. That's horrible," Tara said.

Warren nodded. "I spoke to her on the phone right before you got here. She didn't have anything new to say. She just seemed a bit distraught over what her daughter saw."

"And it's presumed to be the remains of Alyssa White?" Tara asked.

"That's what it looks like, but you can speak to the forensic anthropologist yourself." He motioned to the dunes in front of them, where Tara could see a woman crouched down and speaking to another person.

But then Tara's eyes drifted down the beach to where another part was sectioned off with yellow tape. She had to squint to see law enforcement moving amongst the sand, like ants.

The sheriff caught her gaze. "Yeah, and then we found that body. It's about a quarter mile down the beach." He looked between Tara and Warren. "A young female victim. She was reported missing eight days ago. She's a local, works at a coffee shop—never came home from work."

"You sure there's no other bodies?" Warren asked.

The sheriff nodded. "We've run cadaver dogs up and down this beach for hours. We would've found it by now."

Warren then turned to Tara. They agreed to go speak with the anthropologist, and then they would make their way down the beach to where the second body was found. They walked toward her. The beach was littered with objects thrown from the ocean—seaweed, buoys, boardwalk boards—all tossed there by the strong force of the storm. The remains of a wooden-slat fence lined the sand dunes, showing just how far the water had risen on the beach. What once was used to control erosion, to protect the dunes, was now pulled apart, consumed by the sand it was meant to control. Tara stepped over the slats.

As she and Warren trudged up the small hill, a woman kneeling in the sand looked up. Her dark hair was tied neatly in a knot at the base of her neck. She smiled as they approached. Tara sensed a familiarity between them.

"Warren." The woman beamed.

Warren smiled in return, blushing slightly, something Tara had never seen his face do before. "It's been a while, hasn't it?" he asked.

She nodded before Warren proceeded to introduce them. Dr. Lyn Harris worked for the FBI, specializing in forensic anthropology. She was middle-aged, and Tara had the sense that she'd worked for the bureau for quite a while, as had Warren. Her face looked vaguely familiar. Tara had probably seen her in passing at one point or another. But she could also sense something else. It was the way Dr. Harris's eyes lit up as Warren approached, the way Warren's gaze receded at the notice of her. Warren cleared his throat, as if to ease the awkwardness, and Dr. Harris's face abruptly shifted to a sterner look, as if remembering why they stood there.

Two other forensic analysts moved around them, collecting the markers surrounding the skeletal remains.

"I didn't want to move the remains before you got here," Dr. Harris said. "I've just been taking some pictures. But I am going to have to bring the remains back to the lab soon to do testing."

"Any clue of the cause of death?" Warren asked as he and Tara moved closer. They kneeled in the sand, which was still damp with rain. The wetness seeped through Tara's pants, and she could feel the coolness against her skin.

The bones were fully exposed and intact, the sand carefully pushed to each side. It had the looks of a grave dug into the dune.

Dr. Harris sighed. "I can't tell you a whole lot until I get these remains into a lab. But I did see this." She pointed to a small, V-shaped bone jutting just under the skull. Tara and Warren both leaned in closer and could see a small hair-line break. "Fractures like this are very rare, except for strangulation."

"So you think she was strangled?" Tara asked.

Dr. Harris nodded. "It's very likely."

"Do you know if it's Alyssa White?"

"I just got her dental records sent over. Once I'm in the lab, in a few hours I should know for sure."

Tara turned to Warren. She could see his eyes already wandering down the beach to where the other body was discovered. She knew they both had the same thought, wondering if the other victim was also strangled. But it wasn't just the crime scene that their eyes wandered toward—it was Sheriff Patel, who was headed that way in the distance, his body appearing smaller the farther he trudged. Both Tara and Warren agreed to follow, and after thanking Dr. Harris, they carefully walked off of the dunes and continued down the beach.

The sand had already begun to dry after the storm, making it difficult to walk through, and so they moved toward the edge of the beach, just before the water. Every once in a while, a wave would push the water farther up the beach than expected, causing Tara to step farther up onto the sand.

At first, Tara and Warren were silent, but Tara could sense that Warren was planning to speak. She wasn't sure if it was something to do with the case or her visit to New York, but she feared it was the latter. He kept looking at her, as if giving her an opportunity to speak first. But when she didn't, he opened his mouth.

"Did you get back from New York last night?" he finally asked.

Tara could feel her face begin to redden, but then she reminded herself that Warren already knew the majority of her history. She nodded.

"Everything all right? I was surprised to hear you were heading up there on such short notice."

Tara was getting tired of the incessant questioning, and it only made her feel the need to be more guarded. She knew Warren was coming from a good place, but she didn't like feeling pressured to speak about something she didn't want to. Tara had always been a very private person—and with good reason. So many times as a child she had trusted a friend or an adult, she had allowed herself to be vulnerable—to tell them details of her past, of how it all made her feel. But then they would look at her differently, they would whisper to others, and she would feel the perception around her change.

She knew Warren wasn't like that—he looked out for her, he never once treated her differently after learning her story. Yet she still didn't like feeling pressured to open up, even if it was coming from a good place.

"Yeah, everything's fine," she finally said. She knew her tone sounded defensive—it was hard to hide. "I just had something to take care of," she added, making her voice sound more at ease.

Warren remained quiet, looking up into the distance as they neared the next scene. He squinted as the sun peeked slightly through a break in the clouds. Tara knew he had to have detected her defensive tone, but his face didn't show it. It remained relaxed, almost as if he were expecting that response. He finally nodded as they turned away from the water toward the sand dunes where the other victim lay.

"I'm glad to hear," he finally responded. It was clear that Warren didn't plan to pry any further. Even though he didn't show it, Tara knew he had gotten the hint, and she wondered if she was maybe too defensive.

As they approached the scene, Sheriff Patel looked toward them. He was standing with another detective. Tara knew her conversation with Warren was now over, and she shifted her focus as well as they stepped over the fence lining the dunes and trudged up the hill once again.

Sheriff Patel and the other detective stood around a hole in the sand as they held their shirts over their noses. As Tara and Warren approached, it was evident why. A scent crashed onto them, like a wave of water. It entered Tara's nose and mouth instantly, and she felt her stomach churn. She lifted her shirt too, holding it just over the tip of her nose. Warren did the same.

They stepped closer, and Tara stared down into the crater dug in the sand. She immediately felt lightheaded from the smell and looks of the girl. Her body was a greenish blue from the early stages of decomposition, but Tara could still tell that she was clearly young—a teenager. She could tell by the small curve of her hips—a girl becoming a woman—and from the smoothness of her skin that at even at this stage of decomposition revealed her youth. She wore jean shorts ripped at the edges, a fitted black tank top, and white Converse sneakers that were caked in wet sand.

"How'd you find her?" Tara finally asked. The body must've been buried more than five feet underground.

"A cadaver dog," Patel replied.

Tara nodded.

"Who was the last to see her?" Warren asked as he crouched down, taking a closer look at the body, and Tara did the same.

"Like I said, the last time she was seen was at work. She lives about a quarter mile from there and walked home after her shift. Her boss was the last to see her."

As Patel spoke, Tara and Warren stared into the gaping hole on their hands and knees, still holding their shirts above their noses. The girl's decomposing face was still wincing with pain, and Tara felt a tug on her heart.

Warren reached a hand forward and waved it just below the girl's chin as he looked toward Tara. She could see what he was gesturing at. Just below the girl's chin, the center of her neck was even more purplish-blue, spreading from a clear string-sized center.

"Looks like strangulation," Tara admitted as she finally stood up, trying to get a break from the smell.

Warren stood up as well. "Looks like it wasn't done by a hand either."

He was insinuating that it was a smaller, ligature-like object; string or wire was what Tara assumed.

"That's what we thought too," Patel replied as he looked to the other detective, who then shook his head.

The other detective looked in his mid-forties, but he was fit like a college athlete. The short sleeves of his uniform hugged his arms tightly. Patel quickly introduced Detective Wade.

"You can see similar marks around her wrists," he finally added as he bent down and gestured toward them.

Tara took a closer look and could see similar string-like marks just above her hands. They were less bruised than her neck, but it was clear that they were the marks of ligatures from being tied up. Whoever had taken this girl, whoever had killed her, clearly didn't do so right away. They had tied her up, probably kept her alive for some time before strangling her. *But why?*

"Any way to know if it was sexually motivated?" Tara asked.

Detective Wade shook his head. "We'll have to wait until forensics reviews the body in the lab."

Tara nodded. She knew the statistics. Strangulation was firmly associated with sexually motivated murders, especially in young female victims. The absence of such was rare. And even more rare was strangulation by ligature, but they would have to wait until the body was in the lab for forensics to get an idea of what the actual murder weapon was.

"And no one saw anything?" Warren asked.

It was a question both of them had. It seemed odd that on such a popular beach, with houses not too far from where the bodies were found, no one had seen someone dragging a body.

Detective Wade shook his head. "We spent all this morning going door to door. We didn't get any leads."

"Whoever it was was a careful planner. They must've come in the dead of night," Patel added.

Tara looked around her. It was certainly possible not to be seen. The houses were far enough back that someone could easily be hidden among the beach grass and curvature of the dunes. Plus, in the middle of the night, when everyone would be asleep, it was even more likely.

"Did you speak to family yet?" Tara asked.

"Not yet." Patel shook his head. "We just told them about the news a few hours ago. They were of course really shaken up. We wanted to give them a bit of time."

Tara certainly understood, but she also knew that they could hold some answers about their daughter's last few days that would be crucial in finding her killer. She hated having to interview family. It was always so delicate, and it was always difficult to watch someone in so much pain, especially since she understood it so well. However, she knew that the only way to help them now would be to get justice.

"What about her place of work?" Warren asked.

Wade nodded. "When she went missing, but we couldn't get any leads there either."

Tara turned to Warren. "Start with the family?"

Warren nodded, before thanking the sheriff and Detective Wade. Tara followed him as he turned to the car. They both didn't want to waste another moment.

Chapter Seven

Tara sat in the passenger's seat, staring down at a stack of documents in her lap. They were the case files of Alyssa White. Warren had retrieved them from headquarters before he left for Dewey Beach. He hadn't had a chance to go through them yet, he had told her, but he handed them to her once they got in the car. Now she flipped through them, eagerly reading.

Every once in a while, Tara would look up, but Warren's eyes remained steady on the road. Warren had barely said anything to her since they left the beach. Part of her wondered if it was because she was short with him when he asked about her trip to New York. But she also wondered if he was afraid Tara would ask about him and Dr. Harris, or if his reasoning had to do with both. Tara didn't mind the silence; in fact, she rather liked it. She didn't want to talk about New York.

However, seeing the awkward exchange between Warren and Dr. Harris made Tara realize how little she knew about Warren. Yet he knew so much about her. All he'd ever mentioned about his family was that he wasn't married and that he lived alone. He had told her he was married once, but he had never expanded beyond that. He never mentioned children. It made her feel suddenly exposed. She had told Warren about her mother—something she had told very few people in her life. Yet here he was, completely guarded.

She wanted to ask about Dr. Harris, but the papers in her hand felt heavy, and she knew she had limited time to review them. She looked back down.

The details of Alyssa White's disappearance were similar to the second victim's. Both went missing as they walked home alone. However, unlike the second victim, Alyssa White was not walking home from work. In fact, she wasn't a local at all. She was on vacation with her family, Tara had read. She had met some friends and played mini golf with them that night. And then she had walked home, alone, never to be seen again.

Tara finally looked up. "The killer had to have been stalking them," she said before reading the details of Alyssa's case out loud and reiterating how each victim had gone missing while walking home late at night.

"Whoever it was had to have been watching them. He must've known they'd be walking alone."

Warren nodded. It was the only logical explanation for how they both vanished at the perfect moment—when no one was around, when it was late. He must've been watching them, studying their routine, studying when that perfect moment would be. The thought sent a shiver down Tara's spine. He was living among them, and they didn't even know.

"There must've been someone who saw something," she added as she stared out onto the road ahead of them, dusted with a small layer of sand and littered with broken branches. She knew that if the killer was watching each of the victims, it was likely someone would've seen him and thought he seemed a bit suspicious—that his car was parked too long, that he seemed odd, anything.

Warren agreed. "We'll see what the family has to say. Then I think we head to the coffee shop that the victim worked at. Who knows, he could've even been a customer."

Tara nodded. He was right. The killer most likely knew when she was getting off work. He may even have known her hours. And being a customer, having the perfect opportunity to learn more about his victim while not getting caught could've been the ultimate thrill.

Warren turned onto a side street and then pulled over in front of a house. It was the home of the second victim, and Tara could already feel the unease swirl within her belly. She hated this part, interrupting a family's grieving. But she also knew that families often held more valuable information than they even realized.

They both stepped out of the car as a gust of wind whirled. Particles of sand danced across the stone driveway. The house was small but charming. It was a pale yellow, with a blue front door and white trim. It had the looks of a quintessential beach house, with surfboards strapped to the hood of a Jeep Wrangler in the driveway. Tara wondered how long those surfboards had been strapped there. They had fallen leaves scattered over them. She assumed they were placed there before the storm, before their daughter went missing, before her body was found. The thought gave Tara an unsettled feeling. They had clearly been too stricken with grief even to consider taking them off the roof.

Tara and Warren walked up the front steps, and Tara knocked. Muffled sobbing could be heard coming from inside. But at each knock, the sobbing would die down, replaced by whispering and a sniffle before the door started to open.

A balding man with sun-kissed skin, wearing khaki shorts and a t-shirt that read *Dewey Beach* stood in the doorway. His eyes were red and watery. He looked blankly back and forth between Tara and Warren, as if in a daze, and then a look of reality sank in.

Tara held up her badge. "Do you mind if we just speak with you a moment? I'm so sorry to intrude. We won't be long."

The man's face sank to the floor as he sighed and opened the door farther without a word. The door opened into the living room, where a woman sat on the couch, comforting a child who looked to be about ten. She held him close to her chest, kissing the top of his head as he sobbed into her shirt. The woman looked up as they entered, her face streaked with pain. It was clear she was trying desperately to hold it all in. Her eyes were bloodshot, her face was red. It looked as if she would burst into tears at the slightest trigger, but she was holding it together for her son. She stroked his head continuously, his face still buried into her chest as she cradled him like a baby and looked at them questioningly.

The man motioned for them to sit down, and the woman, realizing who they were, looked down at her son.

"Maybe you should go to your room," she said to him.

He looked up and around him as he slid from his mother's lap and took a seat next to her. His face was swollen and red, his skin as tanned as his parents'. His hair was a light brown, but sun-kissed, which brought out bits of fiery red.

"I want to stay with you," he cried as he looked up at his mother.

She looked around the room for approval, at her husband, Tara, and Warren. It was clear she couldn't bear to tell him no.

"Is that okay?" she asked.

Warren looked at Tara and then back at the woman. "As long as it's okay with you," he replied as he took a seat on a couch next to the one she was sitting in. Tara sat next to him. The house was all light and beachy, from the white furniture to trinket decorations placed throughout the room. A large wooden antique sailboat sat on the table next to the couch.

The husband took a seat next to his wife with the boy between them, still clinging to his mother's arm. The mother and her husband stared at Tara and Warren with concern, cautiously awaiting what they were about to ask in the presence of their son.

"Your daughter was coming home from work when she went missing, correct?" Tara asked.

The woman nodded. "She gets out at ten. She's usually home before ten thirty."

"Do you know of anyone who could've possibly wanted to harm her?"

The woman looked from her husband to Tara as she began to stroke her son's hair again. "No," she started, her voice cracking at the end. "Reese was loved by everyone. I can't think of anyone who would want to hurt her."

"Did she have a boyfriend?"

Again, the woman shook her head, and so did her husband.

"Reese wasn't allowed to date until recently," the father added. "Not until she was seventeen, which was only a month ago." His eyes welled up at his words.

Tara could easily get the sense that they were protective parents, and at that realization, she lost slight hope in her questioning. If she were right, then it was very possible that their daughter kept things from them, unless she was a complete angel, but Tara knew that most seventeen-year-olds were not.

"Have you ever suspected that she might've been seeing someone without you knowing?" Tara finally asked.

The parents looked at her with utter shock and surprise. The boy looked up at his mother as if he too knew it was a question no one would dare to ask. Tara could see just from their faces that they could never imagine their daughter would hide something like that.

"No," the mother replied as she shook her head with full force and certainty. "Reese would never lie to us. She's a good girl."

The father echoed her words, and Tara felt her last flicker of hope die out. She knew she wasn't going to get answers here, but she still covered her bases. She asked about their daughter's friends, about her place of work, if their daughter ever mentioned anyone that seemed off. But each question was only met with a dead-end answer. When they finally exhausted their efforts, Tara and Warren said their goodbyes and stepped outside.

As they reached the driveway and were far enough out of earshot, Warren whispered, "Anyone who thinks a seventeen-year-old wouldn't lie to her strict parents is a bit delusional, don't you think?"

Tara nodded. They were her exact thoughts. "I say we check out the coffee shop she worked at. See if anyone came in there."

After all, they both knew it was the last place she was seen alive. At her suggestion, Warren nodded, reached for the door handle, and slid into his car. He didn't even skip a beat, as if Tara echoed his thoughts as well.

Chapter Eight

T ara and Warren walked down the sidewalk, which was still littered with fallen tree limbs and branches, as Warren ended a call. He had been speaking with Dr. Harris, getting the results of the dental records. As he placed the phone into his pocket, he turned to Tara.

"They match. It's definitely Alyssa," he said.

It was a piece of information they all already assumed, but now they knew for sure, and it was only confirmation that the killer would most likely strike again. Two random killings a year a part. It was just the beginning, Tara assumed, and it made her feet quicken instinctively as they walked toward the coffee shop.

The road was mostly quiet, except for a cleaning crew collecting the remnants of the storm and a street cleaner that swept the road ahead of them. The stores were lined on a long strip, and at the end, in the distance, they could see the ocean.

When they reached the shop, a *Closed* sign hung from the inside of a large glass door, but Tara could see someone moving about within. She knocked. A woman with a mop in hand soon swung open the door.

"We're closed," she muttered. "We don't open for another half hour." Tara assumed she was in her thirties.

She was tired-looking but still young and youthful. She was tall and slender, with piercing green eyes and a loose braid that fell just past her shoulders. She held the mop in one hand, slightly leaning on it, and heaved a tired sigh as she flicked her braid behind her shoulder.

Tara held out her badge, and life burst into the woman's face. It was a look of confusion and concern. But then understanding blossomed, and her face morphed into horror.

"Come in," she said before opening the door wide and then leading the way. Once they stood in the store, her hand moved to her mouth. "What, is it Reese?"

She clearly hadn't known that the body was found, and now Tara would have to break the news to her.

Tara nodded. "Her body was found on the beach this morning."

The woman gasped, closing her eyes tight.

"Did you know Reese well?" Tara questioned.

The woman looked up at her as she steadied herself. She nodded. "I'm the manager here. I've worked with Reese for the past year." She turned to the counter behind her, staring at it longingly. "She was such a sweet girl," she added before bringing her hand to her mouth again in utter horror. She shook her head again, this time in disbelief. "Did you find who did it?"

"Not yet, that's why we're here."

The woman heaved another sigh.

Tara reminded her that Reese went missing after leaving work, and the woman nodded. She had already been informed when the cops first came in after Reese first went missing.

"Did she happen to mention where she was going? Did she mention anyone?" Tara asked.

The woman shook her head again, her eyes falling to the floor as she tried to recall. "No, I already told the police this, though." She looked back up, meeting Tara's eyes. "It was late when she left. She said she was just going home, and I believed it." She paused for a moment. "She has really strict parents, you know."

The woman's words only confirmed Tara's suspicion, but based on her impression, Tara was starting to think that maybe Reese was as obedient as her parents believed.

She asked a few more questions: if she was aware that Reese had a boyfriend, if Reese ever seemed frightened by anyone, if she could think of anyone who would want to harm her. But each time, the woman would just shake her head.

Warren looked at Tara. He could feel defeat surfacing.

"What time did Reese finish her shift?" he finally asked.

She thought for a moment. "I think she left here about eight thirty. The store closed at eight—so yes, she would've been out of here by eight thirty."

Tara and Warren met eyes. Her parents had said ten. Why would she give her parents that time? She was seeing someone. Tara was sure of it.

"Had anyone ever come in here to visit Reese? Anyone who may have been a bit flirtatious?" Tara asked.

The woman chuckled a bit at her question, and then her face fell again at the remembrance that Reese was no longer alive, that the memory was now only that.

"There's Brian," she started, pain tainting her expression. "He's a lifeguard at Rehoboth. He lives around here, though. A couple years older than Reese. He comes in here every day, and he definitely had some sort of crush on her. I think he came in just to see her because he always seemed to come in when she was working. I always thought they would be cute together—but you know, her parents would never allow it."

"And what did Reese do?"

The woman shrugged. "She'd flirt back. She definitely had something for him too, but she was quiet about it. I think they did exchange numbers at one point."

"When was that?"

"A couple months ago, I'd say."

Tara looked toward Warren, and she could see the urgency in his eyes. They clearly both had the same thought. *Could Reese and the lifeguard have had a secret relationship? Did she lie to her parents about when her shift ended so she could meet him?*

"Do you know where we can find him?" Tara asked.

The woman turned to a clock behind her and then nodded. "He's probably at Rehoboth Beach by now. The lifeguards have been working on cleaning up the area."

Tara thanked her, and she and Warren were soon out the door, now with a lead and a newfound purpose in their step.

***

Tara and Warren pulled up along the boardwalk and stepped out into the sandy road. A row of businesses lined the long wooden pathway, creating a barrier between them and the beach behind.

Tara and Warren walked up the stairs and briskly down the boardwalk, scanning the beach below it for any sign of lifeguards. It was early still, the beach and boardwalk were still in need of minor repairs, and the businesses were still closed. The beach was closed too. They were the only people walking about, but every once in a while, a jogger would breeze past them.

"There," Warren said sharply.

Tara looked out onto the beach, and just a few yards in front of them, she could see people in red shorts moving about. They were the lifeguards.

Tara and Warren were soon on the beach as well, moving toward them. Their presence was quickly noticed, and one of the lifeguards looked up and said something to the others that Tara couldn't hear from afar.

Tara knew she and Warren looked as if they didn't belong on the beach. Both in long pants and boots, they clearly weren't dressed for a day under the sun.

The lifeguards looked a bit confused as they got closer. There were five of them, all exceptionally fit teenagers. Two girls and three boys.

"Is one of you Brian?" Tara asked as soon as she was within earshot.

The row of red shorts parted and looked toward a boy in the center. He stepped forward. He was shirtless, his skin bronzed. He had broad shoulders and a perfectly chiseled triangle-shaped upper body, but a sling hung across his chest, holding a casted arm. He confirmed that he was in fact Brian, but he looked startled by the question. Tara realized how odd this must be to him, being approached by intimidating strangers on a beach with no one around. It had probably never happened to him before.

"Are you friends with Reese Tanner?" Tara questioned. She flashed her badge, dissolving any confusion.

His face fell. His bronze skin became flushed in the cheeks. The other lifeguards looked at him and then turned away, moving farther from him. It was as if they knew he would need privacy, that they all sensed something horrible was about to be said.

"Yes," he confirmed. "Is she all right? I've been trying to get ahold of her...I," he stopped himself. He could sense it; nothing was all right. "What happened?" he asked as he stood up straighter, like a trained dog waiting to be told who to attack.

Tara knew instantly that he didn't know, that she would ultimately have to break the news to him. It pained her. He looked sincere in his worry, and she had a feeling that he truly did care for Reese.

Tara sighed. "I'm sorry to have to tell you this," she started. His eyes began to glisten slightly, but then he breathed deeply, holding back the tears. "Her body was found this morning, on Dewey Beach."

He looked around him. He looked as if he might lose his balance, as if he were looking for something to steady himself. The other lifeguards were still listening. They were picking up branches, but at Tara's words they all looked up and then toward each other. Terror flooded their eyes.

"Oh my god," said one, a petite young woman with a rock-solid build. She came scurrying over.

The others followed until they stood just behind Brian. One of the guys, slightly older-looking, placed a hand on Brian's shoulder.

"You're sure?" Brian finally uttered, his tanned face now looking slightly faded from the shock.

Tara nodded. "I'm sorry." She let it sink in for moment. They all looked around at each other in disbelief. "Were you two dating?" Tara finally asked.

Brian stared off into the distance as he scrunched his face in confusion, still trying to make sense of it all. He then looked back toward Tara.

"Yeah, kind of. I guess you can call it that."

"How do you mean?" she asked. It seemed like such a clear-cut question.

"I definitely had feelings for her is what I'm saying," he said. "But her parents would've never allowed her to date me, since I'm nineteen and she's seventeen. We just spoke a lot, really, on the phone, through text. And then we'd meet on the beach sometimes at night, before she had to be home."

"When did you speak to her last?" Tara had remembered what he said in the beginning, that he had been trying to get in touch with her. "You said you've been trying to get a hold of her?"

He nodded. "For about a week and a half, I'd say. She was supposed to meet me that night and never showed. I figured her parents were on to us or something." He shrugged. "Thought maybe she was trying to cut it off."

"You didn't stop by the coffee shop at all after?"

He shook his head. "If her parents were on to us, I didn't want to cause more trouble. I figured she'd reach out to me when she was ready. But I sent one of my buddies over, just to see if she'd say anything to him. You know, if it was over, I just wanted to know." He sighed. "And then I found out she was missing. I just figured she ran away or something, to get away from her parents. I never would've thought—" He stopped abruptly, catching his breath. His friend patted his shoulder, rubbing it slightly.

"Do you remember the exact day you were supposed to meet?" Tara asked.

"It was—" He thought for a moment. "Last Tuesday," he finally said, nodding with certainty.

Tara and Warren shared a look. It was now Wednesday of the following week. The victim had gone missing eight days ago, which would mean he had planned to meet her on the night she went missing.

"And you spoke to her that day?" Warren butted in.

He nodded. "In the morning. Everything seemed good. She was ready to meet me. But then I got held up at home; my mom needed me to watch my brother for an hour. I tried to text her, since she would've already been on her way, but she never answered. And then when I finally was able to get to the beach, she wasn't there."

Tara knew he would be a prime suspect, but if his story checked out, he would have an alibi. Her eyes moved to his arm. "What happened to your arm?"

He looked down at it and sighed. "Fell off a roof. I do roofing for my uncle when I'm not lifeguarding. He owns a company. I broke my forearm…had to get surgery."

"When did that happen?"

He thought for a moment. "It happened last Monday. I went into surgery on Tuesday."

If his story checked out, that would ultimately rule him out as a suspect. Tara and Warren both continued to ask him a series of questions—if she ever seemed afraid, if she ever mentioned anyone. But each answer led nowhere.

"Where were you guys planning on meeting, exactly?"

"On Dewey Beach," he replied. "We meet by an entrance to the beach."

He explained the route. Reese would walk about a half mile down the road, and then she would take a turn by a gas station—Mobile, he said—and then walk straight to an entrance of the beach.

Tara felt a rush of excitement. They could trace her steps. They could possibly find where she was abducted. The gas station. There would be cameras.

Tara thanked him, and once she and Warren were far enough away, he turned toward her.

"Let's make sure his story checks out. And then you thinkin' what I'm thinkin'?

Tara nodded. "Cameras."

They now had a solid lead.

Chapter Nine

Tara and Warren pulled up to the gas station. It was the only one along the road Brian had said Reese walked to meet him. It had to be it; they were both sure of it. They had already gotten a hold of Brian's medical records. He had in fact had surgery two days before Reese went missing. It was enough to rule him out. They both knew it would be too difficult to strangle an individual with an object with only one hand.

They pulled into the lot. It was a large gas station, and cars waited in line for the pump.

"There has to be cameras here," Warren said as they walked toward the gas station store and scanned the area around them. "Ah-ha!" he blurted with satisfaction.

Tara followed his gaze. Just under the awning, above the line of impatient cars, hung a white, round object with black eye-like center—a camera. Another one sat at the other corner. Both faced the road they had just driven on that Reese supposedly walked.

"Let's hope it tells us something," Tara replied.

Warren shrugged. "One can hope."

They both knew that the cameras would only show them a small fraction of the length in which the victim walked. She either reached the gas station, or she didn't. And it was highly unlikely that she was abducted right in front of it. That would be too obvious. But it could help them narrow the area in which she was taken.

Tara and Warren were soon inside. A younger man stood behind the counter, speaking with a customer as he rung him up. He had a piercing in his eyebrow and one in his lip. As he spoke, the metal piercings would move slightly, catching the light coming through the window next to him. He handed the customer a pack of cigarettes, and Tara and Warren stepped forward.

It didn't take long for Tara to explain who they were. At the show of her badge, the young man's eyes flashed with fearful surprise. But at the mention of the cameras, he understood why they were there. After he called his boss to confirm that he could go ahead and show them, they were soon in the back room of the store, looking down at the computer screen.

Warren sat in a chair, rewinding the footage until the day Reese went missing, and then fast-forwarded slowly. They looked for anyone unusual at first. They studied every individual that crossed the camera, but no one sparked their interest. They were all people doing ordinary things—getting gas, parents riding by on their bikes with their kids. Warren then fast-forwarded slowly into the night. The influx of cars into the gas station slowed, the people walking or riding bikes to and from the beach came to a halt. And then—

"There!" Warren burst out, sending a jolt through the room and through Tara. He paused the video, rewinding slightly, and then paused it again. He moved closer to the screen, squinting.

Tara hovered over Warren's shoulder. She could see it too. Upon the street, coming in and out of shadows, was Reese Tanner, wearing her ripped blue jean shorts, her black top, and white Converse sneakers. She walked briskly and was soon out of view of the camera.

Warren swiveled in the chair. "Well, we now know she made it past here."

Tara agreed. They did, and it narrowed the area down quite a bit. It was about a quarter mile, Tara estimated, from where they stood to the beach. Now they knew she went missing somewhere along that route. *But where?* Beyond the gas station was just a strip of homes. They had no other stores to enter to study the surveillance. And Tara thought it was unlikely they would see anything of substance if there were. She had a strange feeling that sat heavy in her gut that the killer perfectly planned this, and then she had a thought...

"I think we should walk the rest of the way to the beach."

She knew it would be the only way to retrace Reese's steps, and maybe she or the killer left something behind.

***

Tara and Warren walked slowly along the road, scanning the ground. They searched for anything, any sign of Reese being abducted, but so far they had walked a quarter mile without anything to show for it.

There was still an awkwardness between them. They had spoken only of the case, but Tara wanted to break the ice. After combing through some brush on the side of the road, she spoke.

"So did you and Dr. Harris date or something?" She knew he would ask, if it were the other way around.

Warren sighed and let out a slight chuckle, as if he knew the question was coming. It made Tara feel more at ease. "How'd you know?"

"Intuition, I guess."

Warren nodded. "I wouldn't call it dating; it was just a date."

They continued toward the beach, still inspecting the ground. A woman on a beachcomber bike came up behind them, and they stepped aside as she passed.

"I guess it didn't go well?" Tara asked over a gust of wind that tried to silence her.

He shook his head. "She's a nice person. I just can't do it."

"Do what?"

"Date."

Tara nodded with slight hesitation, as if she understood, even though she didn't.

Warren studied her, the sun hitting his eyes, causing him to squint in an almost skeptical way. "No one ever told you, did they?"

"Told me what?"

"About my wife." He looked down at the ground as he winced. "And my daughter," he added.

Tara only knew that Warren once had a wife. She had figured he was just divorced. She had no clue about a daughter, and since she was still so new to the FBI, she was just beginning to get to know others in her department. If there was gossip, it was not something that had come up yet.

"No," she replied. She felt a sudden tug on her heart at the sight of him. He could barely look up. It was evident it was a painful topic for him for whatever reason. "You don't have to tell me, if you don't want."

He waved a hand as if telling her not to be silly. He straightened up, sucking in any emotion from his exterior. "No, it's fine," he started. "I forget how new you are sometimes." His face twinged at his words, but then he sighed and continued. "I lost my wife and daughter five years ago. Car accident." He continued to scan the ground, still focused on their mission, as if to distract himself from what he just revealed.

No words could form on Tara's lips. She had no idea, and yet she had spent so much time with him. Her heart ached for him. "I'm so sor—"

"Don't," he cut her off. "I know you are."

Tara nodded, directing her attention back to the ground. She didn't know what more to say.

"She would've been eighteen last week, actually, my daughter," he muttered under his breath with a shake of the head. "That's always a hard one."

Tara understood far deeper than she'd like. Every holiday, every birthday, every new milestone. They all felt empty when she lost her mother. "I know," she replied.

Warren finally lifted his head, placing his hand on her back, rubbing it slightly like a father would.

"I know you do," he replied before pulling his hand back and abruptly shifting the moment. "And so that's why I can't date. Too early. I just still feel married," he added to bring it to a slightly lighter subject. He then looked at her and smiled. "You'll understand one day. When's that guy going to pop the question anyway?" He chuckled slightly.

Tara shrugged. "We shall see." But she knew perfectly well that it might happen soon.

"How's his music going, by the way?"

It was clear that Warren was trying to move their conversation to something lighter. Music was something Warren enjoyed as well. He was a Beatles fan and a guitar enthusiast. He wasn't great at playing, he had admitted, but in his spare time—the little he had—he liked to collect them. Tara had learned that he owned a few Gibsons, a couple Ibanezes, and a Stratocaster that he had signed by Eric Clapton in the seventies. The fact that John was in a classic rock band was something they had bonded over during their car rides. Tara didn't know too much about music, but she did appreciate it, and it was something they had somewhat in common that filled the silence.

"It's good. Keeping him busy," she replied.

But they both knew now wasn't the time to discuss music. They continued their walk, tracing the steps of Reese Tanner. They still had yet to find anything, and Tara thought that odd. No sign of struggle, but they knew it was the path Reese had taken. Homes lined the streets, yet no one heard anything. When they finally reached the path to the beach, they stopped. A wave of disappointment hit them. They knew they were starting from ground zero again. Their lead had led them nowhere. They decided to continue their walk onto the beach, but after walking about a quarter mile, they stopped and turned to each other. They both knew they had reached a dead end.

"It's odd," Tara admitted. "No sign of struggle, and no one heard anything."

Warren nodded. "It's almost as if whoever took her, she went willingly."

Tara agreed. *Could it be possible that the victim knew the killer?* The thought danced in her head. She posed the theory to Warren.

"Possibly," he admitted, but they both knew they had already interviewed her family. They had already gone to her place of work. They already ruled out her secret boyfriend. So, even though they suspected she might have known the killer, they still did not have a suspect. Or did they rule out Brian too soon?

"Could Brian have killed her with one hand?" Tara questioned. After all, Brian was clearly strong. He had an athletic build. He was tall. Could it be possible that even with one hand, he was still able to overpower the victim? Tara asked the question to Warren, who stood pondering a moment. He looked down at his watch.

"Well, let's go see what the medical examiner has to say."

He was right. It had now been a few hours since they brought the body in. Most likely they would have some more information at this point. Tara agreed, and they turned back toward the car, hoping they were finally walking in the direction of answers.

Chapter Ten

Tara and Warren pulled into the parking lot of the medical examiner's office and were surprised to see a swarm of reporters waiting by the entrance. They all stared at the unmarked vehicle until it was out of view behind the building, and Tara knew they would now be fully prepared to pounce on them with questions.

After looking briefly for an unlocked back entrance and failing to find one, Tara and Warren knew it was inevitable that they would have to part the sea of hungry reporters.

As they came around the corner, the news crews were already staring in their direction, eagerly waiting. Tara accidentally locked eyes with a tall, handsome-looking local reporter with perfectly slicked-back brown hair, and within a split second he had a microphone in her face.

"Do you have any suspects?"

His question caused the others to flock around her like vultures, and she was soon unable to see beyond them.

"What do you have to say to the people of Dewey Beach?" another female reporter shouted through the chaos.

"It's too early for comment," Tara replied. "We're following all leads."

She felt Warren's hand upon her back as he led her forward, while asking the reporters to step aside, and they were soon safe within the building.

"Thank you," Tara said as the feeling of claustrophobia subsided. She knew this case would be big, but she somehow forgot just how overwhelming the media could be, and she was thankful to have Warren.

They made their way to the medical examiner's room and were soon met by Fredrick Burns. He was bald except for white hair that lined the sides of his head. They had already spoken to him on the way. He confirmed that he already examined the body, and he was now waiting for them to arrive.

When they knocked, he peered through his thick spectacles at the small, square window in the door, and he hurried over. He greeted them by name.

"I'll give you the rundown," he said as he made his way to an autopsy table centered in the room. Upon it lay a body bag shaped in human form.

He grabbed a set of latex gloves and unzipped the bag. Reese Tanner's body was quickly on full display. She looked the same as she had that morning. He lifted one of her hands.

"First of all, she had ligature marks on her ankles and wrists," he said. This was not new knowledge, since they had already distinguished that at the crime scene. "But it seems to me that given the extent of bruising, she was tied up for quite a while—hours, even."

"So you're saying that she wasn't killed right away?" Tara asked.

The medical examiner shook his head. "Doesn't look like it," he confirmed. "It's a bit hard to know for certain, since the body has already started decomposing, but it seems to me that the ligatures had even been changed a couple times." He pointed to another rope-like pattern on her arm. "This one's a bit thicker. It looks like the killer used something else to tie her, but it's a bit less bruised, which means it might be older."

"Any sign of struggle from when she was abducted?" Warren asked.

The medical examiner pursed his lips and shook his head again. "That's the strange part. I don't see any sign of blunt trauma. No sign of struggle. My guess is she went willingly."

It confirmed what Warren and Tara already assumed, that she knew her abductor.

"Cause of death was strangulation," he continued. "Looks like the killer used something thin, like a shoestring."

"Any chance someone with one broken arm could've strangled her?" Tara asked.

"I'd say that's very unlikely," the medical examiner confirmed. "Her hyoid bone was fractured; it's a bone in her neck. You'd need a lot of force for that, and unless you're the Hulk, it'd be next to impossible to do that with one arm."

It was the same injury that Dr. Harris noted in Alyssa White's skeleton.

"But mainly what I wanted to show you is this." He held up her hand. It was already starting to decompose, but her nails were still intact. As Tara leaned in, she could see the jagged lines where some of her nails had been broken. "It looks as if toward the end she tried to claw her attacker, but oddly, her fingernails were completely clean. No DNA underneath."

Tara and Warren shared a glance. They knew what that meant—that the case was going to be even harder than they expected.

"This killer knows what he's doing," he added. "I couldn't find any fibers, any DNA, or fingerprints." He then turned to Tara and Warren. "I'd almost say this killer has done quite a bit of research or knows crime firsthand."

"Any sign of sexual assault?" Warren asked.

Again the medical examiner shook his head. "Doesn't seem sexually motivated."

Tara and Warren thanked him and soon stepped outside the room. They now knew that the killer might have some knowledge of crime and forensic procedures. They had confirmation that the victim most likely knew the killer. Now they knew why no one on the street had heard anything. The victim was most likely taken willingly and then killed later at another location. And now they knew for certain that it wasn't sexually motivated. All these details made the case suddenly much more complicated, and it gave Tara an uneasy feeling.

"Maybe we should get a hold of the Whites?" Tara suggested. If Reese knew her attacker, it was likely that Alyssa did too. They would just have to find out someone they had in common.

"My thoughts as well," Warren admitted, and they were soon headed to the car.

***

The phone rang on the table in front of them as they anxiously waited for someone to pick up. Tara and Warren sat alone in a room of the police station. It was quiet except for the ringing echoing off the walls and the voices of police officers each time one walked past their door.

They had been given Alyssa White's mother's phone number. The family had moved, they were told, from the shores of New Jersey to a town inland in Connecticut. Tara could only assume that living in the home where their daughter had once lived became unbearable.

The phone had rung five times already, and hope began to slip from Tara's mind. They needed Alyssa's family to answer. If not, then they would officially be at a dead end. But just when Tara was sure it would go to voicemail, a voice was heard.

"Hello?" It was a woman's voice, raspy and tired.

Tara looked at Warren. It did not sound like the voice of someone they would expect. From what they knew about Alyssa's family so far, they were wealthy socialites. Her father was the owner of a commercial real estate company and her mother was apparently a well-known local fitness instructor. However, this woman didn't sound like a fitness instructor at all. In fact, she sounded like someone who didn't take care of herself.

"Mrs. White?" Tara questioned, just to make sure.

She coughed into the phone. "Yes?"

Tara introduced herself, explaining who she and Warren were. "We were just hoping we could ask you a couple questions."

The woman remained silent for a moment, as if contemplating if she should, but then she agreed. "I suppose that's all right," she said. "But I already spoke to police when they told me they found my Alyssa." Her voice shook as she said her daughter's name, and she stopped to steady herself. "It just seems like I've been answering questions over and over again for a year, and still that psycho is out there." Anger swelled in her voice as she spoke louder with each word, and then ended with a coughing fit. "Sorry," she said when done. "I have bad asthma, and smoking cigarettes doesn't help."

Not only did it not help her asthma, but it sounded a bit suicidal to Tara. However, she also understood it was a reflection of this woman's pain, and smoking had been a bad habit to cope.

"Did your daughter ever speak of anyone when she was in Dewey Beach? Maybe a friend she made, or a boy she liked?"

The woman didn't hesitate. "No, and I already told the police this many times. There were a couple of girl friends from our hometown whose parents also owned houses there. She's hung out with them during past summers, but they weren't there that year. They were all getting ready to go off to college, as was Alyssa, but she loved Dewey Beach, and we promised her we would take her there before she left." Her voice trailed off at the end as the remembrance of momentary happiness pulled at her wound.

"You have a son, correct?" Tara asked. She remembered reading it in Alyssa's case file.

"Yes?"

"Did he ever bring anyone around your beach house?"

The woman let out an exasperated sigh. "No, my son has always been more into video games than people. Now, even more so, as you can imagine."

Tara knew what she meant. She had gone through it too. The people whispering in town as she walked by. The children asking questions at school. It was probably another reason why the Whites moved to a different town.

Tara continued to ask her more questions. If her daughter ever seemed afraid. If she could think of anyone who would want to harm her, but each question was met with a simple no and logical reasoning.

Tara shifted in her seat and shared a frustrated glance with Warren before throwing her head back in exasperation. She then leaned forward, focusing again on the phone.

"Was there a place your daughter liked to go to often when she was in Dewey Beach?"

The mother thought for a moment. "Nowhere in particular. Just the beach, I'd say." She then grew quiet, but Tara could sense that she was thinking some more. "Oh," she finally said. "We all used to go kayaking once in a while. She loved it. She actually got a summer job there the year before she went missing, but she never finished out the summer. She said she didn't like it. I was never quite sure why. I think she just wanted to spend time on the beach instead."

"Do you know the name of the place?"

She thought for a moment. "Ocean Paddle, it was called."

Tara asked her where, and she gave an address Tara recognized. It was near the coffee shop Reese worked at. Tara thanked her, and they hung up. She then turned to Warren.

"Let's call Reese's family, see if she has any connection to the shop," Warren suggested.

Moments later, Reese Tanner's mother was now on the call. She sounded tired, but at the mention of the shop, a bit of life sparked in her throat.

"Yes, I've heard of it. Reese worked there in the off-season last year, in the spring, before she got a job at the coffee shop. Why?" Tara could hear the suspicion in her voice, hoping that maybe they were on to something.

"Did you ever visit her at work? Did anyone ever seem off to you?"

"That's actually why she stopped working there," Mrs. Tanner replied. "The owner...he was always a bit creepy with Reese. He would always compliment her on what she was wearing, saying she looked good in it. He'd ask her if she had a boyfriend. He was older too, like in his thirties. It was just weird and concerning, and so Reese didn't work there very long."

Tara looked at Warren, and she knew she had the same look in her eyes that he did. He didn't blink, shock and anticipation reflecting in his stare. It was all the information they needed. They now had a lead. Both victims had worked at the same place. They had most likely interacted with the same creepy owner. It was probably why Alyssa wanted to stop working there. Tara quickly thanked Mrs. Tanner. They now knew were to head next. Tara only hoped that their destination held more answers.

Chapter Eleven

T he kayak shop sat at the edge of a bay. The water lay still and calm. A dock sat at the edge of the parking lot, jutting out atop the water, and boats sat in a rack next to it. It was now the afternoon, which Tara assumed would usually be a busy time for the shop, but today no one was around. The parking lot was empty, and Tara could only assume it was because of the storm. No one in their right mind would go kayaking today, nor would they be allowed to. She just hoped the owner would be there.

Tara's heart sank when they reached the door and saw a closed sign hanging in the window. *We'll have to track him down now*, she thought, *and find where he lives.* But just when the thought crossed her mind, she noticed a light on inside, and then she saw movement. Someone was by the counter.

She knocked, and the movement by the counter stopped. She heard footsteps, and soon a man emerged. His eyes were bloodshot, his hair a mess, his Ocean Paddle shop shirt ripped and tattered, with what looked like a cigarette burn by the pocket. He looked startled as he noticed them behind the glass front door. He opened it.

"We're closed," he mumbled. He reeked of marijuana. Even from a foot away, it trailed up Tara's nose in full force, but she didn't care to bring attention to it. She wanted to stay focused on why they came.

"We know," Tara replied before explaining who they were. She flashed her badge. "We were hoping you could provide us with some information on Alyssa White and Reese Tanner. They both worked here, correct?

His eyes shifted between her and Warren, stealthily. "Sure, what do you need to ask me?"

"Can we come in?"

He remained quiet a moment as he turned his head slightly, trying to look into the store without them noticing, as if making sure that it was indeed safe. "Sure," he finally said as he stepped into the shop, followed by Tara and Warren. A bottle of liquor sat on the counter, and he quickly went over to it, tucking it behind the counter where they couldn't see.

"We don't care if you're drinking. That's not a crime, you know," Warren said.

"I know...I..." he stuttered, as if cautiously choosing his words. "You're right," he finally said with an awkward laugh. "I don't know why I just did that." He took a seat on the chair behind the counter.

He was acting very odd, Tara noted. He was either guilty of the murders, or something else entirely, and she wasn't sure what a bottle of liquor had to do with it.

"It's a shame what happened to those girls," he added with a shake of the head. "I'm not sure how much help I can be, but I'll try."

The whole shop smelled even more of marijuana than him. It was clear what he had been doing, and she could see Warren's eyes wander around the room, trying to catch sign of anything else.

"How long did they work here?" Tara asked.

He leaned hunched over, peering at the ceiling, his lips pursed, thinking. "They both worked here only a couple of months. I think Alyssa was two summers ago." He nodded as he said it. "Yeah, that's right. The year before she went missing."

"And Reese?" Tara asked.

"She worked here in the spring, which is our off-season. April and May." He sighed. "Such a shame. They were such pretty girls."

It was an oddly creepy thing for him to say, given that he was nearly twice their age. It also irked Tara that their looks were the first thing he thought of as why their deaths were a shame, as if that reflected their value.

"We were told they quit because they felt uncomfortable here. Do you have any idea why that would be?"

He let out an awkward grunt and suddenly stood up, gripping the counter. He hesitated a moment and then responded. "No," he said. "I mean, like I said, they were pretty girls. Maybe they felt uncomfortable by the attention they got from customers." He shrugged.

His incessant mention of pretty girls only drove home why Reese thought he was creepy and why Alyssa probably quit. Tara looked toward Warren. She hadn't even noticed that he had moved closer to the entrance to a back room, next to the counter. The door wasn't fully ajar, but Tara could see from where she was standing that it was cracked slightly, with light shining through it into the room they stood in.

The shop owner's head shot in his direction. "Hey!" he yelled. "I didn't give you permission to go back there." His hands gripped the counter tighter.

"I haven't gone back there," Warren replied, still staring into the room. "Why, should I?"

The shop owner grew flustered, realizing he had just created suspicion. "I have a dog back there," he sneered uneasily. "He's uh…he's sleeping, but he's not very friendly."

It was clearly a lie, and Tara knew Warren saw it too. He nodded. Warren would need probable cause to enter the room, and there was certainly something back there that the shop owner didn't want them to see. Tara threw another question at him, helping to buy Warren more time.

"Where were you Wednesday night?" she asked. It was the night Reese went missing.

Redness seeped to the surface of his skin. Tara's questions were making him anxious. "Why?" he asked. "I was here."

"Did anyone else see you here?"

His nails were now digging into the wood. He thought for a moment, as if questioning what he should say. "I was alone," he finally responded.

He had no alibi. Reese had probably walked right by this shop on the way to the beach. He was looking increasingly suspicious.

Suddenly, Warren walked closer to the back room. "Can you tell me why you have chemist's beakers in a kayak shop?" he asked. The shop owner's face grew bright red. Warren stuck his nose in the air, trying to catch a scent he had picked up. Tara moved closer, and after focusing on picking up the scent, she soon smelled it too. Under the lingering smell of marijuana, a potent scent stung her nose. It smelled almost like cleaning products, like ammonia. Tara knew of only one drug that could potentially carry that odor: meth.

Warren walked into the room, while Tara stood by the door frame, keeping her eye on the owner.

"Looks like someone's been cooking meth back here," Warren said loudly.

The shop owner opened his mouth, but he was at a loss for words to defend himself. His face grew redder, and he had now certainly created marks in the wood counter with his nail-digging grip. He stood tense, his eyes shifting between Tara and the front door. He was about to run, she could feel it. But she didn't even have a second to react before...

He hurdled over the counter and took off, springing to the front door. Tara and Warren both whipped around as he flung the door open, fumbling for keys in his pocket. But before he even stepped outside, his foot hit the doorframe, and he went tumbling forward.

It didn't take long for Tara to be on top of him, cuffing him and leading him to the car. He was clearly high. His reactions were slowed, but Tara didn't suspect he was on meth. She knew enough about toxicology to know that he would be acting much differently.

Once he was placed in the car, Warren came out into the parking lot moments later. "Looks like a meth lab. I don't know if it was all the time, though. It wasn't a lot. My guess is he does it here when the shop is closed."

"Did you find anything else?" Tara asked. A meth lab was not what they were searching for.

"I went through everything," he replied. "All the drawers, all the shelving. I didn't find too much, but I did find these." He held out three pictures, and Tara took them. They were each pictures of one single girl. One was Reese, one was Alyssa, and the other she had never seen before. They each stood behind the counter, smiling at the camera. "Seems odd he would keep those," Warren added.

"Who's this?" Tara asked as she held up the picture of the third unknown girl.

Warren shook his head. "I don't know, but I think we should find out."

Tara nodded as they headed to the car. She had her doubts before these images, but now she wondered, could this third girl be next?

***

The shop owner sat in an interrogation room of the police station. They had already learned that his name was Timothy Morris. He had owned the shop for five years, after purchasing it from some guy who wanted to retire.

"And you cook meth out of it in your off time?" Tara questioned.

He winced. He wasn't going to reply, but they already knew the answer.

Tara slid the images found in his desk across the wooden table. "Can you tell me why you had these?"

He looked down at them, terror flashing in his eyes. "They're my employees," he replied. "I take pictures of everyone that works at the shop."

"And these are the only three employees you ever had?"

He opened his mouth to reply but then closed it again. He didn't know how to answer. He knew how bad this looked.

"Well?" Tara questioned impatiently.

He was staring at his hands, clasped in his lap, as he anxiously rubbed them together. He looked up. "I know this looks bad," he pleaded. "But what you're accusing me of..." He paused, looking between Tara and Warren "That's just crazy."

"We didn't accuse you of anything."

He shook his head strongly. "I'm not stupid. I know you're trying to pin those murders on me!" he yelled as he sat up straighter. "I just kept those photos, okay? That's no crime. But I'm not a murderer!" He settled back into his chair.

"Tell me again where you were Wednesday night?"

He sighed, closing his eyes a moment and then looking at Tara. "I was at the shop," he started, and then his eyes drifted off. "Doing what I was doing today."

Tara knew what that meant; he was cooking meth. But he had already stated that no one saw him there. No one knew where he was. She asked him again.

He looked tortured by the truth as he said it. "I was alone."

Warren butted in. "Do you have any cameras outside to show you were there?"

He perked up at the thought, realizing it might save him, but then he sat back farther in his chair in disappointment. "I have one looking out onto the boat dock, but I don't think you'd see my car from it. The

101

other broke a couple weeks ago. I haven't had the funds to get it fixed yet."

Tara sensed he was telling the truth. It was the slight hope at the realization of the cameras, and then the way hope flew away from his eyes when he knew they wouldn't see him in them. If he was lying, then his reaction would be the total opposite of what he just showed. Anyone who was guilty would not hope that cameras caught him in the act.

"Do you remember where you were the day Alyssa went missing?" She reiterated the date.

He stared hard in the distance, his lip curling in deep thought. It was over a year ago, but Tara knew he had to have remembered. It was all over on every news station. Even Tara knew about it, and she was certain that anyone who knew the victim would remember exactly where they were when they heard the news. A sudden thought seemed to strike him. "I was away," he replied excitedly, knowing it could be his saving grace. "In Florida, visiting my mom."

They would have to check his alibi, but if it was true, it could be solid. However, he still didn't have an alibi for Reese.

Tara slid the image of the third unknown girl across the table. "Who is she?"

He stared down at the picture. "That's Lucy. She worked for me a while ago. Around the same time of Alyssa."

"Did they work together?"

He thought a second, looking off into the distance. "Yeah, they did, actually. Not long, I think, only a few weeks. Alyssa stopped working there soon after Lucy started."

His words only confirmed further in Tara's mind that he was just a creep who took photos of young girls that worked in his shop. She now didn't think that Lucy was going to be the third victim. It didn't work in the timeline. Why would he target her now, all of a sudden, two years later? It was unlikely.

However, Tara hoped that maybe Lucy held some information. She knew Alyssa, and she worked with her, even if it was a short time.

"How can we find her?" Tara asked.

"I think I still have her number," he replied.

Tara gave him his cell phone, and he scrolled through it before bringing up Lucy's number. Tara wrote it down. She hoped that Lucy might be able to tell them something, and once it was in her phone, she turned to the door, ready to make the call.

***

Tara and Warren stood outside the interrogation room. A police officer had just removed Timothy Morris from the room they were just in and was now escorting him down the hall to a holding cell. Tara and Warren moved into an office nearby.

"What do you think?" Warren asked.

She could already hear the skepticism in Warren's voice. She knew him well enough now to understand that when Warren asked that question, he had his own doubts too. Tara was doubtful Timothy was who they were looking for. He was certainly a creep, but the way he reacted at the mention of cameras did not coincide with someone who was guilty. There was also one thing in Tara's mind that she continued to question: his motive. There was no sign of sexual assault on Reese's body, and she couldn't see any reason why Timothy would kill if it weren't sexual.

"I have my doubts," she finally admitted.

Warren nodded as he pulled a chair from a round table in the corner of the office and took a seat. Tara sat down as well.

"Me too," he said. "The cameras, right? He seemed hopeful when he thought they might've caught him."

"Exactly, and I'm not sure what his motive would've been."

Warren nodded again. "Let's call that girl, see if she knows anything."

Tara placed her phone on the table. Her name and phone number were still showing across the screen. She pressed the call button and put the phone on speaker, centering it in the middle of the table.

The girl picked up almost immediately. It sounded as if she was just laughing at something. Her laugh trailed off as she said hello. There was a lot of background noise, as if she were at a party.

"Is this Lucy?" Tara asked.

The girl was quiet a moment as the background noise became less apparent. It was clear she was stepping out of the room. Eventually, nothing could be heard at all except her voice.

"Who's asking?"

Tara realized it was probably a rare occurrence for a teenage girl to have an unknown adult call her cell phone. She introduced herself and Warren.

"Is this about those bodies on the beach?" she responded quickly. "You found Alyssa, right?"

"We did. Did you know her well?" Tara already partially knew the answer, but she wanted to see if their familiarity extended beyond the kayak shop.

"I worked with her one summer, at Ocean Paddle. Only a couple of weeks, though. She was cool. We got along pretty well, but I didn't know her too well—only those few weeks."

"Did she tell you why she stopped working?"

The girl was quiet a moment, thinking, and then chuckled slightly. "Yeah, I remember. I think the owner made her feel a bit uncomfortable. He was a little creepy. He'd always tell her how pretty she looked, things like that. He did the same shit to me." She grew quiet again, realizing she just let a curse slip out. "Sorry," she added awkwardly.

Tara brushed it off. Only a teenager would apologize for saying that. "Did he ever do anything to either of you? Did he ever act on his impulses?"

"No, absolutely not," she interjected. "He was a bit creepy, but he definitely never touched either of us or anything like that. Plus, I was always there when Alyssa was there. I'm pretty certain she was never alone with him."

They still couldn't completely rule him out, but Tara was becoming even more certain that he wasn't who they were looking for.

"Do you know Reese Tanner?" Tara asked.

"I've heard of her because of the news and everything. I never met her, though. I live a couple towns over from Dewey Beach, so we didn't go to the same school or anything."

"Did you know she worked at Ocean Paddle for a bit too?"

The girl grew silent again. "No, I didn't," she responded. "I stopped working there about a month after Alyssa."

It was certain Lucy would never have met Reese. Reese started working there about two years after Lucy stopped. And Lucy also wouldn't have been working there while Alyssa went missing. Tara was hoping she could at least have been an alibi for the owner's whereabouts the day Alyssa went missing.

"Were you aware of the owner doing anything illegal?" Tara finally asked.

"Uh, no, why?"

Tara didn't go into details. She asked if she was ever aware of anything going on in the room Tara and Warren had discovered earlier, but the girl only confirmed that the door was usually locked.

Tara thanked her, and the phone call soon ended. She looked toward Warren.

"Let's get one of the cops to check his alibi for the night Alyssa White went missing." He looked at his watch, and Tara looked down at her phone as well. It was now around seven o'clock, and they now didn't have a lead. Warren sighed. "I say we head back to the headquarters and brainstorm a bit." Tara agreed; they would have more access to information in the databases of the J. Edgar Hoover Building.

But Warren's suggestion only made it clearer that he had his doubts as well. And if both their intuitions were right, then whoever killed Alyssa and Reese was still out there.

Chapter Twelve

H e sat in his car, parked on a dead end, staring out onto the road he faced. He would see her soon, walking past. She had a flat tire on her bicycle; he had made sure of it when he walked past it unattended and slashed the tire when no one was around. He had seen her earlier as he drove past, as she fumbled with the tire before realizing she would have to walk the rest of her way home. He hoped she would take this short cut. He knew where she lived, after all. He had been watching her for a few days now, and tonight was the perfect opportunity. There were no houses on the street. Barely anyone drove by at this time of night. Only the crash of the waves could be heard and the rustle of leaves at each passing gust of wind.

No one had seen him. No one would see her.

He waited, his heart pounding, pulsing adrenaline through his veins. Any moment, she would stroll by. Any moment, he would pull out onto the road she walked. He would get to speak with her for the first time. He would lure her. And then he'd have her, and then news would soon break, the exact story he wanted to create.

He stared at the clock, trying to contain himself, trying to make his heart steady. He had to focus on something, and then his eyes moved to the passenger seat. He had forgotten he had the local newspaper, with Reese on the front page. He quickly stuffed it into his glove box.

As he lifted his head again just over the dashboard, he heard movement, and his eyes darted in front of him. She was there, strolling by, with a look of defeat plastered on her face. Her flip-flops slapped the ground at each step. She pushed her bike ahead as the unruly back wheel flopped, trying to veer off-course.

He waited a few moments, letting her pass, just so she wouldn't see him pull out. He would pretend he was just driving by and saw her, and then he would offer her a ride.

Once he knew she was a good distance ahead, he turned the key in the ignition. He turned his headlights on and then slowly pulled out.

As he approached, she noticed the headlights first. Without looking behind her, she stepped farther to the side of the road, pulling her bike closer to her. But then he slowed down, and her head turned toward the car. It was dusk, and her freckled face was spotlighted by the headlights. She squinted. Pieces of her short black hair hung around her face, too short to be held in her high ponytail.

He rolled down the window. "You all right?"

The girl stopped walking as she peered into the car. He could see a familiarity play on her face, but she wasn't sure—it was too dark to see. "Yeah, just a flat."

"You need a ride? It's probably not the smartest to be out here alone right now."

He could see her contemplating his gesture. What he mentioned had clearly crossed her mind as well. After all, a young girl had just been murdered. She peered into the car again, and then her face lit up. "Aren't you—"

He nodded with a warm smile. He knew it was all he needed for her to trust him, and he was right.

"You think you can fit this?" she asked, looking down at her bike.

He reassured her he had room in his trunk, and after he pulled over, helped her take the wheels off, and placed the bike in his trunk, she soon sat beside him. She explained where she lived, and he began to head there, making her feel comfortable at first.

But then he made another turn.

"You're going the wrong way," she said.

But he only stared at the road in silence as he locked the doors.

Chapter Thirteen

Tara stared down at the case files splayed across the table. She felt like she had been staring at them for hours. It was now ten thirty in the evening. They had arrived at the headquarters an hour ago and had been trying to come up with theories since their arrival, but so far they had made little progress.

"It has to be someone with knowledge of forensics," Tara said as she stared down at Reese's forensics report. It was something they had already mentioned, but Tara had a strong feeling that the theory was true, and she couldn't ignore it. *But who?* She couldn't get the thought out of her head, nor did she want to until an answer was found.

The killer was careful enough not to leave DNA behind. He had cleaned the victim's fingernails. He had strangled her, strategically, with something he knew wouldn't trace easily back to him. He was aware of cameras and made sure he wasn't seen by the gas station. And Tara was sure he used gloves.

"Maybe law enforcement?" she questioned.

Warren sat beside her, his arm resting on the table with his hand on his forehead as he stared over Alyssa's report. "It's crossed my mind too," he replied, his eyes not moving from the folder in front of him. "That could also explain why no one heard them get abducted." He then looked up, his eyes moving to Tara. "Like we said before, it seems the victims may have gone willingly. If the killer's a respected cop, that could be why."

Tara nodded. A cop as the killer could explain a lot. It could even be someone who worked close on the case. She got up out of her chair, moving to a computer on the other side of the room. She wanted to run background checks on the sheriff and detective they had interacted with earlier. If she was right, the killer might have had an incident in the past that may not have seemed too alarming. Maybe an angry outburst or even a suspension.

She told Warren what she was doing, and he pulled a chair closer. They looked up Sheriff Patel first. He had been in law enforcement for twenty years. He had no record, only gleaming reviews. They then looked up Detective Wade. He had been with the department for a much shorter time, only ten years, but so far there was nothing on his background check that seemed alarming.

Tara sighed. "I think we should get a list of all cops in the area and get a background check."

Warren agreed. "We can't ask the cops to do it. Maybe Grace?"

Grace was the secretary in their division. She was usually in the office late, and Tara was certain she was probably still in the building. They had passed her on the way in. Tara agreed, and Warren was soon out of his chair, in the doorway, calling to her. Her desk was not far from the office they stood in. She hurried over. She wore a pair of thick-rimmed glasses, her hair in a short bob framing her face. Her eyes looked red and tired, and Tara suddenly felt bad about adding something more to her plate, but they needed it. Warren explained the task.

"Yeah, I can do that," she agreed without hesitation. She had her bags already strapped over her shoulder. She was clearly heading out. "It just might take me until midmorning to get back to you."

"That's fine," Warren replied. They both thanked her, and she hurried back to her desk.

Tara's phone beeped in front of her. She looked down. It was a text from John.

Late night?

Tara looked at the time; it was now almost eleven.

Warren looked up at the clock as well. "I say we call it a night. There's not much more we can do tonight."

Tara agreed, but there was one thought that kept returning to her mind—the motive. *Why would a cop want to kill innocent girls?* She had her own conclusions, but she wanted to see what Warren thought. She turned and asked him.

Warren leaned back in his chair. "I think they'd want to see how much they can get away with. Young girls getting murdered stirs quite the circus. It could all be a game."

Tara agreed; it was her exact conclusion.

***

Tara entered her apartment and was immediately met by John. She had called him on the way home to let him know she was on her way, and now he was in the kitchen pouring a kettle that had just boiled.

"How was your day?" he asked. He placed a plate of food in the microwave

Tara tossed her bag on a table next to the door and then sank onto a barstool, letting out an exhausted sigh. "Tiring," she admitted. She didn't want to go into detail. It pained her that the killer could still be at large, and speaking about it to John would only dig at the wound more.

"How was yours?" she asked, trying to remove the attention from herself.

He shrugged. "Not too bad," he replied as he pulled the plate out the microwave and walked over to give Tara a kiss. He placed a plate of leftover lasagna in front of her. "I figured you'd be hungry."

He took a seat next to her as Tara began to eat. "Since you were getting home late, I decided to go practice with the band after work," he continued. "We got our first gig in two days." He smiled proudly. "Playing some Rush covers."

"That's awesome!" Tara replied excitedly. She was happy for him. Not only was he a huge Rush fan and idolized Neil Peart, but for the first time John seemed to be enjoying his life fully, and she completely supported it. She asked where they were playing.

"Right in town," he replied before naming a local bar. "I really hope you can make it," he added as he stood up to grab the tea that had now finished brewing. He slid a cup across the island counter to Tara "I think it'll be good for you, too, to have a little fun."

It had been a long time since Tara stepped into a bar, and she had to admit a couple drinks and a little fun did sound like it might be good for her. She had been so preoccupied with her job and her past that she had almost forgotten what it was like to let loose and enjoy herself. Plus, she wanted to support John. It was his first gig, and she certainly wanted to be there for him. But she also knew that she couldn't promise anything, especially while in the middle of a case. "I will try my best. I really do want to be there," she replied.

John nodded before giving her another peck on the cheek. He forced a smile as his attention moved back to the cup of tea in his hand, but Tara could still see the disappointment hiding behind it, and it pained her.

In the corner of Tara's eye, a blinking light suddenly caught her attention. She looked up. It was the answering machine of their home phone, signaling they had a message. It was unusual for anyone to call on that phone. They had even contemplated getting rid of it, since they never even used it and it just seemed to attract telemarketers, but John's parents still liked to call on it sometimes.

Tara stood up, moving toward the machine. "Did your parents call?" she asked as her hand hovered over the play button.

"Not that I know of," he replied.

It was probably a telemarketer. She rolled her eyes as she pressed the play button. But once she heard the voice, she stiffened. Her face grew hot, and John stopped eating.

"Hey, Tara, it's me," it began. It was the voice of her father. He sounded rushed, speaking quickly. "It was nice seeing you the other day, but I really don't think you should come back." There was pain in his voice as he said it. "I'm sorry," he added. "I just think it's best for both of us."

Tara didn't move for a moment. Shock and confusion swirled into a haze of questions. Why would he want her to stay away? Her whole life, he had been trying to reach out to her, and now she had, and he didn't want anything to do with her. But she already knew why. It had to be the same reason he cut her visit short. It had to be the questions she asked, the mention of someone else in the room. She spun around to John, who sat, fork in hand, his mouth hanging slightly open in disbelief.

"He's hiding something," Tara said. "Ever since I mentioned the person in the room, his whole attitude toward me changed. He does want to see me. I can hear it in his voice. He's protecting someone."

John nodded. He didn't know what to say, and it occurred to Tara that it was the first time he had even heard her father's voice. It must've been strange.

"It's just so weird," he replied. "Why would he be protecting someone?"

It was the same question that continuously crossed Tara's mind. She had come to the conclusion that if he was protecting someone, it was someone he cared for deeply, or it was someone who held something over his head. But Tara knew the second scenario was less likely. He had already gone to prison for life. What more would he have to lose? She told this to John.

"Did your dad ever have an affair?"

Tara took a seat on the barstool again, resting her chin on her hand. "Not that I know of," she replied. It had crossed her mind before. She had never suspected her father of being unfaithful to her mother when she was a child. But she was only very young, so why would she suspect anything if it wasn't happening in plain sight? "It's possible, I suppose," she added. *Is that who could've been in the room that night?* she wondered. *My father's mistress?* It seemed plausible, but Tara still wondered why, after all these years, he would protect a woman who murdered the mother of his child.

"How did he get the house number anyway?" John asked.

"I gave my contact info at the prison, in case he needed to call. I listed my cell first, and then the home phone."

"And he didn't call your cell?"

Tara shook her head. "He probably knew I'd be more likely to answer it." She knew her father's goal was to leave a message, not to speak to her.

John nodded, and a silence lingered between them before he turned fully toward her. "So what are you going to do?"

Tara didn't even hesitate. "I'm going to find out what he's hiding," she replied as her eyes drifted yet again to the answering machine. Her father's voice still echoed in her mind. She knew him well enough to know that he did not get spooked easily or at all. But the muffled panic in his voice only solidified Tara's feelings that he was trying to keep something buried, and she was more determined than ever to find out what it was.

***

Tara lay in bed, still staring at the ceiling. The room was in total darkness, but she couldn't be more awake. She had too many questions, too many thoughts.

She knew she didn't have time to go visit her father again, not in the middle of this case. But she also knew she somehow needed to get in touch with him. Her only option would be to call. She would do so first thing in the morning, she decided. She just hoped he would speak to her.

Tara knew that he had purposely avoided a conversation with her, which was why he called the house phone in the middle of the day. He had known it was likely she would be at work. But she hoped that no matter what he was hiding, once she called, he wouldn't be able to resist speaking to her. After all, for so many years he had written to her, hoping she would write back or call.

Strange, she thought. After all these years, she now had more reason than a dream to believe someone else was in the room that night of her mother's murder. It was a validation she had never felt before. In a way, it felt good. She wasn't crazy. But it also burdened her with more uncertainty. She had no idea who it could've been, and it troubled her.

All night, she had been digging into every depth of her memory for a clue, but she still couldn't find one. She thought of moments in her childhood, positive memories and negative ones. She thought of moments with her grandmother when she was a child. *Could she have hinted at something?* But no matter what point in time she chose to focus on, she was left without a conclusion. She continued to think of moments in her childhood, but as each memory surfaced, her eyes grew heavier. Eventually, she was barely able to hold them open at all, and she soon faded into sleep.

***

Tara ran, the tall, uncut grass tickling her bare feet. The sky was bluer than she'd ever seen it. The sun was warm against her skin, and it made her smile grow wider. She wore a long pink summer dress. Her mother had sewn it herself, and it flapped against her legs as she ran, faster and faster. She was ready now. She took a deep breath as she threw her hands in the air and then flung her body sideways, letting her hands touch the grass, and then her feet.

"I did it!" she screamed.

A friend at school had been teaching her how to do a cartwheel, but this was the first time she had actually succeeded. She looked around her fenced-in yard, slightly off balance until her eyes met their target. Her mother sat on the steps to their porch. Her smile was wide, making Tara beam with pride. She began to clap.

"Excellent!" she yelled. "That was perfect!"

Tara giggled as she whizzed excitedly across the lawn. Her mother stood up, her arms open. Tara leapt into them. Her mother hugged her and kissed her on the forehead, but then Tara pulled away. She had too much energy to feel constrained. She reached for her mother's hand and then used all the bit of weight she had to pull her mother toward the lawn.

"Now you try, Mommy!"

Her mother laughed. Tara was only five years old, and her mother didn't budge from her pull. "I don't

118

know if that's a good idea, baby," she replied as she smiled down at Tara. "I'm not as quick and flexible as you."

"Please, Mommy!" Tara pulled harder on her mother's hand, and when she still didn't budge, she reached higher, grabbing hold of her forearm. She tightened her grip and pulled hard.

"Tara, ow!" her mother yelled.

Tara instinctively let go, the playfulness immediately dissipating.

"I'm sorry," Tara said as her mother began to rub her arm. This was the second time this week that Tara had touched one of her bruises, and it had scared her just the same. Tara looked at her mother's forearm, which had the marks of a grip held too tight. The bruise was large, spanning half of her mother's small forearm, showing the size of her father's hand.

"You can't pull on people like that," her mother snapped as she took a seat back down. The mood had abruptly changed. It was confusing for Tara, being so young. How could her father grab her, pull her, and even hit her at times? Yet Tara only pulled her mother's arm to play, and she was the one getting in trouble. Even at such a young age, the injustice did not sit well with her.

"I just wanted you to play with me," Tara said sadly, but her mother only raised her eyebrows in scorn and Tara's face fell to her feet. She sat down on the stairs next to her mother. She didn't have the urge to run through the grass anymore. She didn't have the desire to try another cartwheel. There was a sadness in the air that muffled it all, and it hung heavy on them both in silence.

Tara tried to fix it. "What's for dinner tonight?"

"We'll order pizza," her mother replied, trying to force a smile.

Tara loved pizza nights, and her face lit up at the mention. But it wasn't just the food that excited her. She also knew that it meant something else too…

"Daddy won't be home?"

Her mother sighed. "Not tonight, baby, not tonight."

***

Tara's eyes popped open. The room was still dark, and John still lay sound asleep next to her, but she suddenly felt more awake than ever. She knew it wasn't just a dream. She remembered that day, those words—her mother saying her father wouldn't be home. They were words that had been spoken more than once. *How could I have forgotten?*

Her father was a plumber and construction worker, but not the type that would work on building houses. All she understood was that he installed fueling systems. There was a point in time where he worked for a company that required him to travel out of town. It was the reason Tara was given each time she asked why her father wasn't going to be home for dinner, and each time he didn't come home until a couple days later. It wasn't too often, but now, as Tara stared at the darkness above her, she wondered, was there any truth in it at all?

Chapter Fourteen

S ofia lay terrified, flat on the basement floor, her hands tied behind her back. He was nearby, sitting at a computer desk, but his eyes were on something else. A TV was mounted against the wall, and he stared at it intensely. It was the news he was watching, coverage of the girls found on the beach. He had been watching it for hours. It was all taped footage from different channels that he had prerecorded. Every few moments, he would pause it, scribble something down on a pad of paper, and then fast-forward.

It was as if she wasn't even in the room, and the unknown of what he was doing and what was to come next only heightened Sofia's fear. She felt as if she had been lying there for a lifetime, even though it had only been a matter of hours, but how long exactly she did not know. All she knew was that she had awoken in the basement alone, untied, until he heard her and came downstairs. She had tried to make a run for it, but he had stopped her. He was too strong for her to overpower, and he quickly tied her up, duct-taped her mouth, and took a photo of her. Ever since then, he had been sitting at his desk.

Sofia's heart still pounded. Her parents were probably worried about her by now. She hoped that someone would find her, that the cops were already searching for her. But as she looked up at the news he was watching, as she saw each dead girl's face pop up on the screen, a wave of hopelessness crashed into her, and she sobbed. She wanted her mom's home-cooked meal. She wanted her warm bed. She wanted to hear her parents say goodnight. She wanted to wake up from this nightmare.

A warm liquid trickled down her pant leg, and she looked down to see her urine leak out onto the floor. Her eyes welled; her body shook with sheer fear. Her body hadn't even given her warning, and it only signified the reality of her situation. Even her body knew how terrified she was.

Sofia broke out into sobs. She wanted to plead with him to let her go, but her mouth was duct-taped, and all that sounded was a muffled cry. She thought of her school, of her future, how she wanted to be teacher, how she was soon supposed to be applying to colleges. Terror flooded her body at the thought that those things would never happen. She had no way out, nowhere to go. She was completely at his mercy. Her cries grew louder.

Eventually he could no longer ignore her, and he finally stood.

At his movement, Sofia quieted, but he had yet to speak a word. *Is he going to let me go?* she wondered as he moved closer, as he bent down next to her, as he stared at the puddle of urine on the floor.

"Don't be scared," he whispered as he looked from the floor to her face.

His words were almost reassuring, and for a moment, Sofia wondered if he was going to listen.

But then he raised a string in his hands—the same string he tied her hands with—and terror flooded once again through her body. "It's your time," he added. "It's almost over. And I know exactly where I'm going to put you."

He sat atop her legs so she couldn't move. He placed the string around her neck as she tried to plead with him once more. But then she felt the pressure as he pulled, and the words couldn't leave her throat. She thrashed about, but it was no use—his weight was too heavy for her petite body—and eventually her movement slowed as she gasped for air she couldn't find, and the room darkened around her.

Chapter Fifteen

Tara sat in the kitchen of her apartment, staring at her laptop. She had slept very little after her dream and had eventually given up and gotten out of bed. She could now feel the lack of sleep, and she yawned. It was six thirty in the morning. She had been up for an hour, her mind racing.

She had looked up the prison's phone number and was now staring at it, her eyes moving from the number to the time at the bottom of the screen. It was too early to call just yet. She waited another fifteen minutes, and then she dialed. She just hoped her father would speak to her and that the prison would allow it.

Moments later, an operator was on the other end. Tara mentioned her father's name and that she was returning a call. The operator was quiet a moment. Tara could hear the clank of fingers on a keyboard.

"He's allowed limited incoming calls," the woman said. "Are you on his call list?"

"I'm not sure," Tara admitted.

"Your name?"

"Tara Mills."

The woman put her on hold without even a word, but Tara knew she was looking up the call list of her father. A few moments later, she was back on the phone. "Sorry, you're not on his list," the woman said unsympathetically.

Tara sighed. "Is there any other way I can speak to him?"

"You can try coming in, but I can't put you through by phone."

"But..." Tara was going to ask one more time, but the phone suddenly went dead. The operator had hung up on her.

Tara slunk in her chair, defeated. There was no way she would be able to travel to New York in the midst of this case. At that thought, John walked into the kitchen. He yawned as he made his way to the coffee machine.

"Were you able to talk to him?" he asked, knowing very well why she was already up.

Tara sighed. "I'm not on his call list. The only way I can possibly talk to him is by going there, but I have a feeling he'll refuse to see me."

John sat down next to her. "So what's your next move?"

Tara already knew. The dream the night before had stirred the thought. "I want to get hold of the visitation records," she admitted. If he was covering for someone, it was likely they had visited him at one point or another. That might even be the reason why Tara's father pushed her away. He might not want her to poke around and see who'd been coming around when she was already suspicious.

She explained all this to John, and he nodded. It made sense to him too.

Suddenly, Tara's phone vibrated on the counter in front of her. She looked down. Warren's name flashed across the screen, and she immediately picked up. She knew he could either just want to reconvene early, or he could have some important news.

Before she could even say hello, Warren spoke. "Mills," he started, his voice filled with urgency. The next words burst out of his mouth. "Another teenager never came home last night."

***

Within just over two hours, Tara pulled into a parking lot right along the beach. A sea of police vehicles and news vans lined the side of the road. She quickly got out and made her way through the endless questions from reporters. She then stood behind the yellow tape on the sandy beach, peering around for Warren.

When she last spoke to him, a body wasn't found, and she could now see that it still hadn't been. Cops and forensics were tearing apart the beach in every direction. Cadaver dogs were being led over the sand dunes by officers, each in an assigned section spread out for about a mile stretch. She could see Warren up ahead, speaking to Sheriff Patel. She walked over.

"Anything yet?" she asked.

Warren shook his head. "Still no body."

Sheriff Patel said, "We checked for about a five-mile stretch down this beach. If he buried the victim here, he sure didn't do it close to the first two."

"Could she still be alive?" Tara asked.

"It's of course possible."

Tara felt a surge of adrenaline. She suddenly felt as if they were wasting precious time. She could see the same urgency in Warren's eyes.

"What do we know so far?" she asked.

Tara already knew certain details. Warren had filled her in on the way. The victim was Sofia Hernandez, sixteen. She had ridden her bike home from a friend's house and never made it. Sheriff Patel only reiterated those points.

"Did we find her bike?" Tara asked.

Sheriff Patel's shoulders slumped as he shook his head in disappointment, but then he perked up. "We think the killer might've called the victim's sister." It was a new bit of information that Tara hadn't heard before, and she could see it was new to Warren as well; he had arrived at the beach only moments before Tara.

"How do you know?" Warren asked.

Sheriff Patel sighed. "I was over there this morning, interviewing them, and she got the call. She put it on speaker, and someone was breathing really heavy on the other line and then started laughing and hung up. There was something really chilling about it."

A shiver ran down Tara's spine. The killer was mocking them now. "Were you able to trace it?"

Sheriff Patel shook his head. "I tried, but he hung up right before I could, and then he didn't call back." He then looked up, twisting his mouth in confusion. "It's almost like he knew. Like he stayed on just long enough before I could trace him."

Tara and Warren shared a look. It was another detail that made their original theory plausible—that this was someone who knew a thing or two about investigations. Tara spoke to Warren. "I say we go talk to them." They both knew there was no point in hanging around the beach without a body to review. For all they knew, the victim could still be alive, and if that were true, the clock was ticking.

Chapter Sixteen

Tara and Warren arrived at a beautifully large home, layered with cedar siding. A wide-open porch sat on the top floor of the front of the house, directly under the sun. Tara had already called the family on the way. She had asked that the friend who had last seen the victim be present as well, and Tara hoped that one of the three cars in the driveway was hers.

They knocked, and a tall, strikingly beautiful woman came to the door. She had shoulder-length auburn hair and bangs cut stylishly across her forehead. She was older, Tara assumed in her mid-forties, but her skin was still tight and youthful. She looked at them with sheer fear for a moment, until she realized who they were, that Tara was the one who had just called. She most likely assumed they were there to tell her some unfortunate news, but at the realization that they weren't, she sighed. Tara knew immediately who she was: the victim's mother.

The mother was always the easiest person to identify. There was a deep pain that lingered on her face as she faded into herself, trying desperately not to scream.

"Please come in," she said as she moved away from the door.

They followed her across the dining room to a large, open living room with vaulted ceilings. The skylights above shined onto the four people sitting on the couch and in chairs. The woman took a seat on the couch next to her husband and daughter and introduced them all. The other two were the victim's friend and her mother.

Tara and Warren sat down as well. The room fell into silence, but then Tara spoke. "So from what we understand, one of you received a call this morning?" She looked specifically toward the sister, who sat wedged on the couch between her mother and father. She must've been only a couple years older than the victim.

She nodded as she hesitantly raised her gaze from the floor to Tara, who asked her to recount what she heard.

"It was just a lot of heavy breathing, and then he laughed." Her voice began to shake as she said the last words, and her gaze fell to the floor. The event had clearly traumatized her, and her father stroked her back.

"Did it sound like a male?" Tara asked.

"Definitely."

"And did he sound young or older?"

She bit her lip as she thought. "It's hard to tell just on a laugh, but I'd say older. His voice was pretty deep."

The information helped, but Tara also knew that teenage boys could have deep voices as well. "Do you have any clue who it could've been?"

The sister shook her head as her parents did the same, and Tara turned to the friend.

"She never mentioned anything to you? Anyone she seemed afraid of?"

The girl looked as if she wanted to burst into tears at the question, but her mother encouraged her to answer. "No," she revealed with shock still in her voice. "Everything seemed fine."

"Was she dating anyone?" Tara looked from the friend to the parents, but they all shook their heads. "She didn't have a boyfriend," the mother replied. "She was a softball player, and it took up all of her time and interest."

Tara continued to ask more questions. If she knew the other victims. If she ever worked at the coffee shop or kayak rental store, but each question was answered with a no. Tara asked them for some places where Sofia could've gone, and after the mother insisted her daughter didn't run away, she gave some ideas—the batting cages, the softball field. Tara would make sure that the cops searched those areas.

When they finally exhausted their efforts, Tara and Warren stood outside.

"Let's make sure Sheriff Patel knows to check those places the mother mentioned," Warren said. Tara nodded as she reached for her phone in her pocket, about to make the call, but before she punched in the number, they needed to determine their next move. They could both feel the pressure weighing heavy on them, almost to the point of suffocation. They had no lead, and if there was any chance of finding Sofia alive, they needed one soon.

"I have a feeling we were on to something before," she finally said, referring to the theory that the killer was law enforcement or someone who knew a thing or two about investigations. "I think the killer knew how long he could stay on the phone before being tracked, and he knew not to call back. He's clearly mocking us."

Warren nodded. "Let's head to the station," he replied. "We can brainstorm there."

Tara agreed, and they quickly headed to the car as Tara made a call to Sheriff Patel. As she took a seat in the car, the sun shined brightly into her eyes. She pulled the visor down as a frustration bubbled in her stomach. Another day had come, another victim taken, and they did not have answers. She refused to let the sun rise again the same way.

***

Tara and Warren sat in the police station once again, with case files spread across the table. They had called Sheriff Patel, and still no body had been found. They still had some ground to cover, but it was looking more likely that if a body was buried, it wasn't at Dewey Beach. Tara told him of the places to check for Sofia. His team had already checked some, but he agreed that he would have them keep a close watch.

Now, they sat in silence. An immense guilt sat heavy on Tara's conscience. The killer had gotten another victim, and she couldn't help but feel responsible. She stared down at the case files, but her mind was also focused on something else. If they were right, if this killer knew a thing or two about investigations, he would never bury a body in the same place where the others were found.

"Maybe we should have them check other beaches," she finally said. She explained her reasoning.

"I agree," Warren admitted as he reached for his phone and called Sheriff Patel. He was only on the phone briefly before he hung up. "He says they're checking neighboring beaches within a ten-mile radius. They brought in other departments from other towns for the search."

Tara was glad to hear it. They certainly needed help to cover so much ground. But while Sheriff Patel and the other cops were busy searching for a body, Tara and Warren needed a plan to find Sofia and the killer.

Warren sighed. "I think you're right," he started. "We may have been on to something when we were searching for someone with law enforcement experience, or who has some knowledge of investigative procedures." He leaned his elbow on the table, letting his hand hold the weight of his head. His fingers were clenched, almost digging into his scalp.

"Maybe we should do another search," Tara replied. They had asked Patel to expand his search; maybe they needed to expand theirs. "Maybe we need to look at other towns."

They decided to call Grace, who was already working on the initial report—they just needed her to expand her search. But when they called, she was already on it.

"Almost done," she said. "I'm gathering a list of ex-police officers with a record in the past three years in towns within a ten-mile radius."

Grace always thought ahead, always anticipating what an agent would need next, and Tara was grateful that they wouldn't lose any time. Tara thanked her and hung up the phone. They now just had to wait, and while they did, they dug deeper into each case file, trying to find any other connections among the victims. But after going through each, they had yet to find a correlation other than the way they were abducted, how Alyssa and Reese's bodies were found, and the connection in where Reese and Alyssa worked for a short time. They all had attended different schools. Alyssa was from out of town. Reese and Sofia attended neighboring school districts.

After some time had passed, Grace called. She had their results. Tara and Warren moved to a computer and were soon looking over a very short list of names of only two officers. One was a DUI, and Tara immediately scrolled over him, but the second pulled her in: an officer in his late forties who had been on the force for twenty years. He had been fired last spring, right before the summer Alyssa White went missing. Tara read his charge, and her heart rate picked up. He had been charged with assault on his teenage daughter after breaking up a party she was at near Dewey Beach. The cop's name was Officer Terry Brennan, and the assault had occurred on the lawn outside of the party.

She looked over at Warren, making sure he was seeing what she was. His eyebrows knitted, and he sat leaned forward in his chair, glued to the screen.

"What do you think?" she asked when he finished reading.

He sighed. "I think we should find out who was there."

Tara agreed. She would start with Sofia's friend. She had given Tara her number after they interviewed her that morning. Within moments, Sofia's friend was on the line.

Tara reminded her who they were.

"Did you find her?" the girl said abruptly, and Tara's heart sank.

"I'm sorry, but we haven't."

She grew quiet and sighed.

"I wanted to ask you about a party that happened last spring." The girl still didn't speak. Her breathing was suddenly more controlled. "Do you know a cop by the name of Brennan? He broke up a party last spring that his daughter was at?"

She was quiet a moment. "Why?" she asked. "What does this have to do with Sofia?"

"Were you or Sofia there?"

The girl sighed again. "My parents don't know we were there," she said nervously. "But yeah. I remember that party very well. That poor girl was humiliated in front of everyone when her father flipped out." She paused. "It was pretty awful. I just remember him grabbing her by the throat and hitting her hard in the face. He was calling her all these horrible things. I heard later on that he grabbed her arm so hard, he broke it."

"Did you know her?" Tara asked.

"No, but I've heard of her. She was homeschooled. Her dad was really strict. But she'd sneak out sometimes. She had some friends that lived in the area, around Dewey Beach." Tara's mind immediately went to Reese, but then she remembered that earlier, Sofia's friend told her that Sofia didn't know Reese.

"You're sure Sofia didn't know Reese, right? Reese wasn't at that party too?"

The girl hesitated, but then spoke. "I didn't tell you before because I didn't think it mattered," she started. "Me and Sofia didn't really know Reese, but I did recognize her when I saw her on the news and when you showed me her picture." Tara and Warren shared a look as they anxiously waited for her to continue. "She was at that party. I remember her clearly because she tried to help Officer Brennan's daughter after he hit her to the ground, but he just threatened her and she backed up."

"What did he say?" Tara asked.

"Just that she'd be sorry if she got in between them. Something like it was bad enough that she influenced his daughter. And then he said something that I think everyone was shocked about. He said she was a slut, just like every other girl at the party. He said he wasn't going to let his daughter turn into one."

Tara let her words sink in. Could it be enough for motive? Could Officer Brennan have been taken over the edge when he was fired? And then sought out the girls he thought influenced his daughter? It was possible, Tara assumed, especially if he lost more than just his job that night.

"Do you know if Alyssa White was there too?" Tara asked.

The girl wasn't sure. "I didn't know her. Especially because she wasn't local. But it's possible. It seemed everyone was there, and it wasn't just locals either."

Tara thanked her and hung up. She turned to Warren. "I think we should pay Officer Brennan a visit," she said.

Chapter Seventeen

A large multistory apartment building stood tall in front of them. Garbage littered the entrance, and shifty individuals eyed them as they walked past. Two of them were secretly exchanging something, before looking startled as they noticed Tara and Warren briskly walk to the entrance. It was on the more dangerous side of town, and it was where Terry now lived. They had learned, after looking up his information, that he was now divorced, which Tara had suspected. After the incident that night, CPS was called, an investigation ensued, and now Mrs. Brennan had full custody over her daughter.

Tara knew that if Terry Brennan was already a man with a temper before his divorce, it was probably tenfold now. Tara and Warren entered an elevator and were soon on the fifth floor, headed to apartment 525. Tara could feel her gun under shirt, and it gave her comfort as they stood in front of the door and Warren knocked.

It took a few moments, but the door opened, and a tired-looking man stood in front of them. His lip curled in disgust as he saw Tara and Warren. He looked as if he had barely slept in days. The skin under his eyes was red and the whites bloodshot, making him look sickly. His loose-fitting t-shirt was stained with whatever he had eaten that morning, and in one of his hands he held a half-drunk beer.

"Mr. Brennan?" Tara asked, making sure they had come to the right door.

"Yeah, what?" he spat back, confirming it as if it were obvious. He took a swig of his beer.

Tara held up her badge, and a flash of anger appeared in his eyes. "We were wondering if we could talk to you a moment."

He placed the beer down on a side table as he leaned closer to the door. "About what, exactly?" he asked. "What could you possibly want from me?"

"Can we come in?"

"Absolutely not," he spat back without hesitation. He had no care for who they were, and he showed a confidence that was concerning. Tara knew that overconfident suspects were more likely to do something rash, and she was watching all his movements carefully.

He grabbed his beer again and took a swig, his other hand still holding the door handle.

"We are not here to question you about the encounter with your daughter," Tara tried to reassure him, but his face only tightened more in anger at the mention. "But we do have some questions about that night," she added. "We just want to know if you saw any of these girls." She reached in her pocket and pulled out the images of the three victims. He looked at each one carefully, but his eyes fell hard on Reese.

"What does it matter?" he asked as heat rose up his neck.

Tara wasn't sure if he was playing dumb or if he truly didn't watch the news. Almost everyone would recognize their faces by now, since they'd been plastered on every local news station. Tara explained the case and that one of them was missing, but his face didn't change.

"We're just trying to find a connection between the three. We think they might've all been there that night, at the party."

He didn't answer, his eyes still fixed on Reese, until they moved to the others, with the same burning look.

"Do you remember seeing them?" Tara asked again.

"Who the hell knows," he finally blurted as he looked up at Tara with utter disgust. "But you know what, those little sluts probably deserved it if they're going to house parties at sixteen." He went to slam the door, but Warren placed his hand hard against it, holding it slightly ajar.

He was clearly not only controlling, but a misogynist too, and Tara felt a fire flare within her.

"Sir, please, we just want to talk," Warren assured him, but Terry only gave him a fiery glare.

His teeth gritted, he pulled open the door abruptly. "Don't you dare put your hand on my door," he growled. He was about to shut it again, but then a burst of anger flowed through him. "Don't you think I've been through enough!" he screamed. "I lost my damn daughter! My wife! And then you're going to come here and bother me with this shit! Don't you think I know what you're doing?"

Tara's hand casually moved to her hip, closer to her gun. She wasn't quite sure what he was implying. It was either that he was afraid they would bring him up on assault charges for pushing Reese that night and verbally abusing her, or he was referring to something else entirely.

He took one look at Warren and began to laugh awkwardly. "You think you intimidate me?" He moved into the hallway, still holding his beer as it sloshed around, spilling in his clumsy grip. He was clearly drunk.

"We can come back another time," Warren replied.

But Terry's face only contorted with more anger. His lip curled in disgust. "No, you won't. You're both going to leave me alone! Now get the hell out of here." He pushed Warren in the shoulder, an attempt to make him leave, but Warren swatted his hand away.

"Sir, don't put your hands on me." Warren's voice was threatening and stern.

But Warren's words only fueled him further, and his fist flung through the air, heading right to Warren's jaw. Warren ducked and ran into Terry's stomach, causing him to lose balance. He fell flat on his back in the doorway. His beer flew from his hand. Glass shattered across his living room, liquid leaking all over the floor.

He groaned in anguish as he tried to force Warren off him, but he was too drunk. Warren forced him up as Tara came behind and cuffed him.

"You all right?" she asked.

Warren nodded as he pushed Terry forward. But at about halfway down the hall, Mr. Brennan suddenly keeled over. Vomit spilled out of his mouth. Warren shook his head as he waited for Terry to gain his composure and then continued to push him forward. Tara curled her lip in disgust as she followed Warren out to the car. Once he was in the back seat, Tara and Warren agreed to take a look inside the apartment, and they made their way back in.

"What are you thinking so far?" Tara asked as they opened the apartment door. Warren had been mostly quiet, deep in thought.

Warren shrugged. "He clearly has an anger issue," he replied. "Let's see what else we can find," he added as he stepped into the apartment.

The shattered beer bottle still lay in pieces across the living room, soaking into a rug underneath the coffee table, between the TV and pleather couch. Empty beer bottles sat on every space of every surface. It was a small apartment. The kitchen was to the right of the living room, and then there was the bedroom and bathroom at the end of a short hallway.

Tara and Warren looked in every corner for traces of anything that would link him to the crime scene— shovels, tarps, anything to tie someone up—but they were unable to find a single such object. They moved throughout the living room, and then the kitchen, until they moved down the hallway. Tara opened a coat closet. She searched behind jackets. She looked at the bottoms of shoes for traces of sand. But nothing had a touch of suspicion.

They both entered the bedroom. It was dark, with thick curtains covering the windows, shutting out any flicker of the sun. They turned on an overhead light, revealing the mess. The extent of beer bottles had flowed into the bedroom as well. They sat atop the nightstands and dresser and atop a computer desk and filing cabinet in the corner.

Tara moved to the filing cabinet while Warren searched the closet. She flipped through each folder inside. Each were labeled correctly with what they held inside—tax information, birth certificate, social security. Tara sighed as she continued to dig through each one.

One labeled *Family Pictures* struck her amongst the others, and she pulled it out of the bunch. Inside were pictures of him, his daughter, and his wife. Some were Christmas cards, while others looked like photos taken on vacation. Some were them skiing, others were in the tropics with palm trees standing tall in the background. In each one, Mr. Brennan's smile was wide, but his daughter and wife's looked forced. Tara knew that look too well. Unhappiness reflected on their faces at the hands of abuse. Exhaustion could be seen in their eyes, most likely from the endless push-and-pull of control. Tara could only hope that they were happier now, away from their abuser.

Tara put the folder of the images back into the filing cabinet. There was only one more folder left. It was placed at the very back and was the only one that was unlabeled. Tara pulled it out, and dozens of pictures fell out onto the floor. Tara picked one up. It was Mr. Brennan's daughter, walking with some teens on a road late at night. Their backs were turned to the camera, as if someone had snuck up behind them to take the picture. Tara flipped through the rest. Each one was of his daughter, with friends on a beach, or in a park, or entering a house that had the looks of a party going on. Each one was taken late at night from far away, and it was clear that she had no clue a picture was being taken.

Tara already knew that Mrs. Brennan and her daughter had a restraining order against her ex-husband, but it now seemed that it didn't keep him too far at bay. Tara assumed Mr. Brennan's daughter had no idea he was still keeping tabs on her. It was clear he was overprotective and abusive. It was probably driving him insane that he now had no control over who his daughter was hanging out with or what she was doing. *Could following her be a way for him to feel some sense of control?* Tara let that thought roll around in her mind as she looked at each image more intently.

Reese was in almost every picture , standing close to Mr. Brennan's daughter amongst a group. In some, it was just the two of them. *They had to have been good friends,* Tara assumed. They both had strict parents. Tara wondered if that was a commonality they had bonded over, and as a result, tested boundaries together. It was evident that they had been sneaking out of their houses together. On the back of each picture was a time and date. Each taken late at night, after or around midnight. Tara knew their parents never would've allowed them to leave the house at that time.

"What did you find?" Warren finally asked, noticing how intently Tara was looking at them. He moved closer before kneeling on the floor next to her. He picked up a picture as he knitted his eyebrows in suspicion.

But Tara didn't answer. She had found another recognizable face amongst the images: Sofia. It seemed that Sofia knew Mr. Brennan's daughter a bit more than Sofia's close friend had even known. She passed it to Warren.

"Look who it is," she said as she pointed at the girl in the picture. He had already seen Reese. Tara could tell by the way he had gathered each image of her in front of him. He took the photo in his hand.

"Sofia." The name rolled off his tongue. He turned the picture over, looking at the date and time it was taken. He showed it to Tara. It was a few weeks before she went missing. They looked at the dates of all the others of Reese, each taken within months leading up to her disappearance as well. The most recent was taken a week prior.

Could Mr. Brennan had been so insanely controlling that he had sought out his daughter's friends who he thought were influencing her? Tara ran the thought by Warren.

"It's certainly possible," he replied. "I mean, what kind of creep stalks their own daughter?" His eyes washed over the images once more. "The only one missing is Alyssa."

He was right. Alyssa wasn't in any of the images, but it could still be possible that Mr. Brennan's daughter knew her, or maybe he had even mistaken her for someone else. But right now, their biggest priority was finding Sofia.

Warren gathered the pictures back into the envelope. "Grab his car keys. I saw them hanging in the kitchen," he said. Tara knew his intention was to search the car. It would be the only way he'd be able to transfer Sofia, and it could possibly hold evidence, or her.

Tara did as Warren asked, and they were soon headed back out of the building. Tara could see Mr. Brennan in the police vehicle, parked out front. His head was resting against the window. They made their way to the parking lot in the back of the building, and Tara pressed the lock button of Mr. Brennan's car. They followed the beeping noise until they stood in front of a Toyota Camry.

They searched in every corner of the car, in every crevice. They searched the dashboard, the middle console. They searched the trunk. When they finally realized there was nothing more to search, Tara sighed. If he had taken her, he had covered his tracks in the car too. But Tara also knew that there might be evidence they couldn't see. "We'll bring the keys to forensics, have them take a closer look."

Warren nodded, but Tara could see a frustration boiling within him, sadness and anger dancing in his eyes. Something about the case, about Terry, shook him.

"You have to really be scum to abuse your daughter," he said through gritted teeth.

As someone who had lost his teenage daughter, Tara knew this case was striking a delicate chord in him.

He slammed the door of the car as he spun around, making his way to the front of the building. Tara locked it and then quickly followed behind. His eyes locked on the police car as he turned the corner. They narrowed as he saw Terry's head resting on the window.

Just when he was close enough, he swung the backseat door open. Mr. Brennan looked startled as he quickly sat up straight, trying to regain his balance and not fall out of the car.

"Where's Sofia?" Warren barked at him.

Mr. Brennan stared up at him in drunk confusion. "Who?" he muttered.

Warren grabbed her picture from the envelope that was found in the filing cabinet and forced it in front of his face. "Her," Warren said brusquely.

A look of shock crossed his face. His eyes opened wide with fear. He hadn't expected them to find those pictures. At first he didn't answer, swaying slightly back and forth, still trying to hold himself upright. Warren asked him again. He hesitated, but his mouth opened. He was about to say something, but before the words could form, his face turned a shade paler. Tara could see sweat had broken out on his forehead. He continued to sway. He was about to be sick. Warren sensed it too and stepped back just in time as Mr. Brennan hurled all over the ground where Warren just stood.

Warren rolled his eyes as he turned to Tara. "He's going to need to sober up before we ask him anything."

Tara agreed. "I say we talk to his daughter in the meantime," she suggested. They both knew it was likely she held answers. Warren nodded as he made his way to driver's side of the car.

As he opened the door, he looked over the hood. "Let's drop him off, and then we'll go pay his family a visit."

Chapter Eighteen

A row of condos came into view as Warren neared the end of the road. They had already dropped Terry off at the station. The cops there were helping them by trying to get him to sober up. They had also handed his keys off to forensics, and Tara assumed they were now over at his apartment complex, combing through his vehicle for anything of substance.

Now, Tara and Warren were nearing the home of Mrs. Brennan and her daughter. Unlike Terry's complex, this one was on a nice side of town, sitting on a dead-end street, facing the beach. They pulled into the parking lot. A glare reflected into Tara's eyes, and she turned to see two young children riding their bikes around in circles as a father helped one of them gain their balance. Light reflected on the metal rims each time they turned into the sun. Tara smiled. It was refreshing to see a positive parental relationship, when she knew very well she was about to speak of a troubling one.

Warren parked, and they were soon standing two doors down from the father and children. Tara could feel his eyes on them as Warren pressed hard on the doorbell and they waited. A moment later the door swung open. A middle-aged woman with short, curly blonde hair and a toothy smile was in mid-laugh as she opened it. But her face fell upon Tara and Warren standing before her. The smile simmered, replaced with a questionable glare.

"Can I help you?"

A girl moved briefly to the door, as if to check who it was, and then disappeared into the kitchen. Tara assumed it was Terry Brennan's daughter.

"Are you Mrs. Brennan?"

The woman nodded questioningly. She wore an apron covered in white powder, and she wiped a smidge from her cheek. She had clearly been baking.

Tara flashed her badge. "We were wondering if we could speak to you and your daughter," she started. "We know your daughter was friends with Reese Tanner. We were hoping she might be able to help us."

The woman raised her brows in surprise. "Oh," she said, startled. She sighed, shaking her head briefly. "It's a shame. That poor girl. She was a sweetheart." Her mind drifted a moment at her words, and then she abruptly looked back at Tara. "Come in," she added as she stepped aside, opening the door wider.

The condo had a cozy feel, with family pictures neatly placed on surfaces and in frames on the walls. Tara looked at them briefly as she took a seat on the couch. They were of Mrs. Brennan, her daughter, and others, which Tara assumed were extended family. Not one picture had Mr. Brennan in it. A wooden sign hung over the frames with the words *Home, Sweet Home* etched into it.

Mrs. Brennan took off her apron as she walked into the dining room and placed it over a chair.

"I'm sorry, my daughter and I were just baking. My niece's birthday is tomorrow." She was talking to Tara and Warren, but she was now in the dining room, facing the kitchen. "Julie," she called as she waved her hand for her daughter to come near. A shy-looking teenager moved to the doorframe. She locked eyes with Tara from across the room. She suddenly blushed and her eyes fell to her feet. She wore an apron too. She took it off, laying it over her mother's before pushing her pin straight hair behind her ear and sitting on a loveseat across from them. Her mother sat next to her.

"Reese used to come over quite often, actually," Mrs. Brennan said as she looked from Julie to Tara and Warren.

Julie was staring at the floor. She bit her lip at her mother's words, trying to control her emotion. It was clear just from her sitting there that Reese's death had really shook her up.

"You two were close?" Tara asked.

Julie's eyes moved to Tara, and then they closed as they began to well up. She sighed and nodded. "We were." Her voice shook slightly. Mrs. Brennan grabbed her hand.

"Do you have idea who would've wanted to harm her?" Tara asked. She and Warren already had their theory, but she wanted to see what Julie would say. Julie thought for a moment before sharing a brief look with her mother, but then she looked back at her feet and shook her head. In only confirmed that Julie didn't instinctively suspect her father of murder, even though she knew he was violent. But it was something Tara understood personally. As a child, witnessing abuse, she never would've thought her father was a murderer until he was charged as such. Tara's stomach began to churn with sadness at what this girl could soon learn.

Tara reached into her pocket and pulled out a picture of Sofia. She slid it across the coffee table. "Do you know her too?"

Julie let go of her mother's hand and picked up the picture. Familiarity washed over her face and then concern, and she abruptly looked up.

"I do, why?"

It was clear that neither she nor her mother had watched the news that day.

"She went missing last night," Tara said. "She was riding her bike home from a friend's house."

Julie's hand instinctively covered her mouth. Her mother looked at her with sheer concern.

"You knew her too?" her mother asked. It was obvious that she was unaware of the friendship.

Julie nodded, still in shock. "I didn't know her that well, but I've hung out with her a couple of times. Just at..." She paused, her eyes moving to her mother, as if afraid to say what she needed to in her presence. But then she took a deep breath. "At parties," she finished. "We had some mutual friends."

Her mother stared at her, confused. She had clearly no knowledge that her daughter had been sneaking out, going to parties some nights. It was a topic Tara didn't feel the need to address outright, but she also knew that what she and Warren were about to show them would reveal it.

"Do you still talk to your father?" Tara asked Julie.

She and her mother both jerked their heads back. "What does that have to do with anything?" Mrs. Brennan interjected.

Tara looked to Warren, who opened an envelope on his lap. He pulled out the pictures they found in Mr. Brennan's apartment and placed them on the coffee table. It took Julie and her mother a moment for it to register what they were, but then Julie's eyes opened wide. She gasped with a look of total devastation. Mrs. Brennan was quiet as she reached for the pictures. She knitted her brows and squinted.

"I don't understand," she said as she turned to her daughter. "Julie, what are these?"

Julie blushed. It was inevitable now that her mother would know she was sneaking out of the house. "They're pictures of me and my friends, hanging out at night."

Mrs. Brennan continued to stare at them, taking each one in her hand, looking at them intently until moving to the next. She turned each one over, seeing the time and date. She looked at her daughter, not with anger, but with sadness. She sighed.

"I thought you were going to stop with the lying," she said under breath, but her words were met with no response, and then her eyes focused yet again on the pictures. "Who took these?" she asked as it all began to come together.

Warren leaned forward. "We found these in your ex-husband's apartment."

Mrs. Brennan stared at him a moment, trying to make sense of what he was saying, and then she placed a hand over her mouth.

Julie stiffened as terror flooded her eyes.

"But…" Mrs. Brennan started. She picked up the pictures again, one by one, almost frantically. "We have a restraining order." The words fell out of her mouth as she placed another photo down in disbelief. She then looked up at Tara and Warren. "He was a very angry, abusive man. We have no ties with him anymore. He's not supposed to be anywhere within a hundred yards of me or my daughter." She looked at her daughter. "Did you know he was watching you?" she asked, but Julie only shook her head as she too stared down at the pictures in disbelief.

Mrs. Brennan looked back and forth between Tara and Warren as a thought struck her.

"What does this have to do with Reese? Or that other girl?" she asked. You don't think—" She placed her hand over her mouth again, stopping herself before she spoke the words. But it was already clear she understood why they were there.

Julie was still quietly in shock. Tara shared a quick glance with Warren before she spoke. "Did your father ever mention Reese to you? Did he ever talk about her? Or Sofia?"

Julie looked off into the distance and took in a sudden emotional gasp of air. She then looked back at Tara. "My father never liked me hanging out with anyone. He made my mother homeschool me. He didn't want me to have any social influence. That was partially the reason why my mother left him." She glanced at her mother briefly.

"He had a lot of issues. His father was the same way. He was very controlling." Mrs. Brennan sighed. "And he didn't have a relationship with his mother. She left them when he was young for another man."

152

Her words only confirmed that he had a deep-rooted mistrust of women.

"I thought I could help him," Mrs. Brennan added with a shake of her head. "But clearly I was wrong."

Julie stared at her mother as she spoke before grabbing a hold of her hand— the room falling into silence. They were clearly both still healing.

"And how did you meet Reese?" Tara asked Julie.

"I used to go to the coffee shop to study sometimes before my dad got home. I met Reese when she first started working there. That's when our friendship really started. We both had strict parents, so we kind of just understood each other."

"Did you ever tell your dad about her?" Tara asked

Julie shook her head. "I knew if I told him, he would get all concerned about it. He always said I had a personality to be easily influenced." She paused, sadness blooming on her face. Tara felt sorry for her. Hearing those words from her own father had to have affected her confidence.

"And what happened the night of the party?" Tara felt guilty asking. She knew it was a delicate subject, but she needed her to recount her story.

The girl sighed. "My dad thought I was home, but Reese snuck out of her house for a party and invited me. I went. I didn't think my parents would know. But he was a cop and ended up getting called to break up the party." Her eyes began to well up, and Tara knew very well why. It was the same story that Sofia's friend had told them. "He hit me, in front of everyone. Over and over again. He broke my arm." She now couldn't control her emotion as she began to cry. Her mother leaned in closer, wrapping her arm around her. It steadied her.

"Reese tried to stop him. I think he kind of made the connection then. He knew I went to the coffee shop a lot. He used to go in there before work, so he clearly recognized her."

Mrs. Brennan spoke. "I got a call that night when I was in bed. I thought Julie was home, but it was the hospital. She squeezed her daughter's hand. "That was my last straw with him," she added. "I filed for divorce and a restraining order the next morning, and we moved in with my sister."

"Has he tried contacting you at all?" Tara asked.

"Just once," Mrs. Brennan admitted. "He showed up at my sister's house with a box of our stuff a few months ago. He claimed he didn't know we'd be there, but he knew." She rolled her eyes. "He just wanted an excuse to check on us. I told my lawyer that he defied the restraining order, and he never did it again."

Tara looked between Julie and her mother. "Do you think he would've hurt Reese?"

They shared a glance, as if to see what the other thought. They both questioned it; Tara could see it in their eyes. "I would hope not," Mrs. Brennan replied. "I never would suspect him of murder, but I honestly don't even know how he's been this past year."

It was an answer that made him seem even more suspect. His own family couldn't even deny that he was capable of murder. But Tara still had one more question . Did Julie know Alyssa? She was the only victim that somehow hadn't fit into the theory. She looked at Warren, who was already holding her picture in his hand, waiting for the right moment to ask. At Tara's glance, he placed the picture in front of Julie.

"Do you know her?" he asked.

She looked down at it, and Tara could see familiarity flicker in her eyes. But Alyssa's pictures had been everywhere, on every news station, on every telephone pole for a year. Anyone in this town would recognize her.

Julie shook her head, and Tara's heart sank. "Only from the news. I don't think I've ever met her, though."

Tara and Warren thanked them both, and they soon stood in the parking lot. Mr. Brennan seemed like an obvious suspect to Tara now, but the only piece that gave her doubt was Alyssa. *Where did she fit in, if at all?* Once they got into the car, Tara posed the question to Warren. She could see that it was on his mind as well. He was being quiet, as he always was when in deep thought.

"I'm not sure," he admitted as he placed the key in the ignition. He scrunched his face as he stared in front of him. His hand still held the key, even though the car was now on.

"What?" Tara asked. She could tell he had more to say.

He sighed. "I don't know," he said as he turned to her. "Reese and Alyssa do look a bit alike. Could he have confused the two?"

It was a question that hadn't occurred to Tara, but he was right. They were a similar average height. They were both thin with long brown hair. Although Reese's was slightly straighter, it was possible that they could've been mistaken from behind. If that was true, then he had wanted to kill Reese much earlier than he actually did. But Tara also knew that once he captured Alyssa, he would've known. *But maybe it was too late?* She mentioned it to Warren.

He nodded. "I agree. Maybe he knew he couldn't turn back or he'd be caught."

It was possible, Tara assumed, but the only way to know for sure was to get it out of Mr. Brennan directly. "Let's just hope he's sober enough now to talk," she replied as they made their way to the station.

Warren pulled out of the parking lot, and Tara stared at the road ahead of them in silence as she wondered if they had finally caught the killer.

Chapter Nineteen

Tara and Warren entered the interrogation room. They were told that Brennan would now be sober enough to speak. The cops at the station had given him coffee and water until the weight of where he was hit him full-force. He stared at them as they entered. He squinted skeptically, and he sat up straighter, as if ready to take a beating. He had the same arrogance in his stance that he had at the entrance of his apartment, and now it was clear it wasn't just the alcohol that made him that way. It was his core.

His mouth curled into a devious smile as Tara took a seat across from him. She knew what he was thinking. She was a woman. He could intimidate her. It was what he had done to every female in his life, and it amazed her that he still couldn't see it was his ultimate downfall. She gave him the same smile back, with fire behind it, and his smile subsided angrily.

She slid a picture of Alyssa across the table. "Do you know her?"

"Isn't this the picture you showed me at my apartment? I told you, I don't know her. Only saw her on the news." Tara wasn't sure if he was too drunk the first time she showed him, but he had clearly remembered. She asked him again, trying to read his emotion, but once again, his response seemed sincere. Or was he a skilled liar? He was an ex-cop, after all. He knew how to play this game.

Warren took a seat beside her, opening the envelope containing all the pictures found in his apartment. He placed them on the table one by one. Brennan looked down at them, and for the first time a hint of fear surfaced in his eyes, but then it quickly vanished, as if remembering where he was. He had clearly been too drunk to remember Warren showing them to him before. He looked as if he were seeing them for the first time.

"Can you tell me why these were in your apartment?" Tara asked.

He remained quiet as he looked down at them. "I don't need to tell you," he finally blurted.

Tara stared at him. "Your daughter knows that you've been watching her. Her and your ex-wife's lawyer are going to know pretty soon too," she shot back at him. His face fell. "It seems kind of suspect that you've been watching her and her friends, and then suddenly two of her friends go missing. And I'm sure you don't like her hanging out with this crowd, isn't that right?" Tara's head tilted slightly as she stared deep into his eyes. A sudden look of concern swept across his face.

"No," he said, panicking. "She can't know. Wait, what does she think?" He stared down at the pictures again.

Tara pointed angrily at the picture of Sofia. "Where is she?"

He looked up, confused. It was a look Tara wasn't expecting to see. "How the hell would I know?" He then looked from Tara to Warren. "What is this really about?"

Tara couldn't tell if it was all an act or if he truly didn't know that he was being accused of murder. "Where were you last night?"

"I was home," he barked. "Now tell me what the hell this is about!" His frustration caused a vein to pulsate on his forehead.

Tara leaned in closer. She could still smell the alcohol on his breath. She looked him straight in the eye. "Reese and Sofia went missing not long after you took these photos. You know what this looks like? It looks like stalking to me."

Tara looked at Warren, who nodded. "Looks the same to me too, Mills."

Brennan chuckled under his breath. "That's ridiculous," he shot back. "So, what, you think I murdered them? Is that what you put in my daughter's head?"

Tara stood up out of her chair. "I'm going to ask you again. Where is she?" She pointed at Sofia, now leaning over him.

"I said I don't know!" He sighed. "I was just keeping tabs on my daughter, all right?" He leaned back in his chair in defeat. "Since I can't see her and know what she's up to, I try to keep tabs on her somehow." Tara was about to speak, but he stopped her. "I know," he started as if aware of what she was going to say. "The restraining order. But I'm still not physically going near her. I didn't take these pictures." The words fell out of his mouth. It was clearly something he didn't want to admit, but he had been backed into a corner. *But was it the truth?* Tara shared a look with Warren. It was an admission that neither of them foresaw.

"Then who took them?" Tara asked.

He sighed. "I hired a private investigator. I wanted to see what she was up to, but I didn't want her to see me watching her." He looked back down at the pictures. She could see he knew how bad this looked. But his story did sound plausible. It would make sense why Julie never noticed him taking her picture, and he was smart enough to know that if she did, it would immediately be relayed to the lawyers. But now, it would be, regardless. Tara knew, and so did he as an ex-cop that hiring a private investigator would still be considered violating a restraining order.

Suddenly he looked up, as if a thought had struck him. "He was at my house last night, ask him."

***

Tara and Warren stood in a small office down the hall from the interrogation room. Brennan had already given them the name and phone number of the private investigator, and they had just tried calling. But after trying a couple of times, and no answer, disappointment swelled in Tara's belly. Warren placed his phone back into his pocket.

He sighed. "We'll get one of the cops to keep trying or send someone over there."

They had looked up the name of the private investigation agency. It was a legit place, and Tara was beginning to believe that the story would check out, and

so would Brennan's alibi. There was also once piece of
the puzzle that she still couldn't fit: Alyssa White.

She mentioned it to Warren. "I just feel like we're
missing something." He understood without question
what she meant, and he expressed it with a nod. It was
clearly on his mind as well; it had been from the very
start, and they still could not piece it together.

"You think he was telling the truth? That he'd never
seen her before?" Warren asked.

Tara crossed her arms and sighed. "I suppose he
could be lying, but I didn't see him flinch or anything
when I showed it to him."

"Well, he is a cop," Warren reminded her. It was the
same reasoning that had crossed Tara's mind. She
nodded, but she still had a heavy doubt that wouldn't
ease. She could see in Warren's eyes that he felt it too,
but suddenly, Warren's phone rang. He reached for it
and quickly picked it up. Tara waited. At first, she
wasn't sure who it would be, but then it occurred to her
that it could be the Evidence Response Team, that they
could've finished searching Brennan's car. She watched
Warren's face intently, trying to read what he was
hearing, and his expression abruptly changed. They had
found something, she could feel it, and her heart
drummed.

"Hold on, I'm putting you on speaker so my partner
can hear," Warren said.

Tara moved a little closer as Warren held the phone
out for them both to hear.

The man on the phone cleared his throat. "So I was
saying, we found a hair. In the trunk. It's definitely from
a female." Tara looked up at Warren, meeting his eyes,
only to see the same shock. They had their doubts, but

this could make them all subside. If the hair was in fact a victim's, that could be all they needed for certainty.

"Do you know whose it is yet?" Warren asked.

"No, not yet. We'll have results in the morning. Unfortunately, we don't have any DNA for the third victim, but we're going to compare the hair with the DNA of victims one and two. We also just stopped at the Brennans' and got a DNA sample from the mother and daughter so we can rule them out if need be."

Warren thanked him and hung up. He looked at Tara. They both knew there was the potential for substantial evidence, but their only option now was to wait. Warren looked up at a clock hanging on the doorway. Tara spun around. It was now evening. They had exhausted their efforts, but they still had yet to find Sofia.

She looked at Warren. "Sofia," she said. The name rolled off her lips, and there was nothing more she needed to say. Warren understood, for he felt it too. His eyes were glossy from the tiring long day, and sadness swelled in them.

"They're going to keep looking into the night," he replied. He was referring to Sheriff Patel and the army of other officers that were diligently searching on every beach nearby. But Tara could see in his eyes that Warren knew that wasn't all she needed to hear. It was the worry that they might not find her, that she was still out there, alive. But they both knew they had nowhere else to look. Every business was closed. They didn't have a lead. They could only hope that that by capturing Brennan, she was somewhere safe.

"We'll pick up in the morning," Warren said. She could hear in his voice that he was disappointed, but it was their only option now.

They moved to the exit, but all Tara could focus on was another day lost, and as she reached for the door handle, a terrified Sofia haunted her.

***

Tara turned the keys to her condo and opened the door to a room full of darkness. She had arrived home before John. He was still at band practice. Tara had spoken to him on the way, and she was somewhat relieved to have some time to herself. She flicked the lights on, removed her shoes, placed her keys and phone next to the door, and made her way into the bedroom. A hot shower was what she needed. She was exhausted, but her mind was still fully awake, digging at every corner. Sofia was still not found. It was a realization that clung to her mind, unable to let go. It sickened her that she was home preparing for a shower when Sofia could still be out there, when her family was still worried sick.

Tara undressed, turned the water on, and stepped into the shower. The warm water was soothing against her skin. She took a deep breath, letting the steam fill her lungs. It soothed her, but not enough to make her mind stop racing. She knew it wouldn't until Sofia was found and she was certain they had the killer. She had her suspicions about Brennan, but she still wasn't one hundred percent certain. The more she thought about it, the more she felt that he was telling the truth—that he didn't know Alyssa White.

Tara's thoughts were interrupted to the sound of her phone ringing in the distance. It was probably John, she assumed, and she listened as it continued to ring and then stopped. She made a mental note to call when she was done, but then she heard her phone beep. She had a voicemail. John never left voicemails, unless it was important. And if it wasn't John, who else would call her this late?

She hurried up in the shower. She had a bad habit of thinking the worst. Maybe it was John, maybe something happened, a car accident. The thoughts swirled through her head. She tried desperately to shake them off. *He would've called the house phone next*, she told herself. She didn't know why she always thought that way—why tragedy would be her first instinct. She could only assume that it was a byproduct of her childhood trauma, and she hated that she tortured herself with those thoughts.

She stepped out of the shower, dried off, and quickly got dressed. As she exited the bathroom, she heard the jostle of keys in the front door and then the turn of the knob. She instantly relaxed. She knew it was John, and as she entered the kitchen, his smile greeted her at the door. He was still dressed in his business attire, even though he had just come from practice. He was wearing a button-up shirt that was undone from his neck to his chest, his sleeves pushed up his forearm. His hair was slicked over, and Tara couldn't help but marvel at how handsome he looked.

"How was your day?" he asked as he placed the keys down on the counter and leaned over to give her a kiss. He then made his way to the fridge and began rummaging through it. Tara took a seat at the island.

His words instantly brought her thoughts back to Sofia, and her stomach churned into a knot. "Tough," she admitted, but she didn't go into details. She didn't want to, and John understood. He nodded as he took a quick glance at her before taking out a plate of leftovers. He knew her well enough in this career now to understand when something was too much to talk about, and questions were better left unasked.

She changed the subject. "How was practice?"

A smile instantly formed as he placed his food in the microwave. "It was good! I think we're definitely ready for the gig tomorrow. You're coming right?"

She had almost forgotten about John's gig and that she'd told him she'd try her best to be there. But now as the case progressed and was prolonged, she knew it was becoming more unlikely. "I really want to be," she started as his face fell into a frown. "But this case, I really can't promise anything."

He sighed. He was clearly let down, and Tara felt bad causing him disappointment. She truly did want to be there, but she had no clue what tomorrow would hold, and she didn't want to get his hopes up.

He took a seat next to her, his plate of food steaming in his hands. "If you can make it, it would really mean a lot to me. And I think you would really enjoy being there too."

Tara nodded. "I'll do my best," she said.

He smiled weakly, but he still couldn't hide the disappointment behind it. He ate in silence as his eyes remained steady on the food in front of him.

"Everything okay?" Tara asked. He was deep in thought, way deeper than their conversation should've caused.

Her words sent a jolt through his body. "Of course!" The words burst out of him as he suddenly straightened his posture and forced a wider smile.

If Tara questioned his behavior before, she was now fully aware that he was acting odd. She chuckled slightly at the looks of him. Something was on his mind, she was sure of it. She assumed it might be slight anxiety about his upcoming show, although John was never the anxious type. But maybe, she wondered, this was bringing out something new in him.

He relaxed instantly at Tara's laugh, realizing how he looked. "Everything's fine, why?" he said in a normal tone and manner.

"No reason," Tara replied. "How do you feel about having your first gig?" she questioned, trying to see if that was the reason for his behavior.

"I feel good," he said with a hard nod. "I'm excited."

Tara looked at him a moment. He was acting normal again. He would've told her if he was anxious, but Tara wasn't going to push it further. And at that thought, something else struck her.

"By the way, did you call me right before you came home?" She had suddenly remembered the voicemail that came in while she was in the shower. She stood up, moving to the bench by the door, where she had left her phone.

"No, why?" John asked, confused.

She had assumed it wasn't him. After all, he had arrived home right after her phone rang. But if it wasn't John, then who was it? "I had a call…" She scooped her phone up, too preoccupied to finish her explanation. She unlocked the screen to see a missed call and a voicemail from an unknown number. But she recognized the area code as one from New York. Confusion swirled as she pressed play on the voicemail and held the phone to her ear. A familiar voice came through.

"Hi, Tara," it started. "This is Owen Reiner." He paused, as if questioning whether he should go further, but then he continued. "I think I have some information for you. Please give me a call back, only on this number, my cell phone."

The voicemail ended. She pulled the phone away from her ear, staring at the number. Why would Owen, the corrections officer from her father's prison, suddenly call her?

"Who was it?" John asked. She could sense his eyes on her, but she couldn't answer. She was too focused on what she just heard. He had called her a half hour ago. She looked at the time on her phone. It was now nine o' clock, and a flicker of hope stirred. She could still call him back.

Without even a word to John, she briskly walked down the hall. She could feel his eyes follow her. But she didn't have time to explain, and she wanted to make this call alone. She entered the bedroom and sat down on the bed, her phone still sweaty in her grip. She stared at the screen a moment as she took a deep breath. *What could he want to tell me? Did something happen to my dad?* The question stirred a mix of emotions inside her. *No*, she finally said to herself. *He wouldn't have told me to call him on his cell phone.* The only reasonable explanation was that he had maybe decided to hand over the visitation records after all. It would make sense why he called her privately, why he only wanted her to return the call on his cell. It was the last and only thing she had spoken to him about.

Her heart thumped in anticipation as she pressed the send button and held the phone to her ear. Her heart raced as heat radiated on her skin.

The phone rang a couple times, and then—

"Hello?"

"Owen?" Tara asked. She tried to steady her voice, which shook slightly with anticipation.

He was quiet a moment. "Tara?"

"Yes."

"One minute," he said abruptly before the sound of footsteps and the closing of a door. A slightly out-of-breath voice then resurfaced. "I'm glad you called."

Tara didn't know what to say. Everything about this call was strange. She and Owen knew each other, but they weren't close friends; they didn't keep in touch. She knew in the back of her mind that he would only be calling her if he had something important to say, and she just hoped it had to do with the visitation records.

He steadied his breathing and sighed. "I'm really not supposed to be doing this," he said before pausing as if second-guessing the call altogether. "What did you mean exactly when you said something wasn't right about your father's case?"

Tara didn't understand the motivation for his question. Why was he calling her—to ask her a question? "Why?" she asked. "Why did you call?"

"I need to know before I tell you anything more." His voice was stern.

Tara wasn't sure if she should answer. It seemed too personal, and she wasn't sure if she wanted to detail that information to him. After all, they weren't close friends. But she also reminded herself of Owen's character—that he always tried his best to help others. He wasn't the type to use personal information against someone or to judge them. Her curiosity pushed her skepticism aside. If he had something important to tell her, she would be a fool to let him go without revealing it.

"I think someone else was involved with my mother's murder," she admitted. "I think my father's hiding something." She forced the words from her mouth, but as she finished, she felt instantly vulnerable. Her face grew hot as she wondered if she had just admitted something she shouldn't have.

"That's what I thought you might say." He sighed. "I wasn't sure if I should tell you this, but if I was in your situation, I'd hope someone would help me out, and I'm going to trust your judgment as an FBI agent, as a friend." Tara eagerly waited for him to continue. "There has been someone visiting your dad." Tara couldn't believe what she was hearing. Her pulse pounded in her ears. "I think she knows you visited him too. She came the other day, and she went off about how your father was acting odd. She kind of went ballistic, actually. She was demanding to know who visited him. It seems like he was trying to protect you or something and didn't tell her it was you. But she definitely had a feeling, because she said your name." He fell silent as several questions swirled through Tara's head. *Why would he need to protect me? And why would this woman care that I had been visiting him? And how did she know my name?*

"Do you know their relationship?" Tara asked. This woman clearly knew her father well. *But how?* She couldn't think of one person who would visit him, especially a woman.

"She always writes her relationship as a friend," he replied. "But she must be a good friend, because she comes once a week, like clockwork, around noon."

Tara's suspicion was now even more heightened. They were even closer than she imagined. She remembered what John had suggested—maybe he was having an affair—and now Tara was beginning to believe it herself. It sat uneasy in her belly.

"How old is this woman?" Tara asked.

"Forty-two, that's what her license says."

"And what does she look like?" Tara wanted to flesh out as much information as she could get.

"Pretty average-looking, I'd say. But she has curly red hair."

Tara thought for a moment as she remained silent. She did not know anyone that fit that description. Her father was sixty-two. She would be young for him, but it was possible that she was a love interest. In fact, her mother was ten years younger than her father. *Could he have been seeing her all along? Could that be where he went on his work trips?* The ideas spun in her head, and then one other question came forward. "Why are you telling me this?" It seemed odd that he would call her to tell her this, that he would risk his job. For what?

He sighed. "I keep asking myself that too," he said with an awkward chuckle at the end, but then his voice hardened into a serious tone. "I like to think I'm a pretty good judge of character. That woman…" He paused. "I can't explain it, I just get really weird vibes off of her, and it wasn't just that one time. It's every time she comes in. She's jumpy and angry, and then you asking about your dad's visitation records just made me think of her instantly. And then of course she came in and got all riled up about you and then just topped off my suspicion." He grew quiet again, as if thinking of how to solidify why he was telling her all this. "I just couldn't sit by and not say something. It just didn't feel right," he finished.

Tara didn't know how to respond. "Thank you," was all she could say. But she still had yet to wrap her mind around this information or what to do with it. Before she got off the phone with him, she had one last question. "What's her name?"

Owen hesitated. "Mackenzie James." Tara mouthed the name silently before thanking him again and saying her goodbyes.

She sat still at the foot of the bed, staring at the blank wall in front of her. *Mackenzie James,* she mouthed again. She had never heard the name before.

Tara finally stood up. She knew John was eagerly waiting in the next room, still confused. She walked out of the bedroom and down the hall, to see John sitting on the barstool, looking at his phone. He abruptly turned toward her with a look of concerned curiosity.

"Who was it?"

She took a seat next to him, still focused on the strange call. She then turned toward him, shaking her head, still trying to make sense of it all.

"I just received the strangest call," she finally said.

John knitted his eyebrows, the way he always did when he was confused and worried. Tara explained who it was on the phone, what she had just heard, what she suspected. At each revelation, John's eyes opened wider with surprise and disbelief. He just sat quietly and listened. After she finally finished, he looked at her with sorrow in his eyes.

"So what next?" he finally asked.

It was a question Tara hadn't yet answered herself, but it had been on her mind all along. She didn't yet know what her next steps would be. She knew nothing about this woman. She knew nothing about her relationship with her father. She didn't even know if her mother was aware of her when she was alive. After all, Tara was too young to pick up on any of her mother's suspicions, if she had them. But she knew one thing that she was planning to do for sure.

She hadn't even realized how focused her eyes had been on the island counter. She looked up at John. "I'm going to find out who she is." The words burst from her lips as a newfound determination flowed through her body.

John simply nodded, knowing that it was the exact answer she would give.

***

Tara sat on the couch in the living room with only a floor lamp lighting the area surrounding her. She sat cross-legged, her laptop resting on her thighs. It was now close to midnight. John had gone off to bed, but Tara already knew she wouldn't sleep. She needed to look for answers. She had searched for Mackenzie James numerous times, adding every neighboring town near the prison as a keyword. So far, she had found nothing. No articles, no social media accounts, no job hits.

Tara sighed as she scrolled through the results one more time. She was growing frustrated. She knew this woman held the possibility of answers, that she could very well be the person Tara had sensed was in the room during her mother's death. But yet Tara still had no understanding of who she was, other than a name.

She could only assume that her father was having an affair, and it pained her. Not for herself, but for her mother. Her father had already made her mother's life a living hell and then ended it. He had inflicted pain each time he left a bruise on her body. He would belittle her every chance he had, chipping away at every piece of her that made her special. And now he was unfaithful too? Anger boiled up. *How could he do all this to her? And why did she stay with him? Was she ever happy?* The last question caused her fingers to go limp on the keyboard. A great sadness rose up within her, until it crashed on her like a tsunami.

Could it be that the few years Tara had been in this world with her mother were probably the most difficult years her mother had ever faced? Tara's eyes welled, and she sat back in the couch, letting her head rest as she stared at the ceiling. She had been so young, so oblivious.

She wiped a tear away as she tried to picture her mother. At first, she remembered the fights, the abuse, the bruises. But then other memories pushed through, the memories without her father. She pictured her mother smiling, watching Tara play. She pictured her mother's laugh when she did something funny. She envisioned her mother doing arts and crafts with her, baking, going to the museum. Each memory was filled with smiles and laughter.

Tara finally took a deep breath and sat up. *My mother was happy*, she reminded herself. *Because of me.*

173

Warmth flooded through her at the realization; it was love. She suddenly saw everything differently. It wasn't her mother, her father, and her, all living together but distant in their emotions and experiences. She now saw herself and her mother entwined together in a tragedy, with her father standing at a distance.

Tara looked back down at her computer. She couldn't allow self-pity to seep in. She couldn't dwell on her mother's sadness. None of that would help her find answers. Only focusing on the love they shared would, because that was ultimately what drove her. Her mother deserved justice.

Tara laid her fingers atop the keyboard once more. She typed the woman's name in Google over and over again with new towns. She went to Facebook, to Instagram, to Twitter. She searched in every way she could possibly think of. She tried different nicknames she could think of for Mackenzie—Mack, Kenzie, Kenz.

She searched diligently for another hour, each search leading to inaccurate results—same names with different ages, different last names. Eventually, Tara's eyes felt heavy. She tried to push through, to continue to search, but soon all she could focus on was how tired she was. She laid her had back onto the couch. She would just rest her eyes, she told herself, but exhaustion quickly enveloped her, pulling her into a deep, deep sleep.

Chapter Twenty

He took a swig of his whisky, sloshed it in his mouth, and then let the burn hit his throat. He had been sitting in a booth at the restaurant for a couple hours now. He was a few drinks in, the buzz only intensifying the sense of pride he felt at what he had done and what was about to occur.

It was late on a weekday, and the restaurant was relatively quiet. Only a few men sat at the bar—regulars—speaking louder than they realized, sloshing their drinks in their hands at each laugh. It was the type of crowd he had hoped for tonight, because he knew they would never bother him. They wouldn't spark conversation, they wouldn't even recognize him, as people usually did. They were too into their drinks, and he was too concealed in his booth to make a presence.

He stared down at his whiskey, deep into the empty glass, and he smiled. It reminded him of the clues he left behind, the strategy he had followed, and that no matter how close law enforcement thought they were, they too would only be left looking into an empty glass of what once was a lead.

He snapped out of his trance as he sensed movement, and looked up to see the waitress who so often waited on him smiling before him. Her long, slender body was accentuated with an apron tied tight around her waist. "Another?" she asked as she reached for his glass and placed it atop her tray.

Without hesitation, he nodded. He already had a strong buzz, but tonight he deserved it.

"Where are your friends tonight?" she asked, beaming.

"Tired." He laughed. "We all had a long day."

She nodded. She understood. And without another word, she turned on her heels, the smile still plastered on her face as she moved to the bar to place his usual order.

At her exit, his eyes moved to the television, sitting over the bar. The news was on. His story was on, the story he had created. It was everywhere, on every station, on ever television in everyone's home, in every restaurant—it made him glow with pride.

A picture of the girl he had recently buried hung in the corner of the screen as an anchor pleaded for anyone with information to step forward. The station then cut to a reporter standing outside in the dark, highlighted only by the production lights behind the camera and the lights of the search crew that lined the beach behind her.

"I'm here reporting from Fowler Beach, where law enforcement has been diligently searching for any sign of Sofia Hernandez," she started. "So far, no trace of her whereabouts has been reported, and no body has been found, but law enforcement has been extending their efforts."

As he stared at the television, listening to the reporter's words, he knew exactly where she stood, because he had stood there too. The search was closing in, they were getting closer, and his body tingled with excitement. He knew exactly what they were going to find; it was only a matter of time.

Chapter Twenty One

Tara woke up with a startle to her phone ringing on the coffee table. She looked around her. She was in the living room, the floor light still on, her laptop still in her lap. Sunlight was beginning to peak into the room, and it sent a shockwave through her as she realized it was dawn.

She quickly reached for her phone. Warren's name flashed across the screen. *He must have news*, she realized as her hazy, tired mind began to awaken. She picked up.

"Mills," he said before she could even say hello. His voice was tense with urgency, and before he even said his next words, Tara knew what he was going to say. She felt a sudden rush to her head. "They found a body. It looks like Sofia's," he added, confirming what Tara felt in her core but desperately hoped not to hear. Her heart sank as she fully sat up.

"Where?" A wave of guilt rose up.

"Fowler Beach. It's about a half hour north of Dewey." Warren's words were short and rushed. Tara could tell he was in the car. She could hear the constant hum of a motor.

She stood up, placing her laptop on the coffee table. "I'll meet you there," she said. She didn't need to hear more. Warren mentioned where to meet, and they quickly said their goodbyes.

Tara placed her phone on the coffee table. She was about to make her way to her bedroom and get ready, but she lingered momentarily. The laptop caught her eye. In the commotion of answering Warren's call, she had almost forgotten why she woke up on the couch in the first place. Mackenzie James still lingered in her mind, but she didn't have time to focus on that now. This case needed her more. Tara turned away from the laptop and hurriedly made way to her bedroom.

***

Tara pulled up along a dead-end sandy road. Warren's car was already there, parked behind a row of forensic vehicles and cop cars. No news vans had arrived yet, but Tara knew it was only a matter of time.

Unlike Dewey Beach, this one was a bit off the beaten path. Tara had driven about a mile without seeing a single home, and she was almost certain that none lined the beach in front of her. She parked and looked toward the row of beach grass between her and the water. Not a single home could be seen. She knew it would make their job more difficult. Even though there were no witnesses at the last scene, there certainly wouldn't be any here, unless the killer did something foolish, and Tara knew he wouldn't.

She stepped out of the car and made her way to the entranceway of the beach. The wind blew wildly, sweeping up little beads of sand until they struck her face as she walked. She squinted until they passed. And as she opened her eyes wide again, she could see a news van approaching. It bumped along the old road and then turned sharply to park, sending a cloud of sand into the air. The van came to an abrupt halt, and a male reporter jumped out, along with a cameraman, hoisting his heavy gear on his shoulder. It was the same reporter that had shoved a microphone in Tara's face at the medical examiner's office. He made eye contact with her briefly, but Tara quickly turned. She wasn't ready to answer any questions.

Pretty soon, a row of news vans paraded down the street. Another one parked quickly, and a tall brunette swung open the passenger door, microphone already in hand. Tara knew it was only a matter of time before they would hound her. She reached the pathway and stepped over the yellow tape tied to each end of the sand fencing. She was quickly out of his reach, and she was thankful for that.

She focused ahead of her as she hurried onto the beach. She could see Warren up ahead, about two hundred yards away, standing atop the dunes. He was talking to someone, and as Tara grew closer, she could see that it was a cop she did not recognize, dressed in uniform. Forensics personnel were scattered around them, searching diligently in the sand for anything of substance. Warren didn't even see Tara was approaching. He and the officer were staring at the ground between them. Warren's face was tense with pain, and it caused Tara's stomach to twist in a knot. She knew what they were looking at: Sofia's body.

She took a deep breath as she stepped over the sand dune fence and trudged up the small hill. Warren looked up at her presence. A look of sheer horror and disappointment was clear on his face. Another innocent teenage girl had been taken; another life lost. While they were never certain if Sofia was still alive, they had certainly hoped they would find her that way, that they would be able to save her and return her to her family. Now they both knew that another family would never be the same, that their daughter's future would never be lived.

The officer nodded as she finally stood in front of them. She kept her eyes steady, moving between each of them as Warren admitted that he had arrived just before her. Tara couldn't dare look down yet into the gaping hole that she sensed between them.

"Chief Garcia," the man said as he held out his hand. He was short, with a round belly and clean-shaven face. Tara introduced herself as well, but after their introductions a silence fell between them. Warren and Tara met eyes, and then his fell into the hole, reminding Tara that she still hadn't looked down.

She took a deep breath as she followed Warren's eyes. About a few feet deep, Tara could just make out Sofia's face, still covered by bits of sand. Her eyes were closed, but she could see the unmistakable button nose, the curly brown hair. Her skin was now a bluish tint, making the marks around her neck more apparent. They were the same marks found on Reese.

Tara took a deep breath, giving relief to the swell of anger and sadness that had risen up in full force. She looked at Warren and then Chief Garcia.

"When did you find her?"

"I was just telling Warren. Early this morning," he replied. "I've had my cops looking at every beach in the area, and I know others have been doing the same all down the coast in Sussex County." He shook his head at his words, as he tried to stifle his emotions. "I've got teenage girls myself, this one hit home."

Tara looked at Warren. She knew those words would hit him hard after what he had told her about his wife and daughter. She could see the pain surface, but then he shot his eyes to ground, trying to remove any trace of it.

Tara tried not to draw attention to him and bent down, getting a closer look in the hole. She studied the blue marks on Sofia's neck. "Looks like the same marks we saw on Reese," she said to Warren.

He nodded. "Strangulation."

Tara bent down farther, now sitting on her heels. Around Sofia's wrists were the same dark blue ligature marks they had seen on Reese. She scanned the rest of the body. Sofia wore a loose-fitting t-shirt and a pair of jean capris, folded halfway down her calves. Just above her sneakers, around her ankles, the same blue ligature marks were apparent. Tara pointed them out to Warren.

He nodded. "Looks just like Reese too."

Tare looked up. "Do we know an approximate time of death?"

Chief Garcia nodded. "Forensics said it looks she died the night or early morning after she was abducted, between midnight and 2:00 a.m. yesterday morning. He must've buried her pretty soon after that, because we started searching this beach around seven."

His words caused a sudden chill to rise up Tara's spine and then burst into frustration in her mind. Chief Garcia and his officers had possibly just missed the killer. If they had arrived only a few hours earlier, the killer would've still been there, caught in the act of burying Sofia's body. But it wasn't just that missed opportunity that tugged on her conscience. There was something else that tugged even harder—the time Sofia was still alive. She had been abducted between eight and nine, which meant that she had been alive for a few hours before she was killed, but Tara and Warren had failed to find her. The realization sat heavy.

But Tara also knew she couldn't dwell on a lost moment. The killer was still out there. They had to focus on the path ahead of them, carefully deciding where to place their footing. Her thoughts turned to Brennan. She knew it was still possible that he could be who they were looking for. If he had buried the body yesterday morning, he would still have had time to get home before Tara and Warren arrived at his door. An eyewitness was all they would need to be sure, but Tara knew the chances were slim.

"No witnesses?" she asked.

Chief Garcia shook his head with disappointment. "There's not much around here, and no one would be on the beach that late." His words only confirmed what Tara suspected. But then he added, "I was going to tell Warren before you got here that we did find something. I'm not sure what it means, though." Tara's ears perked up, and so did Warren's. He stepped a bit closer.

They hadn't even realized that Chief Garcia was tightly holding an evidence bag. He held it out in front of him. "We found this when we were digging her up," he said as Tara focused on the bag. "It was placed on top of her. Might've fallen out of the killer's pocket." Tara leaned in closer. Inside sat a small black rectangular object. At first she wasn't sure what she was looking at, but then she recognized it. She had seen one before, when John bought her a camera for Christmas one year. It was a memory card.

She looked at Warren. She could tell he recognized it right away, and his eyes lit up. "Have you checked if anything is on it?" he asked.

Chief Garcia shook his head. "We were going to leave that up to you guys. Forensics dusted it but couldn't get a print off it." He handed it to Warren, who then turned to Tara. She could see hope swirl in his eyes. Whatever was on that memory card had the potential to give them clues into who the killer was, or where they could find him. Tara felt a sudden flutter in her chest at the thought. But she also thought it seemed too easy. There were no prints. *Was it possible that the killer strategically left it at the scene on purpose?*

Warren thanked him as he held the bag in front of his face, studying it once more. "Mind if we use your station to take a look?"

Chief Garcia frowned and shook his head, as if Warren's question didn't need to be asked.

Warren looked at Tara. He knew that what he held could be a possible lead, and so did she. After a short goodbye to the chief, they turned on their heels, trudging through the sand.

As they neared the parking lot, Warren opened his mouth to speak, but his phone interrupted. He stopped in his tracks as he pulled out his phone and held it to his ear.

"This is Agent Warren." He grew quiet as he intently listened. He squinted out onto the water.

Tara eagerly waited next to him. She could only think of one person who would call: forensics. It was likely they had the DNA results for the hair found in Brennan's car and that the cops would have checked out his alibi by now.

After a few moments went by, Warren thanked whoever it was and was quickly off the phone. He turned to Tara.

He sighed. "Brennan's alibi checks out," he confirmed, speaking in a low whisper, careful not to be overheard by reporters. Tara nodded with disappointment. She had a gut feeling Brennan wasn't the killer, but it also confirmed that they were starting from ground zero. "He was with the PI the night Sofia went missing," Warren added.

"And the hair?" Tara asked.

"It was his ex-wife's hair," he replied, only confirming what Tara already suspected. She had remembered what his ex-wife had said, that her husband had brought over boxes of her things to her sister's place unsolicited. It was likely that he had put those belongings in his trunk and that her hair was on them.

Warren looked over at the reporters standing yards away from them, by the entrance to the beach. They were too far to overhear, but they were watching Tara and Warren intently.

"We should go," he finally said.

Tara nodded, and they both turned to their cars. They walked in silence as one question continued to dominate Tara's mind. If Brennan wasn't the killer, then who was?

Chapter Twenty Two

Warren and Tara stood next to the computer, hovering over a row of memory card adapters. The police station had given them every device they had that could possibly read the memory card, but so far none of them had worked. Some were too large for the card, others too small, and those that fit caused an error message to flash across the screen.

Tara was beginning to lose hope. She could hear the clock ticking away in her head each time another adapter failed. They needed to know what was on that card, and every moment that they wasted was an opportunity for the killer to plan for his next victim. It sent a chill down Tara's spine.

"I had no idea this would be so difficult," she admitted in frustration. She had only owned one camera in her life, and she knew that memory cards required adapters, but she didn't know that each card was so unique in what it required.

Warren sighed as he shook his head. He tried another, and another, until he was at the last one in the row. He slid the memory card into the adapter and plugged in the USB. They waited, a linger of hope beginning to intensify. But then *Card Error* flashed across the screen.

Warren shook his head again, letting out another sigh as he fully stood up. Tara did the same.

"We'll have to go to a camera store," Tara said.

Warren nodded. They both knew that a camera store was not only where they would find the correct adapter, but they would also learn more information on what type of camera was used. It could also help them narrow down who would own one, or if anyone had bought one in the area.

Tara took a seat at the computer as Warren pulled a chair up next to her. She opened a search engine and began to search for any stores in the area. She started in the area they now were, by Fowler Beach, but after scrolling through a string of results and searching a few different ways, nothing of interest popped up. It was just as Tara expected. There weren't many commercial buildings in the area, from what she could see, and it was hard to envision a camera store.

Her fingers clicked on the keyboard. Her next destination was Dewey Beach. She had a good feeling that she would find something as she scrolled through the results. After all, it was where the murders started. She suspected that it was more likely the killer would purchase a camera in that area. It was also a more touristy area and seemed fitting for a camera store.

Warren leaned in closer as Tara let the mouse hover over a location. It was exactly what they were looking for—a store that sold all kinds of cameras and gear—and it was right in the center of town. Without even a word, Warren took out his phone and put the address in his GPS.

"It's about thirty-five minutes," he said as he suddenly stood up, heading to the door.

Tara was right behind him. As she reached the door frame, she looked down at her phone, tight in her grip. It was now 9:00 a.m., and the realization gave Tara a sudden burst in her step. She knew how quickly time passed. They needed answers fast if they were going to stop this killer before he struck again.

***

Tara stared out the window, watching the beach grass dance in the wind as the car sped past. Warren had insisted on driving, as usual.

They had been in the car for nearly twenty minutes, but they had barely spoken, each too immersed in their own thoughts. Tara looked back down at her lap, where Sofia's case file sat open. She had already gone through each case file twice already, trying to see if there was anything she had missed. But after going through them once more, she sighed and turned again to the window.

She focused on the memory card. If it was in fact the killer's, she could think of only one reason why the killer would have it: to take pictures of the victims. Tara and Warren now knew that there was time between when Sofia was taken and when she was buried. It was possible that the killer had lured his victims somewhere to kill them and document it with photos before finishing them off. The thought made Tara nauseous.

She turned to Warren. "You think the killer could be taking pictures of victims as a trophy?" She knew that it was common for serial killers to take some sort of trophy to remind them of the crime. Sometimes it was just to reminisce. Other times, it was to represent ownership over what they did, like an athlete holding on to a medal as an accomplishment.

Warren nodded. "I think so. We'll know more once we find out what's on it."

He was right. They needed to know what was on it before they could jump to conclusive theories. She knew it was just as likely that the memory card could show images of the killer stalking the victims instead. Either way, the information was valuable. But all they could do now was wait.

Tara turned back to the window as her mind wandered. The name Mackenzie James still sat in the back of her mind. She still didn't quite know what to do with the information, and it pained her.

"You all right?" Warren interrupted her train of thought, and she immediately felt guilty for letting her mind wander from the case.

She hadn't even realized how intently she was staring out the window until she heard Warren's voice. She adjusted herself in her seat, sitting up straighter as she faced forward. "I'm fine," she replied, trying to sound as convincing as possible, but her words hung heavy with her doubt.

Warren picked up on it. "You sure?" He glanced over at her before turning his eyes back to the road, and Tara was careful not to make eye contact. She knew she would give herself away. "I've noticed you haven't had one of your..." He thought for a second on how to word it. "Moments," he finally uttered. "Since the last case."

Tara could feel her face redden. He was referring to the panic attacks she had experienced during her first and most recent case. Those moments had almost cost her career, and she had gone into this case with the fear that they would happen again. It was a sensitive subject. She was lucky they hadn't reoccurred, but she also knew it was evidence that she had worked on herself, that she had gotten to the root of what troubled her. And that root she now knew linked to Mackenzie James.

"Not trying to pry," Warren finally said when Tara didn't respond. "It's a good thing." He smiled at her. "But I have noticed you've been a bit distracted at times."

Warren's words sidelined her. Had she seemed distracted? It hadn't even occurred to her. But if Warren were saying it, she knew she must've. *Maybe it was when he called this morning, when I seemed groggy from falling asleep on the couch? Or maybe when I was short with him about my visit to New York?* Questions rolled around in her head until she realized she had been quiet for too long.

"How so?" She fished for clarification.

Warren shrugged. "I don't know," he sighed, trying to make light of it. "You just seem kind of tired lately and in deep thought." He looked over at her again, but Tara's eyes stayed focused in front of her, and he turned away. "You don't have to tell me. I just want to make sure everything's okay, that's all."

Tara remained quiet. Part of her wanted to tell him what she had been going through. After all, Warren had opened up to her about his wife and daughter, and he already knew about her mother's murder at the hands of her father. Why was this so different?

She hadn't told anyone except John what she had been going through, and it felt odd opening up to someone else. She had no idea how he would react. If she would look crazy, digging into a past that was already put to rest. But at the same time, she almost craved Warren's opinion.

She took a deep breath. "I visited my father," she finally said.

Warren raised his eyebrows, his gaze still ahead of him. "Woah. And how was that?"

"It was…" She paused for a moment. "Interesting. But I think I needed it."

Warren nodded understandingly, but Tara's heart still pounded. She wanted to tell him the rest. It felt as if it were about to burst out of her. "There's just some answers I need from him," she added. It was unprompted, and Warren seemed a bit surprised by the sudden openness. But Tara didn't focus on it. She wanted to finish getting out what she held inside her. "I think I've realized why I had those 'moments.'" Warren looked over at her, his eyes darting between her and the road. "I'm starting to think that someone else might be involved in my mother's death. It's a lot to get into, though."

Warren was quiet. His eyebrows knitted as he tried to make sense of what Tara was telling him. "Are you sure?"

"Yes," she responded without hesitation.

Warren nodded again. It was all he needed to hear. "Do you know who it might be?"

"I think so. I'm determined to find out once this case is over."

Again, he nodded, his eyes moving between Tara and the road. "Good for you, Mills," he finally said. "That takes a lot of guts."

Tara smiled. She wasn't sure how Warren would react, but it was exactly how she hoped. He didn't even need to know the details. He trusted her judgment. He didn't think she was crazy, acting out from some psychological issue.

As he turned onto another road, he shook his head in amusement as he let out a slight chuckle. It was strange, after telling him something so personal and dark. Tara couldn't understand where it was coming from.

"What?" she asked.

He shook his head again. "Nothing, you're just impressive, that's all."

Tara felt a tinge of pride, but she wasn't sure why Warren was complimenting her. In fact, she didn't feel impressive at all. She felt like her psychological baggage was everything that kept her from being impressive.

"Impressive? Why would you say that?"

Warren took a deep breath. "Do you ever wonder why I always want to drive? Why I always insist?"

Tara had never really thought that in-depth about it. She had always found it a bit irritating, but she just assumed it was Warren's strange way of exerting superiority. "I don't know," she replied. "Something to do with your ego?" She looked at him and smiled. He laughed.

"Very funny," he replied, still smiling, but then it faded and he sighed. "Ever since my wife and daughter passed away, I can't stand sitting in the passenger's seat.

And you know what a therapist told me once?" He looked at Tara and back at the road, but he wasn't seeking an answer. "That it's my way of trying to gain control, since I lost them in a car accident." A silence fell around them. She had no idea that Warren's incessant need to drive was deep-rooted in something psychological. It made perfect sense, and she suddenly felt sorry for him. But as she watched him staring intently at the road, she wondered why he was telling her all of this.

"My point being," he continued, "is I stopped seeing the therapist after that. I'd rather be stuck in this psychological war with the road instead of fully letting go. But you..." He looked over at Tara once more with a proud smile. "You get to the root of the problem. You don't let fear hold you back. It takes guts to realize things about yourself and to dig into something that deeply troubles you."

Tara had never thought of it that way, *being brave*. To her it just seemed like a necessity to dig into her past. Not only was it making her life unbearable with nightmares and panic attacks, but she knew it would be a disservice to her mother. She would want Tara to seek freedom from it all, to live her life to the fullest. But she also knew her mother deserved justice, and that was Tara's biggest driving force.

Warren was now pulling into the parking lot of the camera store. It sat in a shopping center amongst a row of other stores.

"I wouldn't call it brave," Tara finally admitted. "It's a necessity for myself and to honor my mother. She'd want me to be happy, and she'd want me to know the truth."

194

Warren had just put the car in park, but his hands still held the steering wheel as he looked out into the parking lot. There was a sadness in his eyes, and Tara suddenly felt bad, but she wasn't sure why. It was as if she had said something she shouldn't have.

He sensed Tara's eyes on him, and he slid his hands from the wheel, still staring in front of him. "Good for you, Mills," he replied with a nod. His words were sincere, more than they had ever felt. But then he switched gears. "Let's go see about this memory card," he added as he finally stepped out of the car. Tara did the same. She knew her words had hit Warren hard for some reason, but she wasn't going to ask. This case needed them now, and so Tara switched her focus as well.

They walked across the parking lot, which was mostly empty. A woman in the store next to the camera shop flipped a sign on the door, making it known they were open. She studied them as they walked past. It was still early, and many of the stores were just opening up. Tara held the evidence bag containing the memory card tightly. They were now so close to finding out what was on it, and it sat like a heavy weight in her hand.

Tara opened the door, and they stepped into an air-conditioned room with display cameras and other gear lining the walls. There were no customers yet, but a man at the counter looked up as they entered. He was tall and lanky, with gray hair on the sides of his head. He peered over his reading glasses, which sat on the tip of his nose.

"Can I help you?" He was unscrewing something on a camera. He placed a small screwdriver down as Tara and Warren approached the counter. He stared skeptically at them until Tara flashed her badge and he cocked his head back in surprise.

"We have a memory card, and we need the adapter for it," Tara said as she slid the evidence bag across the counter.

The man looked down at it. He reached forward, about to pick it up, but stopped himself. "May I?"

Tara nodded, and he scooped up the bag. He turned it in different directions, reading the writing on it before placing it back down. "A C-Fast card reader should work." He walked around the counter to one of the walls. He scanned the wall briefly before retrieving what he was looking for. He placed it down on the counter in front of Tara and Warren. "This should do the trick."

Tara thanked him, but she knew they weren't done yet. They didn't have time to drive back to the station. They needed to know what was on that memory card *now*. She looked at Warren and knew he had the same thought as well. She turned back to the owner. "Could we take a look at this on your computer?" She waved the memory card in her hand as she spoke.

The man sighed. "What are you looking for anyway?" he asked skeptically. "Is this about those missing girls?"

Tara nodded. She didn't even need to plead with him anymore. That was all the confirmation he needed. He shook his head. She could see it troubled him. "If it'll help keep that sicko off the streets, by all means, use my computer." His eyes moved to the entrance of the store before he pursed his lips and turned on his heels. "It's best if you use the one in the back, in case any customers come in." He waved his hand for them to follow him as he walked to the end of the counter and pulled open a door with an *Employees Only* plaque on it. Tara grabbed the adapter off the counter, and she and Warren quickly followed him.

He led them into a small office that contained a computer, a filing cabinet, and loads of camera gear. Tara and Warren stood around him as he powered the computer on and explained how to use the adapter. "I'll leave the rest to you guys," he said before stepping out of the room.

They waited until he was good distance away. They needed to make sure that the evidence was completely sealed, that he had no chance of walking in. And when he finally was gone, they turned back to the computer. Tara felt her palms begin to sweat as she pulled the memory card out of the evidence bag and placed it carefully into the adapter.

She and Warren waited anxiously for the memory card to pop up on the screen. Tara was unable to blink until an icon appeared on the desktop. They both leaned in closer. When Tara clicked on the icon with the mouse, a window popped up, and within it, photo files appeared. Tara heaved a deep sigh as she looked at Warren. Part of her was excited at the possibility that they had found evidence, but another part was fearful. She could see the same pull of emotions dance in Warren's eyes that were steadily glued to the screen.

She let the mouse hover over one of the images as she prepared herself for whatever she was about to see. She knew she was possibly about to see pictures of the victims, in what way she did not know, but she prepared for every possibility. She steadied herself and let her finger click on an image. As it opened, she heaved a sigh of relief. It wasn't a victim. In fact, it was nothing like

197

she expected. Staring back at her was the image of a house, fully ablaze. Flames burned wildly through the roof, tearing it into pieces. Windows were blown out. It looked like a horrific fire, but Tara had no clue what it could mean.

She looked at the next image. It was the same fire, but this time firefighters were there. One of them was helping an elderly woman across the lawn. Others stood in formation, holding a hose, about to extinguish the flames.

Tara was now even more unsure if the memory card had been left on purpose or strategically. The images didn't make sense; they were completely unrelated. But part of her wondered if that was the exact reason why the killer would've left them behind. After all, the card had no prints on it.

Warren caught Tara's perplexed expression "Maybe the killer is trying to throw us off," he suggested.

It was her exact thought as well. "It does seem odd that it had no prints. If it fell out of his pocket or he dropped it, it's unlikely it wouldn't have some sort of forensic evidence on it."

But she still wasn't convinced the pictures were all for nothing. There had to be clues. She looked at two more pictures, each another development of the fire. One was a wide shot of the police activity, the fire almost extinguished. The other was a close-up of the damaged home.

Tara studied both pictures as frustration boiled. They needed something, anything that would give them a lead. They could find where the fire was, have someone help them identify who took the photos. But like Warren said, what if it was all just a means to throw them off track? What if it just wasted precious time? What if these were someone else's photos that were planted at the scene to steer Tara and Warren off course?

She exhaled deeply as she clicked the last image. She waited a moment for it open, expecting to see just another image of the fire. But when it opened, her eyes opened wide. What she had feared all along rose up inside her like a sudden sickness. Warren gasped. Tara looked away instinctively for just a moment as she let the shock subside into a controlled reality.

When she looked back at the screen, she was met by Sofia's terrified eyes. They were bloodshot and wet with tears, and she stared pleadingly at the camera. A chill ran up Tara's spine.

She was lying on what looked like a concrete surface of an unfinished basement or something similar. The picture was taken from above, giving a full aerial view of her on the floor. Her feet were bound with rope, her mouth was duct-taped, and her hands were hidden behind her back; Tara assumed they were also tied.

She turned to Warren, but for a moment he didn't even sense the turn of her head. His eyes remained on the screen, his jaw clenched tight, making it look more defined than it already was. But then he took a deep breath, releasing the tension, and turned to meet Tara's eyes.

"We could find out where that fire was," Warren suggested. "But it could be a long shot." They both knew it would be difficult. The images did not reveal which police department was at the fire. Their vehicles were not included in any of the shots, and neither were the firefighters.

But Tara had another idea. "You think there's a way to identify the type of camera used from the memory card?" If so, they could maybe narrow down where it could've been bought in the area.

Warren shrugged. "Could be possible. Only one way to find out. Let's ask the owner." If anyone could tell them if there was a way to trace the memory card back to a specific camera, it was the store owner. Warren was about to say one more thing, but Tara already knew. She turned to the computer and exited from Sofia's image. Without another word, Warren left the room, only to return moments later with the shop owner.

"What can I help with?" he asked as he stepped into the room behind Warren. He knitted his eyebrows and twisted his mouth in concern. Tara could tell he truly wanted to help, and she was thankful for it. It certainly made their job easier.

"This memory card," Tara started as she pointed to the adapter by the computer. "Is there any way to trace what camera it was used on?"

The man bobbed his head back and forth, weighing the question. "To a degree. You can certainly tell the brand and if it's a high-end camera or not. Like I can tell you already that that memory card is for a Canon. That adaptor I gave you is only used for Canon C-Fast memory cards."

Tara nodded. "Any way to tell what type of Canon?"

The shop owner sighed and shook his head, sending a wave of disappointment through the room. "You can certainly narrow it down. Only certain Canons will use that type of memory card, but you can't narrow it down to one specific camera, or even a couple." Tara contemplated their options. Without being able to pinpoint the exact type of camera used, it opened the door for more obstacles, but it was still certainly possible to track local sales; it would just take more time than she was willing to give. Tara sighed, and the shop owner, sensing her disappointment, perked up, as if to reignite the flame of hope he had extinguished. "I can tell you that the memory card you have is only used for high-end Canons."

"Who would need such high-end camera?" Warren asked.

The shop owner pursed his lips. "A professional, or a really serious hobbyist. Those cameras can run a few thousand dollars."

Tara shared a look with Warren. They both knew it was a bit of information that could potentially help them. The pictures were taken at a potentially newsworthy story. *Could it have been a professional there on assignment?* She knew if that were the case, they would probably come into local shops like this often.

"Do you sell those types of cameras here?" Tara asked.

"No, I only sell the adaptors. I mostly sell Sony cameras." Tara's heart sank. Even though his information so far was useful, she was still hoping to leave with a lead. He tilted his head to the ceiling, giving Tara the hope of another thought brewing. And then he looked back and forth between Tara and Warren excitedly. "I do know a store that does," he said as he turned toward the computer, abruptly opening a drawer at his desk and grabbing a piece of a notepad. He scribbled something down, ripped off the page, and handed it to Tara. "It's only a couple towns over," he added.

Tara took the paper. It was a start, and she thanked him. But then she turned to the computer. She needed an easier way to show the images of the fire if needed without having to insert the memory card.

She pointed at the computer. "Do you mind if I send these images to my email?"

The shop owner shook his head. "Go right ahead."

Tara hovered over the computer as she opened her email and uploaded only the fire images as an attachment. She then quickly ejected the memory card and grabbed the adaptor. They were getting closer to answers. She could feel it in her every bone of her body. She thanked the shop owner again. When she turned around to face Warren, she could see in his wide eyes that he sensed it too. Without a word, he turned to the door. Tara quickly followed.

Chapter Twenty Three

Tara looked up from her phone as the car slowed, turning into a parking lot. *Carter Imaging* was spelled out upon the large awning, hanging over the even larger glass doors. The building was about three times the size of the store they had just come from. It had two stories and was the only building in the parking lot.

The store was about fifteen minutes outside of Dewey Beach. On the way there, Tara had learned from browsing on her phone that it was one of many in a chain, selling all the photography and videography equipment one could ever need, and it seemed like a go-to for any professional. She had already told this to Warren.

"How far is the next closest one?" Warren asked as he parked.

Tara looked down at the search results on her phone "About twenty miles." Her words only confirmed that if the killer was a professional or even a serious hobbyist, it was likely he had stepped foot within this store. Again, Tara felt a slow rise in adrenaline at the possibility of answers moments away. Warren swiftly opened the car door. Her words were affirmation to him as well.

Inside, it was vast, with numerous rows and sections. Tara couldn't even see an end in sight as she looked ahead of her. It was still early, but customers were scattered about, surveying gear and cameras and disappearing amongst the rows. She watched as one customer walked past her to a long counter. It was to the right of her, taking up the majority of the front end of the store. She looked at Warren and bobbed her head in its direction and then led the way.

There was only one person behind the counter. He looked to be in his early thirties, with a thick beard. He helped the customer briefly, giving him directions on where to find a specific item. And when the customer stepped away, he turned to Tara and Warren.

"Can I help you?"

Tara looked around her. There were no customers within earshot, but there were still many present throughout the store, and she wanted to be discreet. She flashed her badge. The sight of it brought a shot of life into the man's face. His eyes opened wide. "Is there a manager we can speak to?" She looked around her again. Another customer was approaching the counter, and she turned to face him again. "In private," she added.

The man looked startled for a moment, as if he needed to make sense of what he was hearing, but then he nodded abruptly. "One moment," he replied before turning to a door behind him and disappearing.

He returned moments later with a middle-aged man in tow. He had a nametag on his shirt that read *Manager*, with his name, Darnell Brown, underneath. He nodded for the younger guy to help a customer standing next to Tara and Warren and turned back toward them.

He was bald, except for traces of black hair beginning to grow in, like a five 'o'clock shadow, across the top of his head. He narrowed his eyes, his eyebrows almost touching from his furrowed brow. He carried a look of skepticism rather than concern.

"I supposed you want to speak in private?" he asked.

Tara nodded, and without another word, he motioned for them to come around the counter and into the room he had just come from. They followed him down a hallway, past different rooms filled with boxes and equipment. Tara's eyes wandered into them as she spotted workers busy unpacking newly arrived items and placing them atop a cart to wheel out into the store.

Once they neared the end of the hallway, he stopped in front of the manager's office and led them inside. It was a small room with a desk, computer, and surveillance cameras of the store. Once the door closed, he turned to face them and crossed his arms. "Well, what can I help you with?"

Tara had been holding the memory card in an evidence bag in her hand. She held it out in front of her, and the manager leaned forward and squinted.

"We're trying to determine what type of camera this might've been used with," she explained.

He reached out, asking to hold it for a better look, and Tara placed it in his palm. He held it up to the light, reading the manufacturer information. "This is a C-Fast memory card," he stated as he continued to turn it in the light, but it was information Tara and Warren already knew. He handed it back to Tara. "I can't say exactly, but definitely a high-end Canon. Could be a Canon IOS or an XC10."

"Do you sell those here?" she asked.

The manager nodded without hesitation. "What's this about, anyway?" He looked between Tara and Warren, trying to find any information in their expressions, but Tara knew he wouldn't find any.

"We're looking for the person who owned this memory card," Tara confirmed. "We think they might be connected to a case we're working on." She didn't reveal any more information. It was unnecessary. She didn't want the full truth to steer him away from admitting what he knew.

He didn't respond. His eyes just narrowed as he nodded once more. He was curious, as anyone would be, but Tara had only given him a small morsel, and he wanted more.

"Has anyone recently come in here to purchase one of these?" Tara asked.

But the manager only let out a small grunt, revealing the absurdity of her question. "This is a popular store. I get people in and out of here all the time buying things like this."

It was clear this was not going to be easy. But Tara knew the only other option to finding whose images were on the camera was by tracking down the fire. If they didn't find answers here, that's what they would do next, but Tara didn't want this visit to be a waste. She knew it was extremely likely that the owner of the memory card had stepped in this store. It was the only one of its kind around. It was well known and a major attraction to anyone seeking high-end equipment, and they sold cameras that used the same type of memory card. Tara knew she had to dig harder.

"Do you get a lot of return customers?"

"Definitely. We get a few, although not a ton since we're outside of D.C. There aren't too many professionals around here, but we do have some photographers and some independent journalists or stringers that come in here regularly."

Tara looked down at the memory card. *Maybe he could recognize the house fire photos, or pinpoint a person who might've taken them,* she wondered. She grabbed her phone from her pocket. "Do you happen recognize any of these images?" she asked as she pulled open her email and downloaded them. "Or anyone who might've taken them?" She stood next to the manager as she scrolled through the images one by one. She watched his face for a reaction. His eyes narrowed, and hope fluttered in Tara's chest at the hope that he recognized them. At the last image, he looked up.

"There is a stringer who comes in here quite a bit. He chases news stories and tries to sell his footage to news organizations." The manager stared into the distance, as if trying to recall a memory. He then turned his head back to Tara and sighed. "Look, I don't really know what this is about." He studied Tara's face for an answer, but she didn't give him one. She knew he was on the brink of revealing something, and she didn't want any revelation of her own to ruin it. His eyes fell from her gaze as he shook his head. He was clearly contemplating what he was about to say, but then he opened his mouth. "I'm not sure what a memory card has to do with any case you're working on, and I really hope this doesn't have to do with those girls whose bodies were found," he started. He studied Tara's face once more, but then his eyes fell again and remained on the floor. "He owns a Canon IOS, that stringer. It would work with this memory card." He looked up to meet her eyes and sighed again. "He was at a story of a house fire two weeks ago, tried to sell it to a local station."

At his words, Tara felt that they were closer than they had ever been. *This is it,* she thought, and it made perfect sense. A stringer, Tara knew, would have somewhat of a professional understanding of crime. He would know not to leave fingerprints. He would possibly know how long it takes to trace a call. Tara turned to Warren and met his eyes briefly. He knew it too; they had a solid lead.

She turned back to the manager. "How do you know? That he was at a house fire."

"He told me. He always tells me stories he's been at without me even asking. It's a bit strange, actually, but I think it's his way of trying to make himself sound important."

"When was he in here last?" Tara asked.

The manager thought for a moment, staring off into the distance. "I'm pretty sure that was the last time he was in here," he replied. It was before any of the bodies were found, and it only heightened Tara's suspicion.

"Do you happen to have his address?"

The manager nodded as he moved to the computer on his desk. He leaned over and began to type something. "His name is Ben Ford," he said as he began scrolling through results. "I order equipment for him once in a while. Here." He stood up and nodded for them to take a look. Tara and Warren hovered over the computer as well. Right next to a recent order was Ben Ford's name and address. Tara typed it into her phone.

"Do you know how long he's been a stringer?" she asked as she finished typing in the address.

The manager pursed his lips. "He's been coming in here for about two years now. He used to work at the local station, WPX9, a while back, but he got laid off from budget cuts, he said, and he's been doing this solo gig ever since." The manager shrugged. "He's pretty young, early thirties maybe, so I don't think he's been doing this for much longer than that."

Tara thanked him. He had been a stringer for what sounded like a year before Alyssa White even went missing. *Could being laid off and a year without a steady job have taken him over the edge?* A hope swirled at a force she had never felt throughout this case. It was a realization that they might be closer than ever. And as they exited the room, she wondered if they now held what they had been looking for all along, and if they were about to come face to face with the killer.

***

They pulled into the driveway of a two-story Cape Cod home on a street amongst others that were all very much alike. The street was quiet, the neighborhood was quaint. It was not what Tara was expecting. It was a rather nice neighborhood, not far from the water, and Tara knew that houses around there were not cheap. For someone who didn't have a steady income, Tara was expecting Ben Ford to occupy an apartment, not a house like this. But there were also two other cars in the driveway.

"Looks like he doesn't live alone," Tara said as the car stuttered to a halt. As she spoke those words, a woman came around the bend of the house, walking across the lawn toward the driveway. She looked to be in her late sixties. She held two towels, and she was just about to toss them onto a clothing line but then stopped in her tracks, her eyes darting to the car. She squinted, trying to make out who it was, but then she began to walk toward them.

Warren took a deep breath. "I guess you're right," he said as he opened the car door and stepped out. Tara did the same as she wondered if they even had the right address. *Maybe we mixed up the numbering of the houses.* They knew little about Ben Ford, but they did know that he was most likely in his early thirties. This woman was most likely not his wife. But then it occurred to Tara that she was maybe his mother.

"Can I help you?" the woman asked. She now stood inches from them. She tucked her frizzy brown hair behind her ears that was rooted in gray as she gazed at them with confusion and concern. She wore cargo pants and a t-shirt, revealing her tanned, wrinkled skin and that she had spent countless years outdoors and under the sun.

"Does Ben Ford live here?" Tara asked.

The woman shot her head back like she had been struck. "Who's asking?" She still clutched the towels, and Tara could see that her grip was getting tighter. It was a strong reaction, she thought. She seemed too defensive and too skeptical, and it only made Tara more suspicious.

Tara flashed her badge, and the woman shot her head back again with a look of pure terror. "What would you want with my son?"

This was not going to be easy, Tara thought. She needed to tread lightly. "We think he may have some information on a case we're working on. We wanted to see if he could help us?" The woman was about to reply but then stopped herself, and her mouth hung open briefly. Tara knew she was contemplating whether to let them speak to him, but Tara didn't want her to think she had the option. "Is he home?"

The woman took a deep breath and slowly nodded. "He's not in any trouble, right?"

"We just want to speak to him," Tara replied. It wasn't a lie. Her reasoning may have been misleading, but they had no evidence against him. They had their suspicions, but they needed to know if the pictures were his before they could jump to any conclusions.

The woman curled her top lip in disgust. She didn't like the idea, but she had no reason to deny them either. She sighed as she looked toward her front door. Tara knew she was contemplating her options. "I suppose I can understand why he might be able to help you. He does work for the news," she admitted. It was exactly what they needed her to think. "He should be downstairs." Her eyes then moved away from the door and fell on Tara, moving between her and Warren. "You can come in," she finally added. She turned toward the house, Tara and Warren right behind her.

They followed her down a short, paved walkway connecting the driveway to the concrete stairs leading to the front door. She opened it a crack and leaned her head in cautiously. "Ben!" she called, but there was no answer. She waited a moment and called out again, louder. "Ben!" But again her voice was met with no reply. She let out a frustrated grunt as she stepped inside and held the door open for Tara and Warren. "You two can come in, just take a seat in the living room." The home opened up into a formal dining room with a long farmhouse table decorated with a centerpiece of brass candles. She motioned for them to follow her and led them down a long hallway, which opened into a spacious sitting area. Sun spilled out into the room through large windows that lined the wall and gave view of the backyard.

They took a seat, and she scurried off back down the hallway, only to stop midway, opening a door and disappearing behind it. They could hear her feet descending stairs. Tara looked over at Warren. She was about to whisper. She thought the mother was being oddly cautious, and Tara wanted to see if Warren felt the same. But as she opened her mouth, Warren put a finger to his lips, signaling to keep quiet. He pointed to the ground, and Tara knew exactly what he was trying to say. They were right below them, and even though Tara would've whispered, if they were trying hard to overhear, it was still possible they could if they got close enough to the ceiling. Tara looked back in front of her, and a few moments later the door to the basement opened.

The mother stepped out first as she looked behind her, her face tinged with pain.

"I'll be fine!" they heard a deep voice bark from behind the door. "Just go upstairs," he ordered her as he stepped out into the hallway. His eyes immediately moved to Tara and Warren, still sitting on the couch, and his face morphed into surprise. He wasn't expecting them to be sitting there.

"You sure you're fine?" the mother asked.

He turned to her, his back facing the living room, and he whispered something they couldn't overhear. Tara assumed he just urged her again that she shouldn't be there, because after he spoke, she sighed and reluctantly retreated the hallway, heading to the front of the house.

He turned to face them. He was tall, with broad shoulders—the tight hallway making him look even larger. He had deep, sunken eyes with bushy brows that created a shadow under them and made him look rather tired. He walked toward them, scowling, and took a seat on a chair across from them. He leaned forward with an air of confidence Tara thought was strange. He was wearing an oversized zipped-up hoodie and tattered jeans that looked like they had seen better days.

"Well, what can I help you with?" he asked.

Tara could hear his mother slowly ascending the stairs. He heard it too, and he looked in that direction and rolled his eyes.

Tara reached into her pocket and pulled out the memory card in the plastic evidence bag. She slid it across the coffee table between them. "We were wondering if this happens to be yours."

He looked down at it, scooped it up in his large hand, and let out a grunt. He slid it back across the coffee table. "How the hell would I know," he barked. "That could be anyone's who has a camera like mine or similar."

"So this does work for your camera?" Tara asked as she placed the card back into her pocket. He had revealed something she hadn't even touched on yet, but it was exactly what she needed to know. He looked startled at her question, realizing he said too much. "Do you use C-Fast cards often?"

"I, uh…" He sat back in the chair, a less confident stance than the one he held before. But then an angry redness seeped to the surface of his skin. "What is this about, exactly? You haven't even told me why you're here."

Tara could hear the floorboards creak above them. The mother was clearly listening, trying to be discreet, but she was anything but that. "We're just trying to figure out who it belongs to. We think they might be able to help us with a case we're working on." He stared at Tara and Warren skeptically. She was stretching the truth. Tara and Warren both knew that whoever owned that memory card was a prime suspect, but Tara wasn't going to scare this guy out of talking. She grabbed hold of her cell phone, clipped on her belt loop, and opened to the photos she had downloaded from her email. She held her phone out, arm's length across the coffee table.

"Does this photo look familiar to you?" It was the first image of the house up in flames.

He leaned in closer and squinted, but then his eyes opened wide, and for the first time his expression morphed into concern. He recognized them. Tara was sure of it. She flipped to the next image, and the next, until he had finally seen each image taken of the house fire.

"Where—" he started, but then he stopped as he stared at the last image on the phone, becoming lost in it and losing his words. Tara pulled the phone back, and he finally met her eyes.

Whatever he was about to say, he stopped himself, his face becoming cold and stern. "Those aren't mine," he replied, crossing his arms awkwardly. "I was at that fire, but those aren't my pictures." He tried to hold a steady gaze on Tara, but she could see a slight unease. He looked nervous. He was lying, she was sure of it.

Warren finally leaned forward. "Do you know whose they might be?"

He looked off into the corner of the room, thinking for a moment, but it was brief, almost too brief. He shook his head. "Not that I can think of. There were a lot of people there." His voice shook at the last sentence.

"This was found at Fowler Beach," Warren added. "Were you at Fowler Beach anytime recently?"

"Why?" Ben shot back, his eyes moving uneasily between Tara and Warren.

"We just want to know if you saw anyone at both locations who might've taken these pictures."

Ben suddenly relaxed slightly. "Fowler Beach," he repeated under his breath. Tara was unsure if he was trying to recall the location, or if he was surprised to hear that the memory card was found there. After a moment, he stiffened and shot his head back to Tara and Warren, as if realizing he let his guard down for a moment.

"This is about those girls found buried on the beach, isn't it?" He waited, and Warren was about to speak, but he continued. "I'm a stringer; I'm at every story. There's tons of reporters and photogs at every one I go to, most the same. It could be anyone."

Tara looked over at Warren before asking a question of her own. "Do you mind if we see your footage from both those days, just so we can see if we spot anyone who might've taken these pictures?"

At Tara's question, a film of sweat began to form on his forehead. "I…uh…I don't think I have that footage with me here. I handed those memory cards over to a station."

"Which station was it? Maybe we can contact them."

His mouth hung open a moment, lost for words, and he unlinked his arms and began to rub his hands nervously in his lap. "Oh wait," he said as he tilted his head in one direction. It was as if a thought finally struck him. "I sold some memory cards last week, from an ad I posted. One just like that." He gestured to the memory card on the coffee table.

"But wouldn't that have been after the fire?" Tara asked. It was a detail he hadn't fully thought out, and she could see the realization flood through his eyes. If he had sold them after the fire, then that could only mean that he was the one who had taken the pictures. His body tensed even more.

"Oh, true," he replied. "It can't be mine then." He began to rub his hands even harder, so hard it was as if he were trying to pull skin from bone.

Silence fell around them. He still had yet to answer Tara's question. "So which station was it?" she asked again. "That you gave the memory card to?"

He refused to meet her eyes, becoming increasingly restless in his seat as he pulled at the skin of his hands. Tara could feel Warren tense up next to her. Ben was becoming increasingly panicked, and they both knew his next move could be unpredictable.

"Uhh…I…uh, I have to take a look. I can't remember at the top of my head." His head was bowed down as he spoke, as if speaking to his hands. But then he suddenly shot up out of his seat. "I need to take a look," he said nervously as he stumbled backward from the chair until he stood behind it.

Tara and Warren stood up as well. "Ben, take a seat. Let's just talk a bit more, and then you can check for us," Tara said. She was afraid he was about to make a run for it.

"What for? What else do you need to ask me?" he asked, his hands now digging into the top of the chair they rested on. "Why is that memory card so important? You think it's a suspect's, don't you?" His eyes moved anxiously between Tara and Warren.

His mother was now standing at the other end of the hallway She was silhouetted against the light of the glass panes in the door. "Ben," she asked. "Is everything all right?"

They all ignored her as Tara stared Ben in the eye. "We're not sure," she began. "But we did find a picture on it that leads us to believe so."

Ben's fingers were about to rip the fabric of the chair from gripping it so hard, but he didn't respond.

"Is this memory card yours, Ben? If it is, you can tell us. There might be a logical explanation."

At Tara's words, anger swelled in his eyes as he gritted his teeth. His hands dug deeper into the chair. "You just want to pin this on me, don't you? I know how these things work." He then looked off into the distance, his expression changing again into fear as he shook his head back and forth and began to pace. "Someone's framing me," he said over and over again as he paced the living room.

It was a strange thing for him to mutter, and it was not the response Tara was expecting at all. "Ben, take a seat, we can talk about this." At Tara's words, he stopped in his tracks and whipped his head, staring directly at Tara's pocket, the same pocket where she had placed the memory card. Without even a second to premeditate it, he hurdled over the chair.

"Ben! No!" his mother screamed, but it was too late.

He lunged at Tara across the coffee table. She darted out of the way, but she wasn't fast enough. He grabbed her shirt as he plunged into the couch. She tried to steady her footing, but his force was too strong, and she fell backward in his grip, their momentum forcing the couch to tumble over.

Her head slammed into the floor, disorienting her for a split-second until she felt the weight of his body on top of her. He was trying to get to the pocket of her pants, but Tara elbowed him right in the chest, and he spiraled back for a moment. He was about to try again, but Warren pulled him back full-force by the collar of his hoodie. "You just made this a whole lot worse for yourself," he spat through gritted teeth as he slammed him face-first into the floor. Tara stood up. Warren sat atop of him, holding him steady by the weight of his body as he cuffed him.

The mother came running in. "Ben, why would you—" she started until she broke out into sobs.

"Someone is framing me!" he yelled as Warren forced him to his feet and pushed him forward. It seemed like a desperate excuse, Tara thought.

"Where are you taking him?" his mother screamed as Warren led him to the car. She followed him out the front door, leaving Tara alone in the house. She rubbed

218

her head where it hit the floor. *Just a bump*, she said to herself. It was nothing compared with the injuries she had suffered before.

The room was suddenly silent, and Tara's eyes focused on the hallway as she walked forward toward the basement door. They now had probable cause to search the house, and she wasn't going to waste any time. She swung the door open to be met by a set of stairs plunging into darkness. She felt around for a light, until she found one and turned it on, lighting the room below her. The fluorescent light almost blinded her as she walked down the carpeted stairs that opened into a large, finished basement. A bed sat in one corner—just a box spring and mattress that still had yet to be made, with sheets crumpled at the foot of it.

A computer was situated at the other end of the room, with bags of what looked like camera gear placed next to it. But as Tara studied the room, something else caught her eye: around the computer, scattered every which way, were pieces of a broken object. She moved closer, sitting on her heels for a closer look as she scooped a piece of the object into her hand. It was a piece of plastic, but then she studied the other pieces around—some little shards of metal, and then her eyes fell upon a larger object sitting under his desk. It was a piece of a hard drive.

Suddenly, Tara heard footsteps behind her and looked to see Warren descending the stairs. "What did you find?" he asked as he reached the last step.

"Looks like a broken hard drive." She slipped on some gloves from her pocket and scooped the larger fragment into her hand before swiveling on her heels and handing it to Warren, who was now behind her.

He turned it around. "Must've happened pretty recently, or he'd clean this up, I assume."

Tara agreed. It seemed as if he were trying to hide something. She spotted a small rectangular window where the wall met the ceiling, and she moved closer for a better look. She stood on her tiptoes as she tried to get a glimpse of the view. She could just make out where the window sat. It was in the front of the house and gave a clear view to the driveway. Ben was a few inches taller than her. He would've easily been able to spot them. She turned around to Warren. "You can see the driveway. He might've heard us and smashed it."

Warren nodded as he moved about the room. The room was large, but mostly empty with only the bed, computer desk, video equipment, and a closet. Warren kneeled down and checked under the bed but then quickly let the bed skirt fall. He looked at Tara and shook his head, signaling that there was nothing underneath. He moved to the closet and began rummaging through it as Tara knelt down by the video gear. She unzipped one of the cases, but only a tripod sat inside. She checked the pockets, but nothing. She moved to the next one, a smaller case. Inside lay a camera. Tara checked the brand—it was a Canon—and began to feel hopeful. She knew it could easily have been the camera that took those pictures, and she scooped it up, switching it on. She tried to look through the video footage, but her heart sank when there wasn't any. She sighed as she looked through the rest of the equipment, but nothing was out of the ordinary.

Warren moved across the room. "Nothing," he said as he shook his head and moved from the closet. He stared across the room at the computer as he moved toward it. "If he's hiding anything, it'll probably be on here. He wouldn't have time to delete everything." He grabbed hold of the mouse and shook it to wake up the computer.

Tara stood up and peered over his shoulder. He opened documents, which revealed multiple folders, each labeled by news story and date. Warren scanned through them. Tara knew he was looking for the images of the fire so they could link the memory card to him.

Tara's ears perked up as she heard footsteps above them, and Ben's mother's muffled cry as she spoke to someone on the phone.

"Ah-ha!" Warren suddenly burst out.

Tara looked back at the screen. She could see he had found a folder titled "Willow Street fire" and dated when the fire had occurred. He opened each image within it. The first ones looked like the exact images found on the memory card. "Looks like someone lied to us," Warren sighed. Tara pulled up the images on her phone and compared them. They were without a doubt identical. Her heart sank. If those images were his, then so was the one of Sofia, which Tara realized now would also most likely be on his computer. Tara braced herself as Warren continued to go through each folder, searching for exactly what Tara was afraid they would find.

He opened numerous folders of car crashes, of press conferences, of court hearings, each one a different scene that Ben had been at, but nothing that looked suspicious. He opened more folders, more past scenes. Tara began to relax as she watched Warren diligently look through all the footage. She was beginning to wonder if they would find anything at all of the victims.

Could the picture of Sofia have been on the hard drive? Could that be why he smashed it? As Warren neared the remaining folders, Tara raised that question to him.

"The hard drive," she said, Warren's gaze still focused on the computer as he opened and closed files. "It could be on there. That would explain why he broke it."

Warren nodded but didn't let Tara's words break his focus. "I thought that too," he said as he moved the mouse in his grip. "If we can't find anything, I'd say that theory would make a lot of sense." He went through two more folders, the last ones in his documents, but nothing, just more photos of a scene that didn't pertain to the victims. Warren sighed. The chances were now slim that they would find something, and after he searched the rest of the computer, he spun around in the office chair. They at least had evidence that he had lied, that the photos of the fire were his. It was enough to link the memory card to him and the image of Sofia.

"Looks like Ben has some explaining to do," Warren said as Tara wondered, was this case now over?

Chapter Twenty Four

B en's gaze lay steady on the floor as Tara opened the door to the interrogation room. He was sitting at a desk in the middle of the room, and as Tara and Warren grew closer, he lifted his head. He looked tired. Even though the day's events had not been long, it had already taken an emotional and mental toll on him. His eyes were red, with dark creases underneath. It was a good thing, Tara noted. She knew that the less mental strength he had, the more likely he was to give in, to lessen his time in that chair.

Tara and Warren took a seat across from him as his eyes fell on Tara with a pleading look. It was as if he hoped for her to spare him, but it only angered her further. All she could picture was the photograph found of Sofia. And at that thought, an image of each other girl—Alyssa, Reese—alone, terrified, and in pain surfaced in her mind. It made her blood boil. The image of Sofia had to be his. If not, he needed a really good explanation.

"You lied to us," she finally spat.

Ben stiffened as he looked between Tara and Warren anxiously. "I," he started, but then he fell silent, his chin falling to his chest as he shook his head. "I knew you wouldn't believe me. You looked through my computer, didn't you?"

"Believe you about what?" Tara asked. "So you admit those pictures are yours?"

He sighed, slowly nodding. "I took those house fire pictures, but I swear I deleted them. I sold that memory card." His voice shook as he spoke. Tara realized he was still playing off that he was being framed.

"If you deleted them and sold it, then how would they be on here?"

"I...I don't know." He fidgeted, his face reddening more in distress. "Someone could've restored them," he blurted as if his life depended on it. "It's possible, with a good restoration software." Tara wasn't sure if that was true, but she still didn't believe him. He seemed to be clawing at any excuse he could find.

Tara opened her phone, pulling up the picture of Sofia. She held it out in front of her. "Was this image restored too?" she asked bluntly. "Is this one of the images you tried to delete?" Her voice was stern and threatening, and as his eyes fell onto the image, his mouth fell open. He leaned back in his chair, shaking his head back and forth aggressively as he pushed Tara's hand and the phone out of his view. "That's not mine."

"Then why was it on your memory card?" Tara asked again.

"I don't know! I swear!" he screamed.

"Is that why you smashed that hard drive in your room? It had pictures like this on it?"

"No!" he yelled again. His face was now beet-red as panic surfaced on every inch of it. He took a deep breath to calm himself and leaned forward. He tried to steady his voice. "Listen, I know what it looks like, but I smashed that hard drive out of anger. I was frustrated because I kept getting denied from these stations. No one has taken my work in months, no one needs anyone full-time. It's been stressful, all right?" He leaned back in his chair again as he heaved a large sigh.

"Well, that still doesn't explain why your memory card was found buried with a victim," Tara reminded him again.

He was growing more frustrated. A vein had begun to pulsate in his neck, but he steadied himself before speaking. "I told you, I sold it. Someone's framing me."

Tara still did not fully understand why he had thought someone was framing him in the first place. They hadn't shown him the image of Sofia at his house, but yet he had already jumped to that conclusion enough to want to destroy the memory card. They still had yet to ask him.

"What made you think someone was framing you?"

"I," he started, looking anxiously between Tara and Warren. He then shook his head. "I knew it was the one I sold once you showed me the pictures. I know how these things work. I've covered many cases. You found it at the scene, you clearly thought it was a suspect's." He paused to catch his breath. "I knew I didn't put it there. Someone else did, and whoever I sold that to was sketchy as all hell."

"Why's that?" Tara asked.

"He called me from an ad I posted. Didn't want to meet me. He told me to leave the memory card in a mailbox, and he left the cash. I didn't think that was too weird because he said he wasn't going to be home, but then a few days later I called him again to see if he wanted something else I was selling, and the phone was disconnected." He heaved another sigh, catching his breath.

Tara looked toward Warren. She wasn't sure if she should believe him or not, but she could tell Warren wasn't convinced.

"What was the address?" Warren finally asked.

Pain crossed Ben's face at Warren's question. He opened his mouth to speak but then hesitated, only making Tara think with more certainty that he was weaving this lie as he went. "It was near Rehoboth, 24 Beach Lane Road, but for all I know, he gave me some random address."

It was as if he were trying to have an explanation for his lies before they even caught him in them.

"Where were you two nights ago?" Warren barked.

"I was home. You can ask my mom, really." But at his words, his face fell. He even knew it wasn't a solid alibi. "Look, I know this all sounds crazy, but someone *is* framing me."

Warren suddenly stood up, his face tight with anger. He placed his hands on the table, leaning inches from Ben's face. "We'll see about that," he said as Ben cowered in his chair. Warren lingered a moment and then straightened before heading to the door. Tara followed behind. It was clear that Warren was convinced that Ben was guilty, and Tara couldn't help but agree.

***

Tara and Warren sat in an office at the police station, a phone on speaker in front of them. They were able to find a land line phone number for the address that Ben had given them, and they were now waiting for someone to pick up.

"Hello?" a woman's voice finally spoke.

Warren cleared his throat. "I'm looking for someone I sold a memory card to the other week. I don't have his name, but he said he lived at this address. I just wanted to see if he'd be interested in some of my camera gear."

"I think you have the wrong number," the voice replied.

"Are you sure?"

"Only Mrs. Westbrook lives her, and me, her caretaker. She's ninety-five. Neither one of us would need a camera." The woman then hung up and Warren sighed, turning to Tara.

"Well, that proves it," he said. "He's giving us the runaround."

Tara nodded. She could tell from Warren's expression that he had no doubt Ben was who they'd been looking for all along. "So you think it's him?"

"I mean, how else would he have those pictures found on the memory card? That picture of Sofia has to be his. He probably dropped it by accident, realized later, and then smashed the hard drive when he saw us." Tara couldn't help but agree. It seemed unlikely that he was being framed, and the broken hard drive in his basement was incredibly suspicious. Warren rolled his eyes as he continued. "And he doesn't have a solid alibi. Of course his mom's going to vouch for him, but even if she did think he was home, he could've snuck out that window in the basement for all we know."

Warren was certainly right. This was the closest they had ever been, and they now had something that linked him directly to the crime scene.

"We have enough to hold him," Warren added. "Of course, a murder weapon would help, but it could still be buried in the beach somewhere. We'll keep the crews still out there a bit longer. It'll be difficult to find, but we'll try."

He was referring to the police who had been diligently searching the beach for the bodies, until they uncovered them. It was extremely possible that the murder weapon had been buried somewhere along the beach as well, but it was just a string they would be looking for. It was not an easy object to uncover.

The cars in Ben Ford's driveway had already been driven to the station as well. Forensics would be searching them overnight. And while Tara believed it was likely that Ben could be the killer, she needed more evidence to be fully convinced.

Warren looked at the clock hanging by the doorway. "It's late," he said. "We'll check back in in the morning." At his words, Tara immediately remembered that John's gig was tonight, and she spun around, looking at the time. It was eight. He was set to go on in an hour. Her heart sank. She knew he would be disappointed, and it had occurred to her that she hadn't even checked her phone since bringing Ben in. She pulled it from her pocket and checked the screen. Just as she expected, a missed call and a couple of texts from John. Tara sighed. She didn't even want to look at them. She just wanted to get there.

"Everything all right?" Warren asked as Tara placed phone down.

Tara nodded. "John's first gig is tonight."

"Ah," Warren replied as he stood up. "This job will be an endless pit of cancelled plans." He shook his head at his words. "But we owe it to our families to always keep trying." He looked at the clock and then back at Tara slumped in the chair. "If you think you can still make it there, you better put some spring in your step."

He was right, Tara realized. She at least had to try to get there, or it would look like she made no effort at all. She couldn't control her missing it, that her job got in the way. But she could still show up, even if it was at the end of him playing.

"You're right," Tara said as she shot up from her chair. "I might as well try."

Warren smiled at her as she made her way to the door. "What's he playing anyway?" he asked.

"Some Rush covers."

Warren's smile grew wider. "Sounds like a good time, enjoy."

But as Tara opened the door, all she could think about was what he said: *an endless pit of cancelled plans*. It made her wonder how much disappointment could John take before he had enough.

Chapter Twenty Five

Tara could already hear the band playing as she hurried to the door of the bar, and hope welled within her. *Maybe I didn't miss it after all*, she wished as she swung open a large wooden door, only to be met by a swarm of people scattered throughout a dimly lit room. An industrial-style lighting fixture hung over a long wraparound bar. People sat on barstools with their backs to the bartenders, drinks in hand, as they faced the band playing on the opposite side of the room.

Tara turned in the direction of the music. She searched among the musicians. She hadn't met John's bandmates yet, and at the thought she suddenly felt a strange disconnection she had never felt with him before. Each face was unfamiliar, and she had no way of knowing if they were his bandmates or not. But one thing was certain: she didn't see John. Her heart sank. It wasn't his band. He was supposed to go on at nine, and it was now ten thirty. The two-and-a-half-hour drive from Dewey Beach had not helped, and if John wasn't still on stage now, it was extremely likely that the band on stage was the next set.

Her eyes scanned the rest of the room. She hoped he hadn't left yet, but as she looked amongst the sea of faces, sadness dropped into the pit of her stomach. For the first time, she felt truly distant from John, and it wasn't a feeling she had expected. They had a great relationship, and she had no doubt that he loved her immensely, but Warren's words had hit her hard. *This job is an endless pit of cancelled plans.* It echoed in her head. She knew John understood that her job was important. This was just his hobby, but it brought him happiness, and there was a part of her that was sad she had such trouble being a part of it. *Is this only the beginning of the rest of our life?* she wondered. *What will it be like when we have kids?* John would be at everything, but would Tara's job always interfere? Would she always be known to disappoint her family?

She hadn't even realized that she had been staring blankly at the band playing when she sensed someone moving toward her, weaving in and out of the people.

"Tara," she heard. It was John's muffled voice, and she spotted his smiling face moving among the crowd. His face was flushed, his hair damp and matted down with sweat, along with his t-shirt. When he was close enough, he wrapped his arms around her waist and pulled her in and kissed her. His touch suddenly made Tara's body relax, and she wondered if maybe she was worrying for no reason. John didn't seem annoyed or disappointed. In fact, he seemed happy to see her.

"Did you see that solo?" he yelled enthusiastically. "How awesome was that!"

Tara's heart sank. His lack of disappointment suddenly made sense. He had thought she was here all along.

She waited a moment as the band finished a song and the room erupted into applause. When it subsided, Tara replied. "I must've missed it. I just got here." She searched his face as his smile dropped into a frown. "I couldn't get out of work. You know I'm in the middle of this case. I…"

"I know. You're sorry." He finished her sentence with a sigh. He was clearly disappointed. After all, he had gotten to perform music from his favorite band, and from his reaction it had clearly gone well. Her absence sat like a pit in her stomach.

But before Tara could even reply to help ease the tension, a man with glasses and slicked-back hair placed his hand on John's shoulder.

"I'm heading out," the man said as he patted John on the back.

His eyes fell on Tara, and John forced a smile as he introduced them. His name was Anthony. "He works in my accounting firm," John informed her as they shook hands. "He happens to play bass too."

John beamed at him as they complimented each other on their respective performances. The same excitement he wore when he first spotted her flooded back into his face, but then Anthony headed to the door and John's face fell once again. It only made Tara's feeling of detachment from John intensify. She had never met Anthony before. She had heard John mention him once or twice, but she had no idea that he played music with him as well.

"You want to get out of here?" John finally asked. "You look tired." She was. The day's events had been exhausting. But she knew John was just trying to change the subject.

"I really wish I could've been here, John. You know I would've if I could."

John heaved another sigh. "I know. That's what you always say." A silence fell around them as guilt swirled in Tara's gut. He stared into the distance a moment, as if contemplating what to say. His eyes then turned again to Tara. "I know your job is more important. It's just frustrating how hard it is to make plans with you sometimes, but I'll get over it."

He forced a smile. Tara was left without words. She didn't know what more to say. She knew that with her job, she couldn't promise him anything, and he knew it too. "Let's go home," he finally said as he placed his arm around Tara's waist. She nodded, letting him guide her through the sea of people toward the door. But all Tara could think about was what Warren had said, and her stomach twisted into a knot. She knew it was only a matter of time before she disappointed John on something bigger. As she stepped out into the summer air, she wondered, what was his limit?

***

Tara sat in the living room, flicking through channels. John had already gone to bed. They didn't speak much more about her missing his show. They both knew there was nothing more to say. It was a reality they both had to accept—that Tara couldn't always be there. He had finally detailed how it went, that they had nailed every song, and the tension had eased between them. It made Tara feel better, but she also knew it was only a matter of time before the same issue would resurface. For now, though, she buried the feeling.

She hadn't even had a chance to digest the day's events, and the more she thought about Ben Ford, the more something didn't sit right within her. She knew he looked guilty, but something about his demeanor made her wonder if he wasn't the person they'd been looking for. He seemed too nervous. He was rash in his reaction to take the memory card from Tara. He didn't seem clever. He hadn't thought out his actions. *The broken hard drive,* Tara thought. He hadn't even bothered to hide the pieces. It was a messy attempt to destroy evidence. Yes, he might not have had time, but the killer seemed cleverer than that.

Tara placed the remote down. She couldn't watch what was on TV. She was too focused fleshing out every thought. She remembered their original findings: *no sign of struggle.* Her and Warren had theorized that the victims went willingly, but why would they get into a car with Ben Ford? He wasn't well known in the community. He wasn't even charming or handsome. It seemed unlikely that a teenage girl would accept a ride from him.

The thoughts rolled around in her head until one struck her full-force. *What if he really is being framed?* It seemed like a far-fetched idea, but if it were true, it was clever, and it was exactly the type of cleverness she'd expect from this killer. Tara's thoughts ran wild, but as her questioning grew, so did her concern that she was getting ahead of herself. She had already taken a step too far on her last case. She was lucky that she was right and kept her job and her life, but what if this time she was wrong? She couldn't bear the thought of losing it all. If she went off on her own, Reinhardt would not be as forgiving. And if she were being honest with herself, the thought of putting herself in danger all over again, without backup, terrified her.

Warren knows what he's doing, she told herself. She needed to learn to trust the people around her, and at that thought she lay down on the couch. She focused on the TV, but as she pushed each new theory away, her mind swirled into a cloud of exhaustion, and before she even had the thought to head to bed, she drifted off into sleep.

***

Tara stared out into the vast ocean, the waves crashing on her bare feet, pushing sand between her toes. She smiled as the warm sun beat on her back and at the sound of children playing on the beach and in the water.

"Tara!" she heard behind her, and she spun around, to see John moving toward her, his hair whipping wildly in the wind. The beach was packed, and John weaved around towels and umbrellas, around people enjoying the day, until he stood aside her and reached out a hand. She grabbed hold of it. It felt warm, a warmth more radiant than the sun. He pulled her forward. "Come on!" he said as he playfully pulled her toward the water. She hesitated because she knew it would be cold, but then she heard another voice call her name, this time out in the water.

"Tara!" she heard, over and over. It was a woman's voice, and as she gazed out into the sea of people, she could see her mother bobbing amongst them.

"Mom," Tara said under her breath. She didn't understand. She looked toward John. He spotted her too. He was staring at her, waving, smiling, and then gave Tara's hand another playful tug. "Let's go," he said as he led her into the water. She walked forward, letting him guide her as the cold water rose up her legs, the warmth escaping her body. She didn't like it; she longed for the warmth, but at each step her mother was closer, and she ached to be beside her.

Deeper and deeper she plunged until the water reached her waist and then her chest. It felt like a bath of ice, and it forced the air from her lungs. But she didn't care. She could still feel John's hand in her grip. She could still see her mother's face as she smiled and waved, now inches away. Tara was now pulling John. She was close to her mother. She could almost touch her. She pulled John harder and harder. But right before she could reach her arm out to hug her, a huge wave formed behind her.

"Look out!" Tara yelled.

Her mother ducked. Tara plunged fully in the water, still holding tight to John's hand. The salt stung her eyes and nose. She could still feel John, but the current pushed and pulled. She could feel their grip growing weaker, and she opened her eyes, but all she was met by was murky darkness. She tightened her grip. The wave had almost passed, and she was about to poke her head up above the water, but suddenly one powerful swell tossed her backward. She tumbled, her hand forced from John's grip. She clawed around her to find him, to feel for him, but each way she felt, her hands just cut through water.

The sea calmed, and Tara gasped for air as she broke the surface. She steadied her breathing. It was just a wave, she reminded herself as she opened her salt-stung eyes. She looked around her, but all she could see was water with no end in sight. She spun in every which direction. John was gone. Her mother was gone. All the people in the water were gone. Panic seized Tara's breathing. There was no land, no beach chairs, no umbrellas to spot. In each direction the water was vast, spanning miles, it seemed, and Tara's mind swirled into a haze of confusion. How could it be? They were all just there.

She looked all around. Land had to be close; it was impossible. She swam in one direction, trusting her instincts. It was this way, *she told herself as she stretched her arms out and swam harder and harder until she needed to stop to catch her breath. She looked in front of her—still a vast body of water with no end in sight, and she began to panic yet again. "John," she screamed. "Mom." But her voice was nothing to the sea. She looked around her again. Desperately, she instinctively paddled in one direction, but then she would stop and try another—each time unsure of her own choices. Eventually, exhausted, she lay on her back, floating, letting the water chose her direction. She stared up at the sky as her tears filled her eyes. She was alone—it was a feeling that ran cold through her body. She knew she wouldn't be found. She knew she wouldn't find land. This was her fate.*

The once beautifully sunny sky now darkened. Obscure purples and blues spread through the white clouds like bruises until it was all that could be seen. They blanketed the sky, lightning crashed, thunder rumbled, and Tara closed her eyes as rain fell onto her now ice-cold skin, meeting the warm tears that formed.

She lay there a few moments until she no longer felt the drops of rain. She no longer heard the rumble of thunder or the crashing of lightning. She opened her eyes.

She was now not in the water. She was looking down at it, at her body floating, the current pushing it in the direction it chose. But her face looked younger, her body different, and she realized it wasn't her body at all. It was a teenager—one that she did not recognize. It wasn't Alyssa. It wasn't Reese or Sofia. But Tara could feel in every fragment of her being that her fate was the same. She wanted to call to her, but as she opened her mouth, she couldn't find her voice. She wanted to shake her, but she couldn't reach her.

Then, suddenly, the girl's eyes popped open. She stared wide-eyed at Tara, but looking past her, at the sky above. The same terror from Sofia's picture flooded through the girl's eyes. Again, Tara tried to call to her. She reached out, but each attempt was useless.

And then suddenly, as if a whirlpool swelled under the sea, the girl was sucked under, until she was nowhere to be seen, and Tara screamed.

Tara bolted upright. It was still night. The sky was still pitch-black through the glass doors of the balcony. The moon still shined brightly, causing everything it touched to glow. The TV was still on. Tara was slick with sweat and heaved a sigh of relief that she was still in her living room. It was a strange nightmare, she admitted. It was obscure, but Tara knew it was emotionally driven. Because now her fear that Ben Ford was not the killer made her skin crawl. Her heart raced.

Her instincts sat in overdrive. And she knew most of all that if she was right and if she ignored them, it would result in the most unfortunate circumstance: another victim.

Chapter Twenty Six

J ustine Wells untied the apron around her waist as she let the door of the restaurant slam shut behind her. She was exhausted. It had been a grueling ten-hour shift, and she was happy to finally be finished. She couldn't wait to lay her head down on her new bed in her new apartment. She was nineteen, and she had just officially moved out of her parents' house and into a two-bedroom apartment with her roommate. Her parents were still mostly supporting her, and they would especially once she started Wilmington College in the fall, but it was still a newfound freedom Justine relished.

She walked briskly to her car. It was late, almost midnight. She didn't like walking to her car at this hour. It had always given her an uncomfortable feeling, but lately especially. She had heard about the girls that had been found buried on the beach, and now each time she walked to her car at night, it was all she could think about. Her parents had even insisted that she text them each time she got home after a shift. She didn't blame them, and she understood. But knowing that they were anxious only heightened her own fears.

She draped the apron over her arm as she dug in her purse for her keys, still not stopping the momentum of her feet propelling her quickly to the parking lot until she could see her all white Jeep glistening under the streetlights. She fumbled in her purse for a moment until she grabbed hold of her keys and pressed the automatic start. The car rumbled, and Justine heaved a sigh of relief. She walked closer, and when she was finally close enough to open the door, she stopped. From the corner of her eye, she could see that her front driver's side tire was sinking into the ground.

"Shit."

She had a spare, but she had only changed a tire once in her life when her father had taught her how to do so. She wasn't sure if she knew how to do it again, but she had to try. She turned her car off, grabbed the key for the spare in the trunk, and then bent down on her hands and knees as she peered underneath. She could see her tire up under the back bumper. She popped open the key slot and stuck the key in, turning it, trying to lower the tire to the ground. But at each turn, the tire did not fall. She tried again and again, but it didn't budge.

She sighed as she looked around the parking lot. There were only four cars. Three of them were owned by customers who were finishing their last drink at the bar before the restaurant officially closed, and the other car belonged to Craig. He was the manager, and there was no way Justine was going to ask him for a ride. It was common knowledge among the waitstaff that he was creepy, and to make matters worse, he had already asked her out on a date. There was no way she would sit through an awkward car ride with him. She knew her even asking for a ride would be seen as interest. It was how he seemed to view every gesture, if it came from a female.

She reached in her purse for her phone as she opened her car door and took a seat inside. She could call her roommate, she decided as she scanned through her contacts and dialed her roommate's number. The phone rang and rang, but finally it went to voicemail. Justine tried again, but just like the last time, her roommate didn't answer, and she sighed in frustration. *She's probably sleeping*, Justine said to herself. Her roommate was known for always putting her phone on silent when she went to bed. It was something Justine had always warned her about. "What if there's an emergency?" she would say, but her roommate was more concerned about getting an uninterrupted sleep.

Justine weighed her options. Her parents lived over two hours away. It didn't make sense to call them, and she didn't want to worry them either. She could call an Uber. She didn't like the idea of renting one alone, especially with everything that had been on the news, but it was either that or asking for a ride from Craig. She opened the app on her phone and put in her locations. She waited for it to find the nearest Uber, and when the app finally did, Justine bubbled with frustration. It was over an hour away.

She shot her head backward, hitting the headrest. She was going to have to ask Craig. It was her only option. Her stomach twisted into a knot.

Suddenly, a knock on her window made her jump, and she spun her head. She wasn't sure who she was expecting to see, but when she saw a familiar face, she relaxed. He smiled at her with his perfectly chiseled jaw and celebrity-white teeth.

She rolled down her window.

"Looks like you have a flat," he said. He was a recurring customer that Justine had served many times. He was well known not only in the restaurant, but in the town as a whole, and he was loved by everyone he met. He was charismatic and charming, and Justine always looked forward to serving his table. He often sat alone at the bar, chatting with anyone who was there. But sometimes he'd come with friends and get a table. He gave good tips. He was kind and handsome.

"I know," she admitted as she shook her head and rolled her eyes. "I tried to get my spare out, but it seems to be stuck."

He ducked under the car as if taking a look himself and then moments later popped back up by her window. "It looks like it's rusted over. That happens sometimes. You'll probably need to take it somewhere."

Justine let out another frustrated grunt.

"Do you have a ride?" he asked.

Justine shook her head. She wasn't even going to count Craig as a possibility.

"If you don't live too far, I can offer you one."

Justine looked over at his BMW parked not too far away. She had always admired it when he rolled into the parking lot, and the thought of being driven in it excited her. She knew enough about him to know that he was trustworthy. No, she didn't know him on much of a personal level, but he was well respected in the community. He was everyone's friend. This was the exact gesture that would be expected of him, and with everything that had been reported on the news, Justine knew it was smarter to go with him than wait over an hour for an Uber.

"If you don't mind," she replied with a smile. And moments later he was leading her to his car.

Chapter Twenty Seven

Tara sat on the couch, staring at a blank TV as she drank her coffee. She had already been up for a few hours. After her nightmare, she had tossed and turned until she finally accepted that she wasn't falling back asleep. Her mind was still focused on the case, on Ben Ford, and her feelings that he wasn't the killer. *It doesn't make sense*, she said to herself over and over again. *Everything pointed to the fact that the girls willingly went with the killer, so why would they go with him? Where would he have taken them, if not to his home? And where is the location where Sofia had her picture taken?* At each thought, her doubts grew stronger, and she remembered her dream. The girl in the water—it was her fear that another victim would be taken because she and Warren had made an error. Her heart stung at the thought.

But as her feelings grew stronger, the same fear of the night before came crawling back into her mind—*what if I'm wrong?* It was a thought that reminded her she couldn't do anything rash. If she were to keep searching, she needed to do so without making it known and without doing anything that could be seen as remotely reckless.

Footsteps interrupted her train of thought as John entered the living room, and Tara spun around.

"I was wondering where you were," he said as he appeared from the hallway. "Did you sleep on the couch?"

He scrunched his face in confusion as he stared at her. He was already dressed for the day in khakis, a fitted button-down shirt, and tie. His hair was already slicked back, and Tara was surprised she hadn't even heard him get up or getting ready. She must've been too enthralled by her thoughts. His question somehow made her feel guilty. She was already feeling distant from him, yet here she was, not even sleeping in the same bed at night, creating a physical distance as well. She knew that part of her dream last night had just been a reiteration of the distance she felt, that she was too preoccupied with her family issues and her job to focus on John. But now wasn't the time to bring it up.

Tara sighed. "I did. I guess I was just that tired."

John only nodded as he walked into kitchen. She wasn't sure what his thoughts were, if he was annoyed that she didn't come to bed, or if he too felt the distance, and his silence only worried Tara more.

"Is everything all right?" he asked skeptically, but it was as if he were afraid of the answer. His back was still toward her as he poured himself a cup of coffee and took a sip.

"Yeah, I'm fine," she lied.

She wasn't going to burden him with her concerns with the case, and now wasn't the time to bring up her feelings of distance. She needed to figure out her next move. She looked toward John as he placed the milk back in the fridge and continued to sip on his coffee, when a thought finally struck her—*the coffee shop.* It was where she and Warren had started. It was where Reese had worked regularly. If Tara's theory was right, if the victims did know the killer, maybe he did visit her at the shop after all. Tara had already asked the owner questions about who visited or spoke to Reese, but she had never asked her about a photographer. At the realization, Tara jumped to her feet and John spun around. He looked at her questioningly.

"I just realized I have to do something for work," she said to him as she briskly walked toward the hallway, her focus now only on the case.

"Tara," she heard, her focus momentarily broken as she spun around to face him. He placed his mug down, pressing his hands onto the island counter. "I really would like to get dinner at some point. It seems like it's been a while since we had some time together."

Tara nodded. "I'd like that," she replied, but his words only gave her an unsettling feeling. He felt the distance too, it was clear to her now, and only she was to blame. But as much as she wanted to discuss it, she didn't have time. If what she sensed was possibly right, another girl could be in danger. Tara pushed the case into the forefront her mind as she walked down the hall, leaving John behind her.

***

Tara pushed the door of the coffee shop open, causing a set of bells dangling from the entryway to jingle upon her entrance. A lanky teenage boy behind the counter looked toward her as he straightened up, preparing to take her order. It was still early, and only one person was in the store, waiting for their coffee to be made by a young female barista.

Tara walked up to the counter. The boy was about to ask what Tara wanted, but she stopped him with her words. "Is your manager here?" He looked confused and startled, as if he were afraid he had done something wrong, but he nodded.

"I'll get her," he responded and turned toward a set of double swinging doors, making eye contact with the barista as he went—the same concern reflecting in each other's eyes—and then he disappeared. As Tara waited, the girl kept glancing over until she was done making the coffee. She handed it to the customer, who turned to the exit, and the girl's eyes awkwardly moved to a TV hanging from the ceiling in the corner of the room.

Moments later, and the same manager Tara had met with days early stood before her. "Ah, Agent Mills," she said as she walked forward. "Surprised to see you in here again." Her long hair, which was braided last time, was tied tightly in a bun.

The cashier and barista relaxed at their boss's recognition, realizing that it had nothing to do with them, But Tara could still see them curiously watching from the corner of their eyes as they tried to make themselves busy by grabbing towels and wiping down the tables.

"I realized that there were a few more questions I didn't get to ask you when I was here last," Tara began. The manager looked at her curiously. "Did Reese ever speak of a photographer? Or did any photographer ever come in here while she was working?"

The manager tilted her head, contemplating the question. "No, not that I'm aware of." She looked toward the two other workers, who looked up at the turn of her head. "Do you guys ever see a photographer come in here?" They both looked toward each other and shook their heads in unison.

The manager turned back to Tara. "Why do you ask?"

Tara didn't want to tell her too much. Interviewing her without Warren being aware could already be seen as insubordinate. She didn't want to stir this woman's curiosity, especially with teenagers present, and have it echo through the community.

"We're just covering our bases," Tara answered. It was a vague response, but the manager accepted it and nodded.

Tara then looked toward the other two employees. "Did they work with Reese?"

The manager nodded. "Roy did for a while," she replied, referring to the cashier. "Angela just started."

Tara turned to face the cashier, who was still washing tables. "Did Reese ever mention someone that would visit her? Someone she seemed friendly with?"

The boy stopped scrubbing and looked up with a frown, shaking his head. "No one in particular. Just her boyfriend, Brian, once in a while." It was a detail Tara was already aware of, and they had already ruled him out because of his broken arm. He also did not fit who Tara was looking for.

She prodded the boy for more. "Anyone else?" she asked, but he only shrugged.

"Not that I'm aware of," he replied.

Tara's heart sank. She wasn't getting anywhere, and she was beginning to wonder if this was a waste of time, if her inner voice was worth listening to. But she also knew she needed to see this through. She didn't want to give up too easily, because if she were right and turned away, she'd be sick with guilt and regret.

She continued to ask them both a few more questions. If Reese ever spoke to anyone on her breaks, if a customer ever seemed to take interest in her, if she ever seemed afraid. They were all questions that she had asked the manager before, but not the boy. But as they both shook their heads at each question, Tara lost the small bit of hope she had left, and her heart sank.

She thanked them both for their time and was about to turn to the door when the manager spoke to her employees. "Oh, look," she said, her eyes glued on the TV. "It's Dan Asher." A large grin filled her face as both employees turned their eyes to the TV.

Tara glanced at the screen. It was a reporter. He looked familiar, and Tara tried to place his face until it suddenly came to her in a rush. He had been at the crime scenes, reporting, and he was also one of the reporters at the medical examiner's office, shoving a microphone in her face, and the one she made eye contact with at Fowler Beach.

Tara turned to the manager. "Do you know him?"

The woman nodded without her eyes moving from the TV. "He's a regular customer. He comes in here quite a bit. He's very nice. He's their crime reporter." She beamed. "Reese had a big crush on him, actually," she giggled before sighing sadly.

But at her words a chill ran down Tara's spine. She looked at the man on the screen again, his hair perfectly slicked back, his masculine, chiseled jaw and dark brown eyes. He was certainly handsome, and Tara assumed equally as charming. Her mind ran wild. He had a news background, he would most likely know a thing or two about how a crime case operates, and he was charming enough that he could lead a girl in his car without struggle. Tara stared at the screen, making a mental note of the station he worked for, and then turned to the door. He was always one of the first reporters at the scene, and at that realization, another chill ran cold through her.

***

Tara sat in her car as she googled the news station on her phone. Could she be on to something? A number popped up, and Tara dialed it. Within a few moments, someone picked up and she realized she wasn't entirely sure how she would approach this. She knew he had been following the story. She could just say she wanted to speak to him about it.

An operator spoke. "How may I direct your call?"

Tara cleared her throat. "Can you please connect me to the news desk?" She had only called a news station a couple times in her life when she was a police officer, but she had remembered how to make sure her call got directed to the correct place.

"One moment," she heard before being placed on hold. Seconds later, a different female voice sounded through the phone.

"This is WDITV. How can I help you?"

"Um yes," Tara started. "I'm FBI Agent Tara Mills. I was hoping to speak with Dan Asher about a story he's working on."

The woman didn't even hesitate. She placed Tara on a brief hold before returning moments later. "His shift just ended an hour ago, but he will be in tomorrow," she said.

"Is there any way I can speak to him before that?" Tara did not intend to wait that long.

"I can give you his work cell number. He's usually quick to respond."

Tara thanked her. "Yes, that would be great," she replied before she reached for a pen and paper in her glove box and the woman began reading off a series of numbers. When she was done, Tara quickly said goodbye.

Without a second to waste, she dialed Dan Asher's number, but her finger hovered over the send button. She wasn't quite sure what she was doing. She still had no evidence to think that he could be the killer other than him knowing one of the victims and fitting a description that she only envisioned in her mind. But either way, she knew it could be worth talking to him. He had been covering the case. He knew Reese. Maybe he had observed something that would be useful.

Tara finally pressed send. Within moments, he picked up. "Dan Asher," he said. His voice was lively and professional, the sound of a true reporter.

Tara introduced herself. "From my understanding, you've been working on the beach murders?"

"That's right." He waited for Tara to elaborate.

"And you knew Reese, I understand, from the coffee shop?"

"Um, yes." He seemed a bit taken back from the question. "I got coffee there often. I recognized her face as soon as I was shown her photo. Such a shame." He paused as if letting his words sink in. "What can I help you with?" he asked, his voice bouncing back into its chipper tone.

"I was just wondering if I could pick your brain a bit." She paused a moment. "Would we be able to meet somewhere?"

The phone fell silent, and an unsettled feeling flowed through Tara, but then again his voice bounced back. "I can give you my address," he said abruptly. "I'm home now."

Tara considered it a moment. She had no reason to believe that he was dangerous, but was this going too far? Was she digging too much on her own? Could she get in trouble? The questions rolled around in her head until another pushed its way forward. Was it also risky if she didn't speak to him? Even if he wasn't the killer, maybe he knew something valuable? *He's a crime scene reporter,* she reminded herself. *There's nothing wrong with seeing what he knows.* At that thought, Tara finally responded.

"Sure, I can head over now." He gave her his address, she thanked him, and they were soon off the phone.

Tara entered the address into the GPS. *I'll have to tell Warren*, she thought. She wasn't going to make the same mistake twice. Someone was going to know where she was. This time, just in case, Warren would have the address. She would call him on the way, but as Tara pulled out of the parking lot, she wondered what Warren would think, and if once again she was going too far.

Chapter Twenty Eight

Justine awoke to a fluorescent light beaming in her eyes. Her head pounded, the light only intensifying it, and she groaned in pain as she turned her head away. Her vision was blurred. She did not know where she was. She didn't remember how she had gotten there, but as she looked in front of her, she knew she was lying on a cold concrete floor. The floor was bare. It outstretched in front of her until meeting a cement wall that was just as bare. A musty smell wafted into her nose. *I'm in a basement*, she said to herself. Her clothes were damp, and so was the floor she lay on, a mix of sweat and moisture trapped in the room.

She turned her head to the other side. She didn't even think to sit up. Her mind was still too clouded by confusion. But she needed to see what was around her. Her vision cleared slowly as she focused on the rest of the room. She could see a desk, a chair, a computer. Images taped to the wall around them, but they were too far, and she was too tired to make out what they were. The light above her was the only one in the room, and it cast a shadow over the wall, making whatever hung upon it less visible. But she needed to see, she wanted to know what they were.

She placed her hand on the ground, pushing herself into a sitting position as the room spun. She squinted at the images as she grabbed hold of a beam in the middle of the basement and pulled herself up to standing. As she stood, she heard floorboards creak above her, and a recent familiar feeling flooded into her body as if to shake her mind fully awake—it was fear. It was an instinct. And suddenly the recent events pierced her mind in fractured memories. *The flat tire. The ride. The...* She stopped herself. She couldn't quite remember what happened next. She remembered a wrong turn and then an excruciating pain in her head. Her hand moved to her temple, and at the slight graze of her fingers, she winced in pain. Her heart began to pound. She didn't know where she was, but she knew it wasn't where she was meant to be.

Again, she looked toward the pictures on the wall and walked toward them, taking a closer look. They were newspaper clippings and printed Internet articles. But as Justine looked even closer, her eyes widened. Each article showed images of young girls that she most certainly recognized. They were the missing girls she had seen from the news, their bodies found on the beach.

Justine suddenly felt sick as she stared at images of the crime scenes, of investigators scavenging the beach for bodies. She stared at the girls' images. *How could I have been so stupid?* she said to herself as she remembered getting into the man's car. *It was him all along.* The realization made her head spin harder. It was hard to believe. She had served him so many times at the restaurant; he was kind and charming, everyone loved him. As the thoughts ran through her head, reality sank into the pit of her stomach. She knew each of the girls on the wall thought the same.

The floorboards creaked above her, and Justine looked up. The sound was just over where she stood. She could hear him pacing, chairs moving, as if he were rearranging. Her heart quickened. It was only a matter of time before he knew she was awake, and she scanned the room for an escape. There was a series of unfinished wooden stairs in the corner of the room. She walked closer, only to see a door leading to the floor he sounded on. It was no use. She needed another way.

Her eyes wandered until they spotted cement stairs leading into a dark crevice. She walked toward it quietly, carefully placing each foot lightly upon the floor, until she was close enough. She gazed up the stairs. There were a set of metal cellar doors, and her heart leapt. She scrambled up the steps. *If I could just open them, I could run,* she said to herself and then stopped in her tracks. She could still hear him moving about above her. He had not heard her, but she knew pushing the doors open would certainly make a sound. She studied the doors. There was no latch; she would just simply push them open, and her heart pounded from anticipation and fear. It seemed too good to be true. But she needed to wait for the right moment, or he would surely hear her.

He had stopped moving furniture around, and Justine felt panic swell at the thought of her opportunity escaping. Only silence echoed from above. She had no clue where he stood, or what he was doing. *Did he hear me?* She was about to just go for it, to push the doors open and run, but then she heard his footsteps again and another push of furniture across the floor. Justine didn't wait; as the movement vibrated the ceiling above her, she pushed at the doors. They opened slightly. She could see light filter between them. She pushed harder, but the doors did not budge further. They were locked, and tears welled in her eyes, and the doors fell back down, their metal clanking together.

It was a sound he had to have heard. She was sure of it. She listened to the floor above her. His footsteps had stopped. He was no longer pushing anything across the floor, and an uncomfortable feeling prickled down Justine's spine. She looked around the room. She had no defense. She needed an object, something to hit him with when he came down. She quietly tiptoed to his desk. She scanned every edge of it, but all that sat upon it was a computer and a mouse. There was nothing she could use as a weapon.

Suddenly, his footsteps quickened above her, growing louder and closer as they approached the basement door. Without any other defense, Justine quickly flattened against the wall where the stairs ended. *I have to try* she thought as a tear trickled down her cheek. She would hit him before he even knew she was there, and then she would have an escape. She could run up the stairs. Her last ounce of hope danced frantically in her thoughts as the door swung open and he descended the stairs.

She could hear his cynical laugh before speaking her name. "Justine," he called. "You awake?"

Three more steps, she said to herself. *Two, one.*

She swung around the corner, already punching and kicking, and she swung at his face, but he caught her arm in his grip. She kicked her leg out, attempting to hit him in the groin, but he bounced back before sending a punch right into her jaw. She stumbled back, falling to the floor as she screamed out in pain and blood pooled from her mouth. She felt her face. Her jaw was now shifted to one side, and she couldn't bear to open it.

"Nice try," he said as he walked casually to her. He bent down next to her. It was as if he were assessing her wound. "They always try to escape but never do," he added. "It's always fun to watch your prey run wild before you catch it again." He let out a sinister laugh as he shook his head. He reached for her hair and slammed her head into the floor.

Justine's mind swirled into a haze. She couldn't move. She couldn't speak. She could hear him move about the room, and he bent down beside her again, grabbed hold of her ankles, and tied something around them. It was painfully tight, and she winced, but she still couldn't move as he did the same to her wrists.

He grabbed hold of a tarp in the room and rolled her into it, encasing all of her. She felt him lift her up, tossing her body over his shoulder, but she had nothing in her to fight back. He carried her up the stairs, through the house, until she heard the opening of a door, of a car unlocking, a trunk unlatching, and she was tossed inside. She now knew her fate, and she wanted to cry, but she couldn't. She wanted scream, but no sound could fill her lungs.

He pulled the tarp down by her face and smiled at her. She could see a string held in his grip, but she still couldn't move. He pressed it up against her throat, harder and harder. Justine gasped for air. She wanted to claw at him, but her hands were tied. She wanted to scream, but she had no air, and her vision faded into blackness.

Chapter Twenty Nine

Tara stared down at her GPS as she placed her phone down in the middle console. She had just pulled out of the parking lot moments ago, and she was already ten minutes from the reporter's house. She waited for Warren to pick up as her palms began to sweat onto the steering wheel. She wasn't sure what he would think. If he would be annoyed that she drove all the way out to Dewey Beach without him knowing. If he would be frustrated that she was still investigating.

"Mills." Tara's thoughts were interrupted. His voice was tinged with urgency, and it caught Tara off-guard. She wasn't expecting it. *Does he already know I went off on my own?* she worried. "I was just about to call you," he added. "Another girl went missing."

"What?" The turn of conversation shook her, and she couldn't believe what she was hearing. Her instincts were right, and at that thought, Tara's blood ran cold. "When?"

"This morning. I just got a call." His voice was rushed, and she could hear him moving about as if he were heading out the door. "She's a waitress, never came home last night. Her roommate called it in." Tara heard the closing of a door behind him. "I'm already headed to the restaurant now. Where are you? Are you driving?"

He could hear the hum of the motor, the distance of her voice on speaker. She knew she just had to say it, and knowing another girl went missing, she now felt more confident with her choices. "I am," she said. "I'm near Dewey Beach." She paused a moment, but Warren waited for her to continue. "I was having doubts last night about Ben. I came out here to ask around the coffee shop again. I think I may have a lead, but I'm not sure."

"What's the lead?" Warren didn't even sound angry. His thoughts were fully on the case, and he wanted all the information she had.

"There's a crime reporter from a local station. He's been at every scene, usually the first one there. I knew he looked familiar. But he apparently goes into the coffee shop a lot, he knew Reese. Apparently she had a crush on him."

"And he's the type of person someone would take a ride from." Warren finished her sentence.

"Exactly, and he would know a thing or two about how to conceal evidence. He's also someone who would possibly have a camera."

"Where are you headed now? I'll meet you there," Warren said, sounding rushed.

"To his house. I called him. He gave me an address. I told him I knew he was following the story and wanted to see what he knew."

"Mills," Warren sighed. Tara could hear the concern in his words. "You need to wait until I get there. It could be a trap."

"I know," she said abruptly. She was now realizing more than ever how dangerous of a situation she was entering. But she also knew she had no time to wait. And it could take Warren close to an hour to get there.

"I can't wait for you," she replied. "But I'll call Sheriff Patel." She knew that he could send backup, which would protect her during the time Warren took to get there. "If that girl could still be alive, we might still have a shot at saving her. If we wait..." Her voice trailed off; she couldn't finish her sentence, but she didn't have to.

Warren sighed again. It was clear he understood. They both knew she couldn't wait for him. She wasn't going to let another girl get murdered. "What's the address?" Tara read it off to him as he entered it into his GPS. "It'll be forty-five minutes," he sighed. "Please just do me a favor and don't go in there before backup gets there."

She agreed that she would wait, and after hanging up, she immediately called Sheriff Patel. He picked up instantly.

"Patel, I need backup," she said without a second to spare.

Patel didn't skip a beat. "Whereabouts?"

She gave him the address before explaining whose home it was and why she was heading there. "There's a strong possibility this could be a killer. I need backup there immediately, but no sirens. This could be a potential hostage situation if he still has a victim. I don't want to raise his suspicion."

Patel understood. "My guys are all out on scenes right now, but I'll rally them up and send them over. Give me ten minutes and someone will be there. You'll see an unmarked vehicle across the street. You'll know it's us."

They quickly hung up.

Tara stared out at the road, her fingers clenched tightly around the wheel. She was almost there, and as the car sped closer, an unwanted memory sprang into her head. It was the previous case she worked on—her reckless decision putting her in an almost fatal position. It surged into her mind like a warning, but Tara shook it off. This was different. Warren knew where she was, and backup was on its way. At that thought, she buried every trace of the voice telling her to wait for Warren.

Chapter Thirty

Tara stood on the doorstep of a split-level home at the end of dead-end street. She did one circle around the block before arriving, hoping to buy backup some more time, but it was all the time she was willing to give. She looked behind her—still no unmarked car where Sheriff Patel said it would be. She looked at the clock on her phone. It was now five minutes past when he said they would be there, and she knew any moment they would pull up. She didn't want to waste another minute. She had waited long enough.

She knocked on a large wooden door with three square window cutouts on the top that were too high for her to see through. She waited a moment. There was no car in the driveway, Tara noted, but she could see a light on, assuming that any car was in the garage.

Within moments, she could hear someone moving toward the door. It swung open to reveal Dan Asher with a smile from ear to ear. He was wearing suit pants, a button-down shirt, and tie. He had just finished his shift, Tara remembered, but his clothes were perfectly unwrinkled, as if he had only worn them for a short while.

"Agent Mills," he said as he put out his hand. His grip was firm and his shake was hard. "Come in," he added as he opened the door wide. Tara stepped into a living room that was immaculately clean and organized. The walls were made of shiplap, the floor a dark finished wood, with dark gray furniture throughout. "Take a seat," he said as he gestured to a couch and sat down on a loveseat opposite.

He was remarkably welcoming, and it made Tara relax as she began to question her suspicion toward him. "Thank you for seeing me," she started. He nodded without hesitation.

"I just hope I can help you," he replied. He knitted his eyebrows in concern as he leaned forward, his elbows on his knees, his hands clasped together. His concern seemed genuine and took Tara by surprise.

"You've been following this case, correct?" Tara asked.

He nodded. "Since the beginning, when Alyssa White went missing." He straightened up, pressing his back against the couch as he shook his head. "It's terrible. The poor girls in this town. Everyone's on edge."

It was a bit of a strange remark, Tara noted. His focus not on the victims but on the terror it ensued in the community, but she didn't bring attention to it. Instead, she pushed forward. "And you knew Reese?"

He sighed and nodded. "I used to order coffee from her." He spoke to the floor as he said the words, and then he lifted his head. "That's as much as I knew about her, though." He shrugged.

"Did she ever mention anyone? Anyone she may have been meeting after work or speaking to?"

He shook his head. "I wish she did. Believe me, I wish I could help."

Tara took out her phone. She still had the pictures of the house fire from the memory card, and she flicked one open. She already knew the images were Ben Ford's, but she wanted to see his reaction. "Do you know who might've taken this photo?"

He leaned in closer, studying it, but only for a moment before he sat back into his seat. "It looks like a house fire we put on the news. I think a couple weeks ago. There were a few reporters there with camera crews, though; it'd be tough to know." His eyes veered to one side of the room, as if to avoid any eye contact as he straightened awkwardly. But then at Tara's gaze he suddenly relaxed and turned to her. It gave Tara a strange feeling, as if he had for a split-second morphed in and out of character.

"Was anyone from your station there?" she asked. Again, she wanted to see what he would say, what his body language would reveal.

He nodded. "It doesn't look like any footage I saw, though. I'm not sure if it came from our station. Were there any other pictures on the memory card?"

He stared at her, waiting for a response, but he hadn't even realized what he had just revealed. Tara's heart quickened as the reality of the situation dropped into the pit of her stomach. She never mentioned a memory card. They hadn't even released that information to the press or public.

"I never mentioned a memory card," she replied.

He stared at her a moment, as if understanding what she just said and what he had just done. She could see a flicker of panic flash in his eyes, until he chuckled, making light of it. "I just assumed. If it was taken at a scene, it had to have come from a memory card, right?" As he spoke, he awkwardly rubbed his knees with his hands, and as Tara looked down at them, she could see swelling and bruising around his knuckles. It looked fresh and new.

"What happened to your hand?"

He looked down at it and then flinched, pulling it toward himself. "I...uh," he stuttered. "I take boxing a couple days a week to stay in shape. Hit a bag too hard." He smiled, stroking his hand. But Tara could tell he was lying. He was witty. He was not someone who would stumble on the truth or even a lie that was well thought out. But on the spot, anyone would.

Silence sat heavy in the room, and for a brief moment a sound echoed in the distance. At first Tara wasn't sure what she heard, but as she looked at his face, it was clear that he heard it too. The same terror Tara saw a flicker of before burst into flames in his eyes.

"What was that?" she asked as she stood up. It was a banging from down the hall, and now Tara could hear it more consistently. She began to walk toward it. "Mind if we go see what that is?" she asked. Every inch of her mind pulled her forward. She needed to see what it was. She could feel the air in the room was now different.

He nodded, but he didn't speak, his charming persona now nowhere to be found. "I don't know what that is."

Tara inched into the hall, but before she took a next step, she sensed him following close—too close. She spun around, his fist already in the air, but she ducked just in time. She charged into his stomach, sending him sprawling backward as he tripped on the edge of the rug, falling flat on his back.

Tara reached for her gun on her belt loop, pulling it out in one swift motion. But just as she took aim, he kicked her legs out, sending her tumbling backward, her gun skidding across the floor. Something shattered and she crashed into something as an excruciating pain shot through her back. Glass covered the floor, every way she looked. She had hit the coffee table, and she could feel a shard in her back as the sensation of warm liquid soaked through her shirt. It was blood, but she didn't have time to assess the damage. He was already scrambling for her gun.

He threw himself toward it, his arm outstretched, his fingertips grazing the grip. Without even a second to think, Tara grabbed a shard of glass, jamming it into his leg. Her hand dripped with blood as she pulled back, the glass still in his leg as he bellowed in agony. His body curled—his focus on the gun momentarily lost. Tara pushed herself onto her knees, about to jump to her feet. She could grab it. The gun was only about a foot away. But just as she got to one foot, she felt a hand grip her other ankle. She spun around to see the shard of glass that was once in his leg now in his grip as he raised it above Tara's leg that he still held.

Tara kicked out her free leg, sending it straight into his chin. He dropped the glass, and his grip loosened just enough for Tara to pull her leg free. She jumped to her feet. Her back was agonizing, but adrenaline gave her strength to push forward. She saw the gun. He saw it too as he jumped to his feet, favoring one leg, and grabbing the shard of glass in the process. Tara scrambled to the gun as he ran toward her, swinging the glass wildly in his hand. In one swift motion, Tara grabbed the gun, cocked it back, and turned toward him, sending one shot through the air. He stumbled back, dropping the glass in his hand, crashing to the ground.

The front door suddenly swung open. It was Sheriff Patel and another officer. They stood with their guns outstretched in front of them, but then they saw the scene and lowered their grip. Warren came hurrying up the steps behind them. Sheriff Patel and the officer stepped aside as Warren burst into the room. He saw Tara, gun still in hand. He saw Dan Asher flat on the ground, blood oozing from a wound, and he lowered his gun.

Warren stood shell-shocked for a moment as he looked at Tara. Her mind was still spinning as her eyes focused on the man on the ground. "Is he dead?" she asked as she tried hard to steady her breathing.

Sheriff Patel bent down by the reporter. "No pulse," he said.

Warren was still staring at Tara as he walked toward her. "Are you all right?"

She was perched up against the kitchen counter, her hands resting atop behind her. She could still feel the pain in her back, and as she caught her breath, all she could think about was the banging. She didn't even answer Warren's question before she pushed off the counter and hurried down the hall.

"Call an ambulance," Warren said to Sheriff Patel, who already held his phone to his ear and nodded. Warren then caught Tara's movement. "Where are you going?" He hurried after her down the hall and then gasped. "Tara, you're bleeding."

But she didn't pay attention to his words. "Shh," she said as she held her finger to her lips. "I heard something." Warren quieted down, but he couldn't help staring worriedly at Tara's back. They crept along the hall. The banging had stopped. Tara held her gun in front of her, for she had no idea what she was about to discover. "FBI," she yelled, and suddenly the banging began again in full force.

Tara turned to Warren. He heard it too, and they both barreled down the hallway until they reached a door where the sound emanated. Tara swung it open. It was a garage. A BMW sat parked inside, and it shook at each thump from within the trunk.

"We need keys," Tara yelled toward Warren, who quickly turned on his heels, running back through to the kitchen. He returned moments later with keys in hand and pressed a button. The trunk popped open, and Tara opened it wider. Inside, a blue tarp covered a squealing body. Tara unwrapped it to reveal a girl, her eyes wide, her mouth taped shut. Tears fell down her cheeks as she stared up at Tara. Warren ripped the tape off the girl's mouth, and she gasped for air before uncontrollable sobbing overcame her.

The ambulance could be heard in the distance, growing louder as it approached. "You're safe now," Tara told her, as she too felt a wave of emotion. The victim was alive, and for the first time, Tara knew the case was officially over.

Chapter Thirty One

Tara stood on the porch of Dan Asher's home, bandages now wrapped around her core and hand. The ambulance still sat in the driveway as the EMTs prepared to leave. Warren and Sheriff Patel stood nearby, speaking, before Warren turned to Tara.

She was lucky. Her wound was not serious. She would only need a couple of stitches in her back. He had not dug too deep, and for that Tara was grateful. Her hand was fine. She was concerned that she would need time to recover, like she did after the trail killer case, when she had injured her arm. But this was merely a scrape in comparison, and she knew it would heal quickly.

"How's Justine?" Tara asked as Warren stepped onto the stoop. Justine's ambulance was now far gone, but she knew Warren had just received an update from Patel. Last she heard was that Justine suffered asphyxia from strangulation, but she had yet to learn if there would be any permanent damage.

"EMS thinks she should be fine, but she'll need a CT scan."

Tara nodded. She was grateful that they had gotten to her when they did. Dan Asher had clearly tried to kill her but didn't know he was unsuccessful. If Tara had gotten there any later, if he discovered that she was still alive—Tara couldn't even finish the thought as it stirred a swirl of emotions.

She turned to the door and pushed it open. They hadn't even searched the rest of the house yet, but they were aware of the basement. It was a small bit of information they were able to get from Justine before she was taken off to the hospital. She was kept there, she had told them, but that was all the information she was able to give. The house had already been cleared by Sheriff Patel and his officers, but now Tara and Warren were ready to do a more thorough sweep.

They entered the home, walking past forensic investigators who were placing yellow markers around the blood spatter, where Dan Asher's body was removed from moments ago. Once they reached the hallway, they turned to a door just past the kitchen and Tara turned the knob in her gloved hand.

The stairs creaked as they descended, the room opening up into a musty, dark unfinished basement. There were no windows. The room was dimly lit and bare except for a computer and television, and a wall of newspaper clippings. Tara and Warren moved closer, as they both peered at each clipping on the wall.

"Looks like he's been keeping tabs on this whole investigation," Warren said as they stared at the dates, all from last year, when Alyssa went missing, to now. He must've had every newspaper clipping ever printed regarding the case on the wall. It made Tara shudder. Some were developments in the case, others were pleas for details on the missing victims. But then her eyes fell on another—one that was old and faded. She leaned in closer, squinting to make out the date on the article. The lettering was almost too faded, but she could just make out the two and the three zeros. It was from the year 2000, twenty years ago.

A young girl, who looked to be the same age of the victims, stared back at Tara. It looked like a yearbook picture. She was posed and smiling—just a headshot. Tara began to read

The Newbury Police are asking for your help in finding a teenage girl that had gone missing Friday night at approximately 7:30, on her walk home from volleyball practice at Newbury High. Leslie Asher was expected home soon after but never arrived.

Tara pulled her eyes away from the paper. "Asher," she said under her breath. It was the same last name as the killer. She had gone missing in an almost identical way. *Was he recreating a personal tragedy?* Her heart pounded in her chest as she turned to Warren, but he was fixated on something else.

A pocketed folder was flipped open in front of him, papers pulled out as he scattered them across the desk, looking at each one intently.

"What is it?" Tara asked.

She looked down at the papers as well. They were hand-written notes—bullet points—each one a detail of the case. Next to some in red ink he wrote *Don't report yet*, and then others he had crossed out the same wording and recorded a date for when that information was released.

But Tara followed Warren's gaze to a detail marked at the bottom of one page. *Dewey Beach: Sofia*

Hernandez was scribbled across it. But it wasn't the place or name that caused him to stare. It was what was written next to it. Scribbled in red ink it read *Ben Ford's memory card. DO NOT REPORT.*

Tara pulled back, and so did Warren as they both shared a glance. It was clear now: he had planted the memory card. But there was another realization that sat heavy in the room.

And then Warren spoke. "He was creating this story all along, intentionally."

Chapter Thirty Two

T ara and Warren sat across from Reinhardt in his office at the J. Edgar Hoover Building. It was now late in the afternoon. It had been a long day, but one that they were all proud of, and Reinhardt had a smile from ear to ear, but Tara still sat at the edge of her seat.

They now knew that Dan Asher had created the news stories, most likely to further his career. They knew that he did indeed frame Ben Ford. But there was one piece to the puzzle that Tara still didn't fully understand—the news clipping of Leslie Asher—and she knew that Reinhardt had called them in to tell them what he now knew.

"First and foremost, how's your back?" Reinhardt asked as he looked at Tara.

"Not too bad," she replied. After she left Dan Asher's home, she had gone to the hospital and gotten her stitches. They would dissolve in about a week, she was told.

Reinhardt nodded and then sat back in his chair, placing his hands at the base of his neck. He shook his head. "No one would've ever suspected this guy," he said. He leaned forward again, slapping a piece of paper on his desk and reading it. "Local reporter for the past three years, very well liked and respected at work and in the town." He shook his head again. "His career really took off when he covered this case. He was the main reporter covering it, and well, it was a huge story. Doesn't sound like a coincidence to me."

Tara and Warren nodded in unison. Reinhardt was hinting at exactly what they had already concluded—that he had created the story to further his career. It sent a shiver down Tara's spine at how he was there all along—in plain sight. And it had occurred to her just how dangerous he actually was. He was charming, likeable, and intelligent. He had been at crime scenes, watching them, on TV, getting a thrill out of spinning his own narrative. He had been pulling the strings the whole time, and Tara knew he could've easily gone undetected.

"And the girl?" Tara finally asked. Leslie Asher was still in the forefront of her mind.

He sighed as he reached for a file on his desk before pulling out a missing person report and placing it in front of them.

"We found her file. Leslie Asher was Dan Asher's older sister."

But what does it mean?

"Sixteen years old," Reinhardt continued. "Her body was found weeks later gagged and buried in the backyard of her volleyball coach."

Tara shared a glance with Warren as she tried to force the pieces together. She could see in his eyes that he was doing the same. Dan Asher had to have been no older than thirteen when the disappearance and murder happened. It was something that no child should ever have to experience—the death of a family member, let alone a murder. But it all suddenly made sense.

"I'm assuming it really shook the town," Tara said, and Reinhardt nodded.

"So much so that the family relocated," he replied.

Tara sat silently, absorbing it all. Dan Asher had witnessed a tragedy just like the ones he created. He chose adolescent girls. He kidnapped them, burying their bodies. It wasn't a coincidence; Tara was sure of it. She remembered the news coverage when her mother was murdered, reporters waiting outside her house, wanting to get a glimpse of the poor child that had lost her mother at the hands of her father. Her grandmother shielded her from it as much she could, but Tara knew why they were there.

But Dan Asher was older, much more aware when tragedy struck his family. And it was a missing person case—it would've stirred more attention. He had seen at a young age the effects of the media, and it suddenly made sense why he chose it as a career path. It was the same reason Tara chose to be an FBI agent—to be on the other side of a tragedy, to be in control.

Tara's stomach churned at the thought, at the connection. But then another thought pushed forward, setting them apart. The career had never been enough for him. He craved more. He craved murder. And instead of using his career to prevent what he had witnessed, he craved creating the only story he knew best.

"Everything all right?" It was Warren's voice, and Tara snapped out of her thoughts to see him and Reinhardt staring at her.

"Just a lot to absorb," she replied.

Warren nodded. "Sounds like he had some deep psychological issues that motivated him."

Tara agreed, more than Warren would ever understand.

Reinhardt slapped the folder closed on his desk and sighed again. "You two are pretty impressive together, I have to say." He looked from Warren to Tara. Warren looked over at Tara and smiled as Reinhardt grew silent and stood up, leaning over his desk. He stared right into Tara's eyes, and then Warren's. "You two did an excellent job," he added before a smile burst on his face and he reached out, shaking both their hands. Tara's heart swelled. It was the exact ending to the case she had hoped for but had feared it would not come, that her instincts were wrong.

Reinhardt then looked behind them to the glass wall separating his office from the rest of the floor. "You guys are becoming famous around here," he joked as he motioned for them to look behind them. Tara turned around to see each agent was out of their cubicle, standing in the aisle, clapping and whistling.

"Go on," Reinhardt added with a flick of his wrist. They were done for the day, and it was his way of saying to enjoy it, to savor the moment.

Tara and Warren both stepped out of the office, and the floor burst into a roar and clapping. Some agents came up to them, patting them on their back, shaking their hands, congratulating them. It was a feeling like no other and a reaction Tara had not expected. A smile broke out on her face. When it finally simmered down, Tara turned to Warren. The same satisfaction that Tara felt reflected on his face as well.

"I wish we could get a drink to celebrate," he said to her.

Warren had never asked to get a drink with Tara, and it felt like a newfound bond and respect had formed between them. But she also could sense that it was a segue to something more.

"You can't?" Tara asked.

He shook his head, still with a smile. He lowered his mouth to her ear, as if telling her a secret. "I have a date," he whispered. He pulled back, his smile even wider. It was contagious. Tara had never seen him so happy, and she smiled instantaneously.

"With who?" But at that very moment, Warren's eyes wandered and his smile beamed even wider. Tara followed his gaze to see Dr. Harris opening the large glass doors of their division, and as the door swung open, she met Warren's eyes. She waved at him before continuing down the hall. "Dr. Harris?" Tara whispered. She had remembered that Warren dated her before, but he refused to pursue it further. It was too painful for him.

He nodded as he turned fully to Tara. "And thank you," he added. Tara had no clue what for, and she was about to ask him, but he stopped her. "For reminding me that my wife would want me to find happiness." At his words, Tara recalled their conversation in the car on the way to the camera store, when she had mentioned that she dug into her past for her mother—for justice and because Tara knew she wouldn't want her past to plague her. It was something that had clearly hit Warren hard.

Tara nodded. "Good for you, Warren."

He smiled again at as he looked at his watch. "She's going to be out of work soon, I better go home and take a shower after today's events." He then looked back up at Tara. "What are you going to do?"

The recollection of their conversation only reminded Tara that she had something to do of her own. "I think I'm going to New York," she replied. It had occurred to her that if she were to find out who that woman visiting her father truly was, she was going to have to come face-to-face with her. She already knew what time the woman visited him, and Tara was ready to confront her.

"You sure you're going to be all right?" he asked.

Tara wasn't sure, but she knew that the only way she could be okay for good was to get to the bottom of who this woman was and what she had to do with her mother's murder. "Yes," she replied. "It's the only way I will be."

Chapter Thirty Three

Next morning

T ara sat in the parking lot, her car turned off as she waited for someone to enter the building. She had booked the earliest flight out to New York and rented a car, and now she sat right outside the prison. She only knew that this woman was forty-two, had curly red hair, and that she came everyday around noon, but Tara was beginning to think it was a long shot that she would spot her. It was now a half hour past twelve, and every person that had entered the building did not fit that description. She had only spotted one person so far that seemed reasonably close, but once Tara stepped out of her car and said "Mackenzie," the woman did not turn around, and Tara realized that her hair was actually a light brown, not red.

As Tara waited, she stared down at her phone to see a text from John. *I'd love to take you out to dinner when you get back*, it read, and Tara sighed. He had been trying so hard to spend time with her, and at every moment she had, she had picked up and left on a mission of her own. He had understood why she left again this time, but she could see the disappointment on his face when she told him. She owed him that dinner, and so she replied that she would love it, which she would. She desperately needed time with him too.

As Tara placed her phone down, she spotted a woman walking to the entrance. She looked like she could be in her forties. She had red, curly hair, and Tara's heart began to pound.

Before the woman reached the door, Tara rolled down her window. "Mackenzie," she yelled. The woman stopped in her tracks. She spun around, a confused and fiery glare scanning the parking lot. Tara felt her palms begin to sweat as she stepped out of the car.

"Mackenzie James?" Tara asked.

The woman glared at her skeptically as she cautiously began to walk closer. She was around Tara's height, 5'6". She wore form-fitting jeans and a t-shirt that accentuated her slender build. She had dark brown deep-set eyes, and as Tara looked into them, for a moment it felt as if she had seen them before. But then she scanned the rest of her face—her petite little nose, her porcelain skin. She was remarkably pretty and looked relatively young for her age, but Tara was sure she had never met her.

"Yes?" the woman said once she was close enough.

Tara had been in her car, contemplating over and over again how she would approach her. She would ease into it, she had told herself. But in that moment, as she stood in front of her, everything Tara had planned blended into one, and she was unable to pull the pieces apart in chronological order.

"How do you know Richard Mills?" Tara asked. It was blunt and straightforward, and at the question, the woman stiffened. Her eyes narrowed into a cynical glare.

"Tara," she said under her breath, suddenly realizing who she was. Her eyes opened wide with panic at the realization. "He's my friend," she spat. "Is that a problem?" She was trying to sound tough, but her voice shook. For some reason, Tara's presence was making her increasingly anxious.

"You must be pretty close friends then, since you visit him almost every day."

She stayed silent a moment. The bit of information had caught her off-guard. "I suppose so," she replied. She stared Tara straight in the eye, as if afraid to turn away, or as if too afraid to show her nerves, which she had already revealed.

"How do you know my name, anyway?" Tara asked, but the woman didn't answer. Tara sighed. "I'm not trying to start trouble with you. It just seems odd that my dad has such a close relationship with someone that I know nothing about, and I don't see why it's such a big secret."

The color suddenly drained from the woman's face. "We're friends," she muttered again, but her voice shook even more.

"Romantically?" Tara questioned.

But the woman didn't respond. It was as if she wasn't sure if she should say any more. And as Tara stared into her eyes again, the same familiarity washed over her. It was as if she'd seen that same terrified look in the same eyes before.

"I think we're done here," the woman finally uttered as she turned away from Tara and began to walk to her car.

"You just got here," Tara called after her, but it didn't stop her. She opened her car door and quickly got inside. "Wait!" Tara yelled, picking up into a run as she ran toward her. Tara knew she most likely would not get this opportunity again, and she suddenly regretted coming at her so strong. "I just want to talk," she yelled again, but it was no use. The woman wanted nothing to do with her. The car sped through the parking lot to the exit, and before Tara could even capture a plate number, it made a left turn and barreled down the road until it could no longer be heard at all.

Tara stood in silence, defeated. She had traveled all this way, and now she was leaving just the way she had come—empty-handed. The only bit she gained was a face to put to the name, but without knowing where she lived or anything about her, that bit of information was useless. But as the woman's face surfaced into Tara's mind, a thought suddenly burst through. The reaction—staring at Tara dead in the eye as Tara asked her questions, afraid to pull away, and then quickly leaving when it got too difficult—she had seen it before. It was the same reaction her father had, and at that thought, another one came crashing down. The deep-set, dark brown eyes. The look of terror—it felt as if she had looked into them before. And then it occurred to her: they were identical to her father's.

Tara stared out into the street as she pieced each thought together, trying to make sense of it. *Am I just searching for a connection?* she wondered, but as she thought it, she knew it wasn't true. The resemblance was all too real, and it could only mean one thing: they were related.

Chapter Thirty Four

Tara and John walked along the path of Jones Point Park, his arm wrapped around her waist. Tara had arrived back in Washington, D.C., earlier that day, and John had insisted that they go out to dinner that evening and for a short walk before. He said she needed it, and Tara couldn't resist. She knew she owed it to John. He wanted so badly to spend time with her, and he was right; she needed it too.

She had already told John what had happened that day when she met Mackenzie, and he had agreed that the whole scenario seemed odd.

"You sure she looked like your dad?"

"It was an uncanny resemblance," she replied with a nod of certainty. "I just don't get it. If she's related, who would she be?" Tara had already tried to connect the dots as best she could. Her father only had one sister, but Tara knew she had passed away, and Mackenzie most certainly was not the same person. "Maybe a cousin?" she questioned, but at the thought, she knew it would be unlikely for them to have the same eyes unless they were immediate family. And then another thought surfaced—one that had been reoccurring—but she kept swatting away. Could her father have had another daughter? The thought sent a chill down her spine. Mackenzie was nineteen years older than Tara and twenty years younger than her father. It was certainly possible, but Tara buried the thought. "I don't know," she finally sighed. John kissed her cheek as a warm breeze flowed, making the coolness of his kiss linger as he pulled away.

"You will find answers," he told her. "You always do."

Tara looked out onto the water that glistened under the setting sun. She knew there was no more to say. She would have to keep looking, keep searching. There were answers out there. She just had to find them. She felt John's hand pull away from her waist and then inch into her hand until he clasped it tightly. He gave it a gentle squeeze.

"But I think you need to let go sometimes, even if it's just for a moment or a day. You owe it to yourself to clear your head," he added.

Tara nodded. He was right. She owed it to herself to relax. And she owed it to John. Her mind had been spinning in full gear for as long as she could remember now, and she couldn't recall the last time she actually enjoyed a walk or a dinner. "You're right," she said with a smile. "Let's just enjoy this."

He gave her hand another squeeze as they continued their walk. Tara watched runners go by, people on roller blades, an older woman feeding the seagulls, and it occurred to her how much she always missed from not being in the moment and how much there was to see. She stared out onto the water, marveling at the beauty of it all, at the clouds bursting with fragmented light, at the water shimmering.

She felt another pull on her hand as John slowed to a halt, and she turned around to face him.

"What's wrong?" she asked, but then she stopped herself from asking more. The sky danced in his eyes, his smile beamed from ear to ear, and she knew nothing was wrong at all.

"Tara, I love you with all my heart," he began. His eyes were filled with emotion, and Tara didn't quite understand why he was telling her this all of a sudden.

"I love you too, John," she replied.

"We've both grown so much, and I truly think it's because we have each other to lean on. We make each other better, don't you think?"

Tara nodded. It certainly was true. Part of the strength she had in coming to terms with her past was because John supported her and encouraged it. He had also always been there each time Tara doubted her abilities as an agent, cheering her on, never once giving her reason to feel discouraged. And it was with Tara's encouragement that John had gotten back into music.

John suddenly bent down on one knee, still holding Tara's hand as her heart fluttered. "I've been waiting a long time to find the right moment." He chuckled. "It hasn't been easy."

She knew what he was about to ask, and it all suddenly made sense—why he was growing frustrated that it was so hard to spend time with her, why his mother was acting odd at dinner that one night, why she was so nosey about Tara's sudden trip to New York. With the case and her personal issues with her father contently at the forefront of her mind, she had almost forgotten that she had sensed this all along.

He let go of Tara's hand, reached into his pocket, and pulled out a little black box. Tara's eyes widened as he pulled it open. Inside, a large single diamond caught the sun and shimmered.

"John," Tara gasped.

"Will you marry me, Tara Mills?" He looked more handsome than ever, the remaining bits of sunlight captured in his blonde hair.

"Yes," she gasped.

A huge smile formed on his face at her words. He pulled out the diamond ring and slipped it onto Tara's finger. But her eyes stayed focused on him. She grabbed him by the hand, pulling him up onto his feet, and wrapped her arms around his waist. His folding around her—his embrace feeling safer than it ever had. He was hers. She was his, and nothing else mattered.

Epilogue

Tara turned onto Tenth Street as she balanced a coffee tray in one hand and clutched a bag of bagels and John's favorite breakfast sandwich in the other. She had woken up early. John was still asleep, and she had decided it was about time she did something nice for him.

She looked down at her hand gripping the brown paper bag—at her ring sparkling in the morning sun—and a warm feeling spread throughout her body. They had only been engaged less than twenty-four hours and Tara was still in awe. All this time, she had worried that John was feeling too distant from her, but in reality, he was just trying to find a time to propose. Tara knew now she had not made it easy for him—the trips to New York, her mind always on the case or her father.

She wanted to enjoy this moment, to soak it up for all it was worth. John was right. She deserved to live in the moment—to take a break from all that her mind constantly worked to solve. She not only owed it to herself, but also to her relationship with John. She had just finished a case. For now, she had a slight break from work. And finding out who Mackenzie James was could wait. She wanted to enjoy this little bit of time with John as much as she could.

Tara pushed the large turnstile door of her apartment building and walked over to the mailboxes, placing her coffee and paper bag onto the floor. John was usually the one to grab the mail, but since they were both home late last night, neither of them had. She unlocked the box with her apartment number and pulled out a few pieces of mail. She looked through them quickly. They were mainly junk, and one electricity bill, but she stopped on one last envelope. It had no return address, but it was handwritten and addressed to her. She wasn't expecting anything, and Tara rarely received a letter in the mail unless it were a bill or something of that sort. She ripped it open. Inside sat a piece of folded paper. One edge was ragged, as if had been ripped out of notebook. She unfolded it, and for a second Tara lost her breath as she stared down at two words scribbled across the page. *STOP DIGGING.*

Tara looked around her. It seemed like a sick joke, but she knew no one could've put it in her mailbox. It had Tara's address on it. It was clearly mailed, and Tara's blood went cold. It wasn't her father's handwriting, and she only knew of one other person that could've sent it: Mackenzie.

Tara folded the piece of paper and placed it back into the envelope as her mind raced. She knew it could only have been sent for one reason: desperation. Mackenzie James was hiding something, something terrible, that she wanted to lie dead forever.

ONE LAST UNVEIL
(A Tara Mills Mystery—Book Three)

**ONE LAST UNVEIL is book three in the FBI
mystery series by debut author Sarah Sutton.**

**A true-crime podcaster is found brutally stabbed to
death in her home after walking her child to the bus
stop. At first, all fingers point to those closest to her.
But when a friend and fellow podcaster digs into her
obsession—a cold case laid to rest for fifteen years—
and later turns up dead, local police realize that a
serial killer dubbed the Silent Stalker could be
striking again for the first time in years.**

With the FBI called in and no leads to follow, they
quickly realize they need a brilliant mind to crack the
case: FBI Agent Tara Mills. But Tara is reluctant at first.
The case reminds her too much of her mother's, when
it's revealed that the victim's daughter—a selective
mute—lost her mother at the same age as Tara. But Tara
is compelled as she realizes it is only a matter of time
before he strikes again. As she peels back each layer,
she falls deeper into the darkest depths of her mind and
into the nightmares she had tried so hard to escape.

Meanwhile, Tara digs deeper into her past, obsessed
with revealing the mystery woman visiting her father in
prison, which leads to a shocking discovery. As she

battles her own psyche and more victims go missing, Tara realizes that the key to solving it all could be what she finds most triggering: her connection to the victim's daughter. As she takes a path she fears to travel, deep into the depths of her mind, she unveils a truth she never expected.

Book #4 in the series will be available soon!

BOOKS BY SARAH SUTTON

TARA MILLS MYSTERY SERIES
ONE LAST STEP (Book #1)
ONE LAST BREATH (Book #2)
ONE LAST UNVEIL (Book #3)

Printed in Great Britain
by Amazon